A MELODY IN THE WILDERNESS

A MELODY
IN THE
WILDERNESS

Leena Sarma

LIFI PUBLICATIONS PVT. LTD.
NEW DELHI

Published by:
LiFi Publications Pvt. Ltd.
211, 2nd Floor, Gagandeep
12, Rajendra Place, New Delhi–110 008, India
Phone : (011) 2574 1000
E-mail : info@lifipublications.com
Web : www.lifipublications.com

ISBN 13:-978-93-82536-54-3 ISBN 10: 93-82536-54-X

First published in 2014

Cataloging in Publication Data—DK
[Courtesy: D.K. Agencies (P) Ltd. <docinfo@dkagencies.com>]

Sarma, Leena, 1961–
A melody in the wilderness / Leena Sarma.
p. cm.
Novel.
ISBN 9789382536543

1. Women, East Indian--United States--Fiction. 2. Culture shock--United States--Fiction. 3. Indic fiction (English). I. Title.

DDC 823.92 23

Printed in India by D.K. Fine Art Press (P) Ltd., Delhi–52

To Aranyak, my dear son and his doting father

1

<u>*3rd June, 2001*</u>

A motley crowd has been watching from a specially erected glass chamber, the final moments of Timothy McVeigh like a bunch of wild teenagers cheering or jeering at all the antics of this ghastly drama in a brazenly passionate manner. Timothy McVeigh! The villain of Oklahoma bomb blast! His Face has been full of sweat, eyes giving out a rigid gaze and that sullenness has been engulfing his entire body with such ferocity that it is on the verge of becoming still in a few seconds time. Why on earth should they show an iota of sympathy for him? For someone who, probably in an apoplectic fit, had blithely snatched away the near and dear ones from their orbit of life?

I'm the master of my fate
*I'm the captain of my soul!**

Timothy McVeigh's last quote, his philosophy of life! Do you have any last wish? Any last words to say? The prison official's

* from the poem 'Invictus' by William Ernest Hentley (1849–1903)

hushed voice is audible. Seemingly stumped Timothy hands him that crushed slip of paper in what appears to be a pre-meditated act of a bewildered person going to bid adieu to this world shortly. Isn't it strange that it was coming from someone who is in a weird sentience of being and not being at the moment, the mind should have been numbed and the body is shortly going to be subjected to the annihilation of death?

Gayatri tries to recite the verse, slowly and with a lot of devotion as if she has been inhaling something puzzlingly sacred. I'm the master of my fate! I'm the captain of my soul. Am I the master? Am I the captain? She is not sure, not at this absurd, insensate phase of life when so many things have been happening and that too in such a rushed pace. Probably she would have liked to believe it fifteen years back when she had stepped into the soil of the USA as a gullible, young bride from that land of Red River and Blue Hills of northeast India with hopes and only hopes forming a lucid blanket all over her beautiful, cherubic face. But all those winged hopes, those elixirs of life which were singing lullaby to her frayed feelings many a times in the irrefutable, languid past have vanished now. She knows it for sure.

A long, circuitous queue with a medley of crowd jostling for space in front of a coffee shop! Different varieties of multicolored pastries adorn the gleaming glass-covered shelves, preparing themselves to be devoured by this ravenous crowd. Jubilations can be sniffed all over! Gayatri feels like switching off the television. A death is a death. Why should there be celebrations over someone's end, even if the victim was an abominable criminal accused of committing the most heinous crime of snuffing out lives of about three hundred odd unsuspecting people?

But this is America. Siddhartha would have said brusquely like he was telling her in Punxsutawney for the first time after her arrival in America.

Punxsutawney. Yes, it was in Punxsutawney only. A small, sleepy and adorable town in the state of Pennsylvania. The day was 2nd February. The town, with tiny doll-like houses, was full of fog that morning. A white sheet of ice was covering the ground and snowmen of different shapes and sizes were welcoming the tourists who trooped into the town before dawn. The sleepy groundhog was pulled out of the hole, his holy abode during this entire winter, amidst an uproar. The day being a cloudy day without a trace of sunshine, the shadow of that tiny creature was not going to fall on the ground.

'Be prepared for an extended winter.' The tall man shouted at the top of his voice like a soothsayer. The roaring cries of applause of onlookers pierced the sky. 'It's a Native American belief. When the shadow of a sleepy groundhog is seen on the ground, on a particular day, it's believed that winter is going to be over shortly. It's going to be an opposite scenario, if the shadow doesn't touch the ground.' Siddhartha briefed her before this trip was planned.

'Why there's so much excitement over a sleepy animal's shadow? What's so funny about it?'

'Look, they're enjoying life. And think about the business opportunities! The entire town is on the street selling something or the other....'

Siddhartha was always trying to explain this awesome entity called America to his new bride whenever there was an opening. Sometime he was an anthropologist, sometime a historian or sometime a tourist guide with a veritable treasure-trove of information! He had to showcase America! 'This is America.' His favorite quote! Whenever there was a puzzled look on his wife's face, this one-liner was flung flamboyantly to quell her swelling seas of confusion.

That day, on that fog-filled morning, Gayatri was listening intently to Siddhartha while savoring a groundhog shaped brownie in Punxsutawney made by some Punxsutawney housewife. At the same time she was coveting a groundhog shaped cute key ring hung in that makeshift shop for her house like a little child eyeing a candy. And probably some more, as mementos from this curiously pretty and petite town of America, for her friends back home in India! She would narrate this story about groundhog and many other fascinating tales about this new land to her friends and relatives there. Most of her acquaintances who had amassed some half-baked information about America would simply be wonderstruck at these parables.

Her mother, who never had an inclusive view about that great puzzle called life, would be thoroughly amazed and stupefied by this intriguing fact that the useless rodent which, so far, had been identified with only destruction in her own household could assume the role of a clairvoyant in a small town in a different country!

It was another matter that when she actually went home, she forgot to talk about Punxsutawney and an intensely cold fun-filled morning there. All those mementoes which she bought with lot of excitement in that idyllic tourist spot were left behind at the last moment when so many other things had to be tied up in a swirling sea of immense confusion.

A sigh comes out of her. A sigh of utter despair!

The bizarre death scene of Timothy McVeigh has come to an end and the make-believe judicial hearing by Justice Joe Brown has been going on in its place there. Why should her mind constantly waver like a pendulum between an unpleasant past and a not-so-invigorating present? Why should reminiscences of the past fifteen years of her life keep propping up at the slightest provocation?

The TV screen in front of her eyes is the reality at present.

Her mind must be reined. She must take charge of her life.

The African-American lady wails like a child in desperation. 'I have got enough proof to show that my husband has been indulging in infidelity during the entire period of our married life. He should suitably compensate me for those loathsome acts of cruelty, My Lord!'

'What can I do my lord? My wife feels that physical relationship is for procreation only. She dubs it as an impure act. I'm a healthy man and I've got desires. How can you blame me if I go to other women to satisfy my desires?'

There is a look of defiance in his dark, brooding eyes. His image in the close-up illustrates his petrifying insolence, something like a menacing evil about to stomp out of the virtual screen to the world at large. Justice Joe Brown now looks at the crying lady and then suddenly his sepulchral gaze fixed on the man. An intent, meditative gaze! What is he going to say now? He might feel empathy with the husband and say, 'Yes, you are right. Your wife has denied you of your rightful share of pleasure.' Or he might snap at the chap and talk of the values of blissful togetherness.

Justice Joe Brown might say anything.

Very intimate stories of joys and woes have been bought and sold for a few dollars. What would have been Siddhartha's reaction if he was present here now? 'This is America.' He would have said matter-of-factly.

'The same things are happening in India also. Imaginary stories are sold on Indian Television too in the garb of reality television these days. No difference between your West and my East on this account.'

Her brother would have proclaimed, with a straight, belligerent face, like Siddhartha was doing on so many other similar occasions.

Justice Joe Brown must have pronounced his verdict during this small spell of her mental hibernation. The lady, the estranged wife, seems to be ecstatic. The man has slowly gone out of the room wiping his face vigorously by a white paper napkin making it look like a crumpled piece of paper in the process. Gayatri switches off the television and the much dreaded silence engulfs the entire room immediately.

Silence! A frightening word! A chilling proposition!

She felt it immediately after her arrival in America. At dawn Siddhartha would hastily push off to the workplace and from there an all-pervading silence would take over the entire household. She would open the window and there was no stirring of human life anywhere. Only the endless streams of cars of all shapes and sizes would whir past her and announce the reign of those machines in a state of perpetual flux.

'Why we never get to hear the sound of horn?' Siddhartha has got every reason to get irritated at this foolish question. 'Honking means bad manners here. If you want to show anger on someone then you do it, but otherwise...!'

'Why do we get to see so few people around here? In India, oh, so many of them. Life's so dull in this place!' Siddhartha was clearly annoyed. You want varieties in life? Where do you find that in India? In the haggard-looking beggar-woman in a Railway Station or in the furious flood-water ravaging the countryside in the north-eastern corner of India? He thought peevishly as was evident from his puckered brow.

'Look, this is a vast country, three times as big as India with one-third of India's population in the other hemisphere. Please stop looking for India here.'

She remembers one occasion, a rare one, when she was thrilled in those initial years of her settling down in America. Probably that was her second year in this country. She was in Atlanta City, the Las Vegas of East Coast. They went to the massive, seven-storied Taj Mahal Casino built by Donald Trump, the billionaire entrepreneur, in the style of the seventh wonder of the world.

It was that cohesive group of people: Siddhartha, Gayatri, their friends Anjali and Arup. She put a twenty-five cents coin in one of the machines and the machine, like a juggler, was churning out ten twenty-five cents in quick succession. Next time another twenty-five cent coin was put. But this time the machine remained inexplicably quiet after gobbling up the small, adorable coin. Another twenty-five cent coin followed by another spell of ominous silence! She glanced sideways; she could see a glass-covered huge hall full of people. They were looking intently either at some fixed machine or at some revolving wheels like the Meditating Buddha in the quest of something deeper, something more meaningful.

'I want you to see an interesting thing.' Anjali was inching, like a tempest, towards the door virtually dragging Gayatri along with her to that small souvenir shop opposite the Taj Mahal Casino.

'I don't want to buy anything.' Gayatri's voice was sounding like a whisper in that vast, over-powering silence in an exotic ambience. Anjali was laughing heartily, almost like a mad woman. 'My poor little girl! Who told you to buy? Just wait and see the fun.'

Your things are bought and sold here. No mortgage. The glow-sign proclaiming the business ethics of the shop was loud and clear.

One elderly blowzy woman was seen hurrying to the shop. Her wrinkled leg-skin was cleverly camouflaged by a pair of long, skin-colored woolen stockings. Her soft but desperate words were audible.... White-gold necklace... 20 carats... 10 dollars for 12 hours.

She was showing something to him so frantically as if in she was in utter desperation. The shopkeeper was glancing at that impassively. A picture of sheer contrast!

'Didn't I tell you that they were in mortgage business? That bold proclamation outside is just a hoax, an eye-wash!' Anjali told her in a hush, 'This lady must have lost everything in the casino. I bet she'll come again in the midnight to give away her wedding ring and go back to that mystic place to earn some money. By the time she goes back in the morning she might not even have enough to pay for her gas.'

There were too many things inside the glass-encased tiny chamber – lots of ornaments made of gold, silver, diamond, one place occupied exclusively by sparkling diamond souvenirs. So many Holy Crosses made of precious metals adorned that corner! Gayatri felt a sudden surge of pain. How could someone be so heartless to throw those divine crosses away?

Her eyes suddenly caught the sight of a *mangalsutra*, the holy sign of marriage for a Hindu woman. The black-colored sparkling stones were singing a tune of harmony with the gold beads while lying cozily side by side. The smiling face of the Lord Krishna was staring at her from the locket of the necklace. 'Look, it's a mangalsutra. How could someone throw away a mangalsutra like this?' Anjali was not prepared to share Gayatri's anguish. '...Must be some woman who has been trapped in a love-less marriage or some desperate man who has got no qualms in throwing away his wife's honor! A crazy Indian! Doesn't deserve much thought.'

Anjali was on the driver's seat during the backward journey towards home. Gayatri was surreptitiously eyeing her. They had come from the same place with the same middle-class Indian background and values. But Anjali had adjusted to this alien culture like a fish to water. She was brimming with confidence at that point of time also. Her slender fingers were on the wheel and her eyes were on the fast receding road ahead. 'Next time when I come here I won't restrain myself. I'll play till my heart stops craving for more!' There was an unfathomable desolation in Anjali's shrill voice. But Gayatri's mind was repeatedly bouncing back to the sight of that glittering mangalsutra lying abandoned at one corner, the face of the smiling Krishna with his flute was almost popping out from the locket of the necklace and creating an inexplicable hollowness in her inner self.

The memory of that forsaken mangalsutra has come back to haunt her after so many years at this forlorn moment.

✦

'The groom works in America.' The voice of her mother laden with so much pride while inviting people for her daughter's wedding still rings in her ears.

'Can you cook fish well?' Her mother-in-law was asking on their first meeting. 'He has given us this awesome job of selecting a girl for him. My son, a jewel, doesn't believe in love marriage. He feels an arranged marriage, a time-tested system is only going to succeed.'

Gayatri couldn't miss a clear hint of smug satisfaction in her would-be-mother-in-law's sweet voice where conceit was wrapped up by layers of affable words.

Siddhartha Borthakur, the Associate Professor in biotechnology in Pennsylvania State University, a name to reckon with in his field was proud of his achievements. Like many other immigrants of his generation he wanted to make it big in his dream country and he was not apologetic about it.

'America is the Paradise on earth.' His eye-balls were rolling upward as if to trace out America among the celestial bodies. She was listening to those incantations like an obedient child and trying to look beyond at the parapet of the sky following his pervasive gaze. 'I'm not sure about the existence of an elusive paradise where virtuous people are supposed to flock after death. I don't know whether I've done enough good work to find a place there later on. But I must have really done something outstanding during my last birth to find a foothold in this man-made heaven. My karma in the last birth ensured this for me.'

Quietly she was also trying to comprehend that overwhelming entity called America at that point of time. She was striving to unify within herself this young man's espousal of seemingly dichotomous concepts of rebirth and karma with that modern monolith called America by prowling every patch of her cerebral jungle.

Then she was married and there was her brush with loneliness, her prolonged period of camaraderie with overwhelming silence and her muffled disenchantment with this new impersonal surrounding!

But there was soon a change also. All the silences were drowned in the cacophony of sounds of varying shapes and sizes. Two children in quick succession, their ever-increasing demand for food, attention etc., and hectic schedule of Siddhartha, all these brought about a total transformation in her life. The strident chanting of hymns by Siddhartha in the makeshift puja-*ghar* in the backyard, the loud noise of the cartoon characters in the TV where Gaurav, her three-year-old elder son was always glued to, the constant wailing of her infant daughter before being put to a night-long sleep! Ah! There were down pouring of sounds.

'Can't you put her to sleep fast? This baby! Spoilt and rotten!' Siddhartha was fuming. How could she make her husband understand that she was dead tired looking after and feeding the little one day-in and day-out, finding out tricks to fend off ever-increasing jealousies of little Gaurav for this new intruder in his exclusive realm, making an elaborate breakfast and an equally lavish lunch-pack for

Siddhartha in the wee hours of the morning and not letting up any effort to prepare an enjoyable evening meal for all of them?

Gaurav was totally absorbed in "Winnie the Pooh". That was the time to feed his dinner. He would be thoroughly involved in the different antics of that cartoon character and gulp down everything that would be forced down his throat without realizing, albeit in his own interest, that a trick had been played on him by his dear mother.

The baby had slept, Gaurav was fast asleep and now she would be all alone with her husband. That was their time. A time to be otherwise cherished between two young people, but that was never the case here. Siddhartha would talk to his parents in India, ask about their welfare, Gayatri would chip in, talk to her sister-in-law for a while and hung up. Then Siddhartha would talk at length about his laboratory, office, colleagues etc. without leaving much time or space for Gayatri to share her world with him. That was their routine.

But that was an evening when Siddhartha was in no mood to talk to his people back home. He was not going to talk about his office either. He was opening an envelope with an unusual flair and a handwritten mail was promptly coming out from that sanctimonious envelope. 'Father has sent the baby's horoscope and a name. She has a strong horoscope with all the auspicious planetary constellations.' A broad smile of satisfaction was spreading on his face.

There was a pause. 'Father has also sent a name for her. Katyayani. Her zodiac sign is Virgo and her first name should start with Ka. How do you like it?'

'Kaa-tyaa-yani!' She was trying to inhale that name in her senses. 'Don't you think it's going to be a bit difficult for people here to pronounce?'

'Why should it be? If we can pronounce something like McCartney or Schwarzenegger, why not Katyayani? And how can we discard a name given by our father to his granddaughter simply because people here might find it difficult to utter?'

'Landing of people on the moon in 1969 was a hoax – a carefully crafted story planted on an unsuspecting world by this superpower to score a brawny point over arch-rival Red Russia. Look at this photograph...the flag of America is fluttering on moon's soil. Is it possible in a vacuum? Tell me, convince me....' The gray-haired gentleman with drooping eye-lids, might be a veteran scientist with NASA, was desperately trying to prove his point. He was raucously supported by a group of younger-looking people.

'Don't listen to all these crap. How could fraud of such a massive magnitude take place in this free country? Look at his face! Frustrated guy!'

Siddhartha seemed to be too annoyed with the man who was questioning a rare technological feat of the country where he had planted his incisive feet to chart out a higher life for himself.

'You're a biotechnologist. You put everything under a microscope, observe their behavior and come to a conclusion. There is no place for invisibles in your lexicons. But why do you believe in destiny, the conjecture of working of celestial bodies on our day-to-day lives? Where is the proof? You take birth under some stellar conjunctions and your entire life is pre-decided. Unbelievable!'

She must have transgressed her boundaries, her limits so assiduously earmarked for her in this relationship. Siddhartha was not happy and he was not making any effort to hide it either. 'This is our tradition. The legacy of a great civilization! Traditions, beliefs, cultures are not tangible things which can be put under a scanner and dissected.'

She was planning earlier to talk about Irena, her Italian neighbor to her husband. But he was in a foul mood. He always resented her intimacy with Irena and Dominique. 'These Italians! Hauler of mafia culture to this country....' His hatred for her friends, whoever they might be, would invariably culminate in the condemnation of an entire nation.

Should she recount her chance meeting with Irena that day in the community gym? Irena was just back from her work and was swinging her body on the treadmill. 'We don't want our children to grow up in an alien culture. We're going back the day we feel we have a decent saving.' Profuse sweating, coming out of her delicately sculpted body as a result of those rhythmic movements, couldn't camouflage her determined look. 'People in Italy have flocked to learn English. They all want to land up in America, their ultimate dreamland and you can find mini Americas springing up everywhere in Italy. But there has also been a parallel movement against American culture in some small towns in our country. Why do we need that quick-paced life of America where there is no time even to wait and breathe in peace? They have asked. Let us enjoy life in our own gentle pace. We may take a stroll, meet people on the way, ask about their welfare and sip coffee with them at our leisure. Believe me Gayathri, there are many takers for that kind of argument also in our country and their numbers are swelling.'

Gayatri wanted to tell all these to Siddhartha. That young lady, herself a lonely foreigner who craved for home-made pasta and macaroni, opened up a whole new world to Gayatri, a world weaved together through incongruously varied factors like loneliness, nostalgia, rebellion and a desire to disentangle.

'They want to go back...not now...but probably after a few years.'

'Who? Those Italians? Huh! Who's going to beg them to stay?'

'No one has asked us to stay either!'

'America needs us more than we need America.' His voice was stern.

'...How could all the three astronauts of Apollo 11 come back to the earth in the pink of their health when solar-spots were at their peak during that period...?' There was no stopping of that elderly-looking gentleman on the television screen.

Siddhartha switched off the television in haste, in a show of total fury. This inert object had no defense but to bear the brunt of his indignation, like a vulnerable child at the mercy of a heartless adult.

'Now this matter is between me, the two people I love most: my wife and our daughter, and our God... It's nobody's business but ours. Even Presidents have private lives...'

Lara Sinclair, the professor of Effective communication of Pennsylvania State University switches off the DVD player.

'Look at his arrogance! There's sensation everywhere and this man with who the hell are you to meddle in my life attitude is declaring that only God and his family are privy to his personal affairs.'

A naughty, effulgent smile creates an ethereal ripple on the cream and peach complexion of Lara Sinclair, her twinkling eyes sweeping the entire classroom in one sideways glance. Her supple body with enviable curves has been coruscating a spectral charm through a body hugging Lacoste sweat-shirt and a pair of faded Levi jeans.

Everyone in the class has been listening with rapt attention the famous "Map Room" speech of Bill Clinton delivered for his countrymen after those infamous escapades with Monica Lewinsky.

'What do you feel about this speech? Do you think the President of the most powerful country in the world can afford to claim that there is a distinct line of demarcation between his private and public lives...?'

Lara is looking for an answer.

'The President of the USA is a public figure and the people of America have got every right to know what is going on in his personal life.'

That is Jacob, an otherwise jovial boy, with an injured, deflated look at this moment. Both his feet are up on the desk. He is about to gulp down the remaining portion of the liquid from a one-liter Pepsi bottle. His blue-dyed wavy hair, silver nose-stud and silver earrings in conjunction with faded blue-colored jeans have imparted a bohemian image which is in total contrast with the earnestness with which he conducts himself in each class and answers each question with lot of contemplations.

Gayatri talked to him on the very first day of the class. It was biting cold outside and as soon as she entered the warm classroom it had an immediate effect. She gave out a loud sneeze, an embarrassment. She looked here and there. Why should it happen to her in the classroom and that too on the very first day itself?

'God Bless You.' It was Jacob. He was smiling.

'I'm not an American by birth and I'm not familiar with most of your customs. How am I supposed to respond to your God Bless You?'

'You just say Thank You.'

'Thank you.'

'You're welcome. I'm Jacob. And you?'

'Gayatri...from India.'

'Gayaatri...Gye! Where's India? Is it in Africa?'

A student of a graduation course and still not aware of a country which is carrying one-fifth of the humanity in its womb!

'I know about India. It's near China. I've heard about Mahatma Gandhi and Indira Gandhi. Were they man and wife? Great leaders, great couple, both of them!'

It was Janet, the girl with red, curly, unkempt hair with her innocent toothless smile. Both the front teeth were conspicuously missing.

Gayatri came to the class with lots of trepidation. Room No 111, Sheffield Building, teacher Lara Sinclair. She found out about this class through the internet. Effective Communication. Yes, this was what she was looking for.

She was a new bride then. The telephone was ringing. 'Hi!' The feminine voice on the other side was not familiar but effusive. The words were coming out in quick successions. She decided to take the easiest way out. Yeah...yeah...yeah.

Whatever the lady at the other end was saying was met with this one-word response. After some time, she heard somebody knocking at their door.

'Hi!' Two tall, well-built men on her doorstep. 'The tickets for the horse-show. Fifty dollars each.'

'You ordered on phone.' They were polite but firm with "Don't try to mess up" look. 'I don't need tickets for horse-show.'

'You ordered for it.'

She was baffled. Her voice was almost trailing off. 'No, I didn't...'

They were adamant. The taller one raised one finger dauntingly, 'Okay, one ticket, fifty dollars.' There was some kind of finality in his hoarse voice. She developed a sudden bout of dread. In appearance, at least, he had seemed capable of murder and bedlam. She cowered in fright and bought a ticket.

Siddhartha was aghast. 'Fifty Dollars? Do you think it's a joke to part with fifty Dollars just like that? It's more than two thousand rupees in India.'

Ever since Siddhartha left her all alone, realization dawned on her that for her very survival in this society she would have to be in sync with it, she cannot afford to shuffle herself out. Doors for going back to her roots for an isomorphic identity with the people there were closed for ever.

Anjali goaded her to go on with life, 'C'mon Gayatri, it's futile to live like a wimp and that too for a leech like Siddhartha. Let him pass his time with that scientist and her extended family of cloned snake, vampire, falcon, dracula and what not. Let his blood be sucked by all of them. But you must fight it out.'

Now she is in this Effective Communication class to improve her communication skill and get a professional degree in the process. She once told Lara about her inability to talk in rushed, abbreviated American English. Lara dismissed it as something very inconsequential, 'You'll pick up very fast. Just give some time to yourself. You see, that's not very difficult. I mean the typical American English or words whatever you may say. Going to is gonna...You are is ya...Want to is wanna... Come here is C'mere...Oh my God is Omigod.... This country of ours has no time even to utter a complete sentence, everyone is in such a big hurry....' Lara's smile was so reassuring!

Her eyes are burning. She was working in McDonald for the entire night. It is a handsome earning, eight dollars per hour. As soon as the class is over she is rushing to the Hamilton Building to work there as a receptionist. Gaurav, called Garry by his friends, is going to the High School next year. Katyayani, known as Katie among her friends, is in middle school. Rents of her tiny apartment, gas bill and telephone bill are to be taken care of. Suddenly she finds herself in the cauldron of a lot of messy things in this big, dyspeptic conundrum called world from which Siddhartha promised to keep her diligently away.

Gayatri glances outside. The classroom has a glass wall. The undulating greenish-blue ground outside the wall has merged with a small faraway hill and created an illusion of a fairyland. Miles and miles of virgin land without any trace of human settlement has produced an aura of amazement inside her.

'Which thing has first struck your mind here? Ceaseless flow of vehicles or the cute, postcard like houses all around?' Siddhartha asked her on her arrival in the country.

'No fencing, no wall, no discernible mark of demarcation between the houses! It is amazing.' Her unrehearsed reply was bound to elicit strong response from her husband.

'Boundaries are clearly marked on the papers...'

'I have made a yummy banana cake for you. Let's have it.' Gayatri's mind is now back to the class after this mouth-watering proposal of partaking a home-made cake.

Lara always brings lot of goodies for her students here.

Her banana cake is delicious.

Lara comes at a quick pace towards Gayatri and places a paper-napkin below her chin. Then she bends downward and starts picking up the fragments of the cake scattered below because of Gayatri's hurried eating.

'This is the American way of telling you that you've done a wrong thing.' Siddhartha told her long time back when they landed up in Detroit Airport as newlyweds. She was thoroughly exhausted after her long day-and-night flight to America. The food in the aircraft was tasteless and she was famished. She wanted to sprinkle some cold water on her face.

'Where's the toilet?'

'There.' His finger pointed towards a direction. RESTROOM. She opened the door of HER. She was startled at the dazzling scenario inside. Rows and rows of wash basins with a huge mirror spreading across the entire wall on one side!

She opened the faucet and sprinkled some cold water on her weary face. 'Hi!' A pretty lady greeted her with a wide grin. Why should this stranger greet her? She had never met her. Only much later she realized that strangers should also greet each other in this country with "Hi" when they just happen to meet on the way.

That pretty lady took out one or two rolls of paper napkins from a nearby rolling-machine and wiped out the water scattered on the basin and then threw them in the nearby waste-paper basket. She accomplished all these work in a few minutes time and scurried away quickly.

'This is the American way of giving you a mouthful. This is not India where you can treat any public place with as much contempt as possible...' Siddhartha reprimanded her on that day.

At this moment too her mind has gone back to Siddhartha. She could find a synergy in Lara's palpable disapproval in her action with the probable admonition her action would have invited from Siddhartha.

She must get a respite from the phobic clutches of Siddhartha's make believe commands.

She must be on her own.

'Yeah Gayatri, what do you think about this speech? And about the man? An arrogant one?'

Lara's eyes are locked with hers. She must come back to the class.

'He was the most powerful man in the world at that time. The leader of the most powerful nation! In spite of that, he didn't discount the role of his wife in the matter of heart....'

She pauses for a while. There has been an avalanche of memories rushing down her soul.

'...This speech shows that Clinton is a human being who is open to remorse for his actions, at least, to the near and dear ones. You don't find even that much of humility with many other people.'

'True! This speech touched the chord with many, precisely, for that reason.'

Lara Sinclair too pauses for a while.

'The triumph of a speech depends mostly on the impact it makes on the audience. If the recipient group laps up a speech on the perceived ground of honesty, truthfulness or anything of that sort, then the speech is a success. A person maybe a prolific speaker, he or she may be in total command of the subject, he or she maybe oozing out oodles of confidence, but audience may reject that speaker for some inexplicable reason. People didn't like Al Gore's speech during the presidential debate because of an apparent arrogance. It's like a game of dice, this liking part...'

Lara is silent for a while. Her eyes sway again, probably, with some enigmatic internal rhythms. Time is going to be over soon and suddenly she gives out an inscrutable smile. 'Bye. Thanks.' She murmurs and with that she rushes out of the class leaving behind a sweet fragrance.

✦ ✦ ✦

2

'It's the time for *Rongali Bihu* festival in our place in India. Spring is imminent and people back home are going to welcome this queen of seasons with songs, dances, a whole lot of exotic dishes and lots of gaieties.'

Gaurav has just opened the window. He apparently responds to the gushing enthusiasm of his mother with a certain amount of disdain. His gaze is fixed outside. 'Winter is going away.' Disappointment clearly rings in Gaurav's voice as if he is being pushed towards a dark catacomb of despair called summer. He is passionate about winter and totally in love with snow.

The huge pond outside their flat looks like a vast stretch of blue. A crowd of Canadian geese playing across its calm water has been the only visible sign of life there at this moment. Some people have gathered outside Zackary's flat on the other side of the pond. A typical scene during the last few days!

Zackary, a classmate of Gaurav, has started a queer protest by waving a placard sitting in front of his house, 'Give me the right to live my life the way I want.' His parents got divorced recently and the court has given his custody to the mother. He is aghast at the decision. Why should he go to a woman who never bothered to show the slightest hint of affection to her son during his growing up years?

Richard has been sitting by his side. Richard, Zackary's father, has always been there in his life. How can he erase from his memories all those exclusive moments of warmth when his small body, shivering and shriveling with shooting fever, was hugged with a load of assurances by this caring man in many a cold and lonely nights?

His mother has been equally appalled. 'The man, who has been enjoying all these years on my hard-earned dollars while I was slogging for the comfort of the family, wants now to assume the role of a martyr...!'

'Has he been attending school? Your friend?'

Gaurav's face is expressionless. The cold, blank stare doesn't spew any emotion. 'No. Not of late.'

Gaurav's father has left them for another woman. Why has there been no stirring in Gaurav? Gayatri sometime feels tempted to provoke her teenage son, 'Look, your father has deserted all of us. Why can't you sit in a protest against this desertion like your friend?'

No, she is not going to tell him anything.

Every Sunday Siddhartha calls up the children and takes stock of their life inundating them with lot of questions. Gayatri is curious to know whether Siddhartha, her life-companion for more than a decade, has ever bothered to ask about her.

Ever since he left her for Nora Roberts, his fellow biotechnologist and an exalted figure in the realm of stem-cell research, on the ground of intellectual incompatibility, she has been living on this edge of hope that he would come back one day to the inviting warmth of the home-zone.

A few days back, she could not contain herself. 'Tell me, what all you and your dad talk about? Do you mention about our visit to the library every Sunday and that we all play computer games and carry loads of books back home? Do you talk about my working long hours away from home most of the nights...?'

Gaurav was silent.

Katie was enthusiastic. 'Of course I told him about our library trips.' She could hear her heart pounding. 'Daddy is so happy. He told me that when Nora would be here she would also take us to interesting spots.'

Last winter Siddhartha came. She received that much-awaited phone call, 'I'm coming there.'

Is he coming back to her? What is she supposed to do now? Should she show all her pent-up emotions to the man who was almost throwing her out on the street without any prior warning and said with a cold finality 'No, there is no place for you in my life...?'

Or forgive him for everything and accept him complacently back here?

Her hands were frantically moving up and down over her mangalsutra, the sacred sign of her union with Siddhartha. This was given by Siddhartha immediately after their marriage. That was the time when the Dot Busters were issuing threats to the Indian immigrants, 'We've been living here since ages and you bastards, the infants in this country, are going to take away all our high-paying jobs...?' Indian community was identified by the sign of that Dot, the small vermilion circle put on the forehead by a married Hindu woman, and they became the object of sporadic vitriolic attacks. Most of the Indian Hindu women stopped wearing that vermilion mark after those senseless attacks born out of an unbridled, collective xenophobia.

Siddhartha told her to obliterate all signs of that mark and wear the mangalsutra, the necklace with gold and black beads instead, in this country. She has been clutching on to that mangalsutra since that day.

'Are you with me?' Siddhartha's voice on the other side.

'We'll be staying in a hotel.'

'We?'

Her hopes dashed, like a candle that had fizzled out, spouting smoke and ashes of dejection.

'Yeah, Nora and me. We're going to take a break and roam around in the State College with the children.'

They came and asked her to come with them to Mount Nitany, a small hillock with lots of caves where dinosaurs seem to have roamed around in plenty once upon a time, to spend a few hours of solitude in the lap of Mother Nature.

'I'm still very old fashioned, Siddhartha. I cannot reconcile myself to sharing space with your mistress.'

Since morning she had been making a number of delicacies for the picnic-goers.

'Don't put your trademark spices in the chicken curry. Nora is not used to spicy food.' That was Siddhartha. Gayatri did not miss the subtle hint of sarcasm in his voice, his usual way of reducing another person in his vicinity to shreds. She remained calm. 'I'm making some eatables for the kids.'

Children were going away waving at her, steadying their gaze at the road ahead when they comfortably settled themselves on the backside of the huge SUV. They were, obviously, excited at the prospect of all the fun and frolic associated with this outing. Clearly an escape from their hitherto humdrum existence!

She remembered Linda, precisely, at that point of time. There was a get-together in the Springtown Natural Park for all the foreign students, teachers and scholars of the Pennsylvania State University. Linda, the tall, thin, almost emaciated and quintessentially dry-skinned lady came to her and gave her a bear hug. 'We're going to be your host-family for some time till you feel comfortable in this new land. University people asked me if we could adopt an Indian family, a newly-wed couple, to familiarize them with American culture. I jumped at the prospect.... Come, I'll introduce you to my family.'

Gayatri was virtually dragged to a small, apparently cohesive group. 'This is Jeff, my boyfriend. She's Emily, Jeff's daughter; look at this tall, beautiful girl! Victoria, my daughter and here is Adams, my son and a student of this university who stays in dorm; Monica, Jeff's ex-wife and her Romanian husband Pollock. My ex-husband Bill, a professor of Mathematics in Penn State. This is my big family. And guys, this is Gayathri, from India, we can call her Gye. Can we?'

Gayatri nodded her head vigorously.

She was amazed at this chaotic scenario and felt tired after some time in trying to keep pace with this medley of relations stretched to a ridiculously expansive extent. But Siddhartha was not amused. 'These are crazy people. Boyfriend, girlfriend, ex-wife, ex-husband, children from all these permutations and combinations, what a mad scenario! Please keep away from that woman.'

Siddhartha called up university foreign-scholars Division to inform them that they were in the lookout for a different family.'

'Is there any problem with Linda? Last year the Korean family liked her a lot.' The lady at the other end was inquisitive and a little bit concerned.

'Linda is a great lady. We were, otherwise, so comfortable with her. But Linda has pets, a dog and a beautiful, furry cat.' Siddhartha paused for a minute, 'My wife has fur allergy.'

'Oh! We're so sorry about it. Ok, we'll look for someone who doesn't have pets to be your host family.'

'Thank you. Yeah, a family without pets is welcome.'

Gayatri never had any problem with Linda and her enormously big family where one was tied to the other like beads in a round, infinite but beautifully designed necklace. When the initial weariness was over, she started enjoying that sprinkling of liberalism where feud being closeted with camaraderie in the definition of a family. But Siddhartha being Siddhartha, the matter had to be pursued urgently to bring about an immediate and logical way out for an apparently weird imbroglio, much to the dismay of his wife.

Kenny and John came to their life at that point of time. A pleasant family with husband, wife and three grown-up children. Kenny and John had been married since the last thirty-five years.

'You have been married for so long. Isn't that a unique thing in this country?'

'We met one American lady who introduced us to a whole horde of girlfriend, boyfriend, ex-wife, ex-husband, children from all these liaisons as one family.' Siddhartha's interjection to Gayatri's polite broaching up of the topic was too blatant.

'There was obviously no tension among these conflicting relations. I think that is the norm in this country and yours is an exception.' Gayatri's earnestness to gather some inputs about this new land was not offensive.

But there was a lot of resilience in Kenny's strong denial. 'That's not true. There are still many families in America where that villain of peace called divorce, hasn't crept in. And there are tensions in all those relations called ex-husband and current husband, ex-wife and current-wife, stepmum, stepdad etc. Some people show it, some don't. Americans are human-beings and they are not above all the weaknesses a normal human-being is supposed to have.'

'That's exactly what I wanted to tell my wife...but she resolutely refused to believe me....'

'Once upon a time you called Linda, our host, a crazy person for stretching the concept of family to an outrageous extent. What do you think? Have I become as crazy as Linda in your eyes to buy her theory of family and be happy at sharing my space with your girlfriend?'

She was at the doorstep with Siddhartha. He immediately looked away. What was there in his look? Indifference? Disdain? Embarrassment? Or remorse? She shared a life, a life replete with many small ups and downs, with this man and she was dying to know what had been going on in his mind and heart, exactly, at that moment of his going away.

She can suddenly see Zackary breaking into an impromptu protest jig in front of a recording camera. A playful child throws a red ball to the huge pond and the abrupt splashing of placid blue water makes the resting geese scurrying for cover. The tranquility is gone.

Nora called up Gaurav and Katyayani. She is taking them out during coming Thanksgiving holidays.

Thanksgiving! So many memories are ingrained in this word! Memories for a great country like America and memories for an ordinary woman like Gayatri!

During the last part of sixteenth century, some Englishmen were unhappy with the oppressive religious policy of England and left English seashore to be with their American brethren at New England in America. Some navigational miscalculation here and there made them to land in Boston in Massachusetts and not in New England where welcoming friends were supposed to be waiting for them with open arms.

It was the month of November. A vast landscape of an alien barren land was unfolding before their eyes. A bitter cold-wave was sweeping the valley and half of the new immigrants perished in that ravaging cold in that valley of death.

Before the onset of the next winter the survivors devised a strategy. They learnt the art of cultivation from the Native Americans and together built a prosperous agriculture. A huge reserve of food swept away the fear of starvation and death from their minds. Now it was the time for celebration for the immigrants and the native people.

The fat turkeys roaming around the areas were roasted in the fire and sweet jams prepared from cranberries and apple-pie were also prepared to be savored along with the feast.

That was the way to say thanks to the almighty for their survival and for the rich harvest which ensured their continuation in this new world.

Gayatri heard this narration from Siddhartha as a part of his effort to imbricate all the nuances of American life for the convenience of his new wife when she had arrived here from India several years back.

'The present day Americans celebrate this Thanksgiving as a tribute to God for their birth in this great country. Those who do not believe in the existence of God also celebrate this as homage to America for giving them a unique life with abundance of everything.... This is a post-harvest festival like our own *Magh* Bihu, Pongal or *Lohri*.' Siddhartha explained to her before her first Thanksgiving in America. 'People gather in their ancestral homes and take food together like we do in our own country during Bihu. It's a much-cherished home-coming for the majority of people to partake mama's cuisines.'

Anjali called up in the morning itself to invite them for dinner and stay. 'A large-turkey is being baked in oven. I have a coal-oven here.'

Gayatri's first Thanksgiving in this country. An occasion for real celebration and a sumptuous feast! That's what her friends made her to believe.

When they reached Harrisburg, the capital town of Pennsylvania, after a two-hour drive, the entire town was resplendent in colorful lights of different hues. The small garden in front of Anjali's house was decorated in blinking lights which seemed to be playing a naughty game of hide and seek with a fog-filled white darkness. Anjali was wearing a richly-embroidered silk saree in place of her usual T-shirt and trouser. A bunch of fresh jasmine flowers dangling from her wild hair accentuated her feral beauty. The dining table creaked with the weight of an assortment of bowls where brown bread, shredded cauliflowers fried in oil and chilies, finely chopped cucumbers and radish in sweetened yogurt, cashew and raisin studded mutton biriyani and so many other delicacies were safely ensconced. A huge baked turkey with lots of spices over it was the prima donna of the dining table.

Another Assamese family joined them in the late evening. Jiauddin Ahmed and Ashifa *bou*. With a rich texture of salt and pepper hair, a smooth, glowing, gray complexion and that omnipresent smile on his face, Ahmed dada was an epitome of happiness and confidence.

'So boys, what are your plans? Are you going to stick to this foreign shore forever or going back home?'

'We're going back. That's for sure. Look at the lifestyles of all those corporate people in Bangalore or Hyderabad! What's the point in staying back when you get everything there in your homeland?' There was no ambiguity, ifs and buts, in Arup's voice.

Ahmed dada's smile was nostalgic but somewhat quizzical. 'Very difficult Arup. Your children were born and brought up here. They've acknowledged this country as their own. They've accepted George Washington as the father of their nation. India is a distant land for them, an alien one. This country which is a foreign land for you is the country of your children.'

Siddhartha was pouring Diet Pepsi in his glass. Siddhartha was always conscious about his health. Diet and Pepsi! What a contradiction! Like this scientist who could think of horoscope and stem-cell research in the same breath or loving and discarding India for greener pastures at the same time.

'I've never considered going back. Why should I go back to India? Fund-constraint will sap my baby, my research on stem-cell totally.'

There was no spangle of humor in Siddhartha's voice. Ahmed dada was impressed. 'You do not have any pang of guilt about bringing up your children in this country! This is great. The feelings should have been the same with scores of other Indians. Why should there be apprehension? They're Americans and accept them as Americans. All problems are over.'

'No. My children will be Indians only.' Siddhartha's voice stiffened so much as if he was delivering a verdict in a court room full of people. "They'll be brought up here but Indian values will be superimposed on them. They'll go to temple once a week, they'll visit India once a year, they'll learn age-old Indian values and get married to Indians when they grow up.'

'Very difficult proposition Siddhartha, very difficult. What do you want? That they will be celebrating life in American society taking with them an invisible, almost simultaneous, craze for India inside! Look, it's painful to stay here, for someone like me. Very often when I'm fast asleep, I dream about my walks along the river Brahmaputra as a child and then on waking up I realize that I'm in an alien land. I can't go back because of my daughter. She belongs to this land, totally and inalienably. I cannot go back because one part of me also belongs to this land. Living here, I cry for that country and if I go back, I'll cry for this country...'

Ahmed Dada's pain seemed to have engulfed all of them, a collective entity sewn together by an irretrievably lost past and an equally mystified future.

The one person who remained unfazed by all these discourses was Ashifa bou, a vibrant, beautiful, radiant lady with unassuming manners. 'When we came almost thirty years back, we looked hysterically for an Indian face here and there. It was such a rare sight at that time. Indian grocery was not found anywhere. I cried for my favorite dal. Once I saw a saree-clad lady from a distance and without wasting any time ran towards her. I grabbed her from behind. Oh! An American girl, a Hare Krishna disciple and a drug-addict. She asked for some money for her marijuana and I happily gave away some.'

She was belching out a hearty laugh. 'Of course, time has changed. Now, so many of us are here. People there too have got access to everything unlike in the past. Last time, when I took some crème and lotion bottles for my relatives there, they seemed to be not interested.'

That was the first Thanksgiving in Gayatri's life. Next year they went to John and Kenny's place with little Gaurav.

It was their thirty-fifth marriage anniversary and also the Thanksgiving day.

And it was really a warm and wonderful evening. Kenny was glowing with all the adulation she received from her family. When John initiated the Thanksgiving prayer to the Almighty, before the sumptuous feast so painstakingly prepared by his companion for the last thirty-five years, the radiance emanated from his face conveyed his love for his wife and this beautiful family surrounding him.

When they departed from Kenny's house that fog-filled wintry evening, John and Kenny were there at the doorstep waving at them. The kind, elderly couple looked like two fragile fairies floating in the air epitomizing an all-pervading love which transcended all perimeters.

Thanksgiving had always been a period for going out on long holidays for Siddhartha and his family. Sometime they would go by air and sometime by road. It was real fun to go by those sleek, black-topped highways of America. Gayatri would carry the road map with her and Gaurav would read out the names of the streets.

'We'll have to go through Devon Street which is 8 miles away from Princeton Street.' Gayatri would announce.

'It's Princeton Street.' Gaurav would yell.

Siddhartha would take his car towards Princeton Street.

Gaurav sometime wanted to eat chicken-burger and fries in the Burger King. Gayatri would prefer vegetable-roll in the SUBWAY. Siddhartha looked for well-cooked Chinese food in some decent outlet. There were disputes. Sometime all of them would end up eating chicken-burgers, sometime American Chop suey would fill their bellies and sometime vegetable-roll would come from the omnipresent SUBWAY. But there was never a murmur of disquiet. There was happiness in giving up also.

Siddhartha left home during the last Thanksgiving with the unspoken threat of never returning again to their small nest called home. Gayatri roamed around on the roads, with Katie in tow, the entire day in a state of total despair. They had their dinner in the nearby church. Gaurav too had gone out that evening to his friend's place to have dinner with them.

Why Nora is going to take away her children during this Thanksgiving? A feeling of loneliness grapples with her entire being making her to go numb at that very moment. Is there any place in this desolate land where she can dump her loneliness for a while and cry her heart out?

She looks at her mobile and after a brief pause dials a number. She could hear that familiar hello from Kenny's sweet, unpretentious voice.

'Can I come to your home during this Thanksgiving?'

Dr. Mrs. Shakuntala Kundan is sitting in a swivel chair in front of an oval-shaped black wooden table in that bright, sparkling room. With a mauve-colored silk saree draping over her slim, tall, smooth body and a well-coiffed hair adorning her forehead, she is the perfect image of a graceful lady who must be striding ahead in her 40s. A satin-smooth cloudy skin texture has added a mystic element to her very palpable oriental look. The tiny diamond earrings have been emanating a silvery radiance and bestowing its glow in full on her luminous face at the moment.

'How many years have you been staying in this country?'

'Fifteen years.'

'I've been here for thirty years. A long spell of time, isn't it? I came here as a 20 year old medical student and then completed medical education in this country. Later on, I specialized as a counselor in psychotherapy. It was a virgin field at that time with lots of potential.'

This beautiful lady with smooth, flowing complexion is fifty-year old! Gayatri is truly amazed.

'You have some real problems, I presume. An Indian origin person doesn't usually come to us. Americans are a different breed altogether in these matters. An American rushes to us when he sneezes twice in succession.'

Mrs. Kundan's beautiful, charcoal-colored eyes gaze at her without giving her that uncanny feeling that she is under some kind of microscopic scrutiny.

Anjali suggested that she should come to this lady, a leading-light in the field of psychotherapy, to find a way out for stemming her unabated tide of depression.

'Why should I go to her? Have I gone mad?'

'Yes. Very soon, you're going to go mad. Look at your face in the mirror. Layers and layers of tensions are merrily playing over it.'

She dialed the given number to fix an appointment with this lady.

'Tell me Gayatri.' She told in chaste Hindi.

'What should I tell?'

'Anything.'

'I cannot sleep. Sleep eludes me completely.'

'What else?'

'I want to pour acid on my face, burn my hair, take a sharp knife and stab my limbs.'

'Your face is like that of a blooming rose. Dark, wavy cloud would pale in front of your thick, playful, serpentine hair. And your eyes! It's a divine gift. Your entire soul is mirrored in those bottomless eyes. Your beauty is not meant for annihilation, dear.'

Gayatri's eyes are fixed on the bronze image of Kali; the nude and angry goddess with protruding tongue, her husband, the mighty Lord Shiva prostrating himself under her feet till her anger is subsided. A beautiful woman turning herself into a bizarre figure when injustice was heaped on her!

'She's angry.'

'Who?'

'Why? You're enamored of her, I can see that. I'm also impressed by her. She was insulted and she transformed herself into an irate, fuming deity out to exterminate injustice. Look, even Lord Shiva, the God of destruction in our Hindu pantheon and her own dear husband is under her feet. If a woman is angry, she can shed her clothes, her armor of modesty and the ultimate sheen of feminine beauty and can trample anyone, even the mighty lord of destruction.'

Mrs. Kundan can talk with passion.

'You can see both creation and destruction embodied in her. How true! Creation and destruction are different facets of the same entity called life. Most of the westerners do not understand this contradiction inherent in our thought-process. I explain it to them and they're amazed. You know Gayatri, I was brought up in a small town in northern India in a loving, sheltered atmosphere. My mother would give me a hug whenever I demanded attention. She would tell me bedtime stories of beautiful prince and princess in the backdrop of a strange, snowy country. Whenever father visited us from his place of work, he'd inundate us with lots of chocolates and toys brought from that big city. One day our pet dog Jodie was trying to take me out of the house and I was resisting his effort. But at one point of time I thought why not play games of ball-throwing with him! As soon as I was out of the house, the house collapsed like a pack of cards and my mother, the loving mother who used to tell stories about charming prince and princess in majestic castles, was no more. It was a major earthquake. In one stroke, there was a big chasm between the past and the present. I had to shift to

Bombay to be with my father in that concrete jungle. Later on, another woman joined the family as stepmother. I remained as aloof from her as possible. In one moment, the protective veneer called Mother vanished and the next moment my transformation from a child to a woman or rather my birth as a woman was completed.'

It is role-reversal. She has come to narrate her story and here, sitting on the other side, she has been listening to Mrs. Kundan's tales. Some people have the knack of story-telling. Earthquake is not an alien thing for Gayatri. She was born and brought up in Assam, a province of north-east India, where earthquake was always a part of life.

But an earthquake of a very different magnitude shook her own life in this country. She lost the ground where she was very firmly planted once and the roof overhead was also blown away in that calamity. She could not get a whiff of what was coming. She has been stripped of her honor. Should she also assume the role of the livid goddess Kali now to retrieve that long-lost prestige?

'Tell me about yourself.'

Gayatry looks at Mrs. Kundan, wide-eyed. Where to start? With all those humiliating statements directed at her by Siddhartha during their decade-long married life? Or with his verbal tributes to Nora for her manifold virtues?

'The name of your husband is Siddhartha?'

She nods her head in approval.

'Thousands of years ago, when the world was just opening it's portals to History, a prince called Siddhartha left his pretty, young wife in her sleep to start a long journey in the quest of truth.'

'My Siddhartha left me when I was wide awake. I was told, in unambiguous words, about my incompatibility with his great intellect.'

'You accepted all those rubbish Gayatri?'

'It was a monologue. I was made to stand there as a convict and death-sentence was pronounced.'

She related all the things to Dr. Kundan about how Nora would drop in some evenings and relish the Indian delicacies prepared by her. Nora would talk about her research-work.

'My work centers round stem-cell. When a fetus is aborted, we can keep the cells of such a fetus alive under a congenial environment in the laboratory. Such cells, which are called Embryonic Stem Cells, can be nourished to grow into some particular useful organs like liver, kidney, heart, lung under specific laboratory conditions. Those organs can be transplanted in case of failure in a human body.'

Nora was trying to transport Gayatri to her cryptic world of cells, bodies, fetus and ultimately to the vast canvas of life itself. She never built a wall around her work to bar Gayatri's entry in that highly intellectual universe.

'You know, this stem cell research has invited a lot of flak on ethical issues. Many people feel that use of cells for this research might encourage abortion. Some believe that a fetus has also the right to live. The policy-makers are perplexed at the vexed issue of the beginning of life. When does life actually begin? At the zygotic stage or in a full-grown fetus or in a child just after birth? My work has been facing fund-crunch because of that baffling situation.'

Nora rested her head on the sofa-back. Her eyes were giving a faraway look. Perfectly tousled dark-blond wavy hair, melting-Cherry-Mash chocolate eyes and her gleaming white teeth ready to go for an Oral-B commercial, she was matching more with the mental image of the Greek Love Goddess Venus than a boringly serious scientist ready to innovate something esoteric.

'With that mystic aura around her look, Nora should have frolicked in front of arch-light instead of wasting herself in front of a dingy microscope.' Gayatri, later on, told Siddhartha.

'Nora is fond of taking up challenges. Her predilection to do something in a particular field goes up if the impediments are more there.'

Nora's penchant for challenges was, probably, flowing to Siddhartha. 'Nora was a trophy to be won. A coveted trophy, a difficult feat!' Gayatri tries to give a plausible explanation to Siddhartha's drifting towards Nora so that Mrs. Kundan can comprehend the scenario.

'Do you have any solution for my problem?'

'You come to terms to a No-Siddhartha-Life. Sooner the better.'

'I've been deserted by my husband and a long, winding and inert road to the future is lying ahead.'

'Your description about your future is totally wrong. You've a beautiful time ahead. Look, I'm not going to prescribe some anti-depressants to you like most American psychiatrists would have done in your case. There're lots of chaos and disorderliness in the country where I was born. That has come as a boon in my present vocation. When people in trouble come to me, I talk to them, probe about their personal lives, listen to them with utmost curiosity, and suggest some ways to wriggle out of quaint situations like a loving friend. These things are not written in any book on medical science. These remedies are not suggested in any classroom lecture. But a caring heart can really do wonders for a bruised soul. Most of the people coming to me are America-born Americans. They feel relieved to find someone who is prepared to listen to their travails. In this country you don't get people to talk to...'

Mrs. Kundan suddenly looks pensive. 'So many people come with so many varied problems. Many depressed people come to me for being too fat. They want to shed weight but can't say no to food. I asked one of the women who came for help, What do you eat for different meals? With a straight face she told, Burger, chips, Pepsi...for all meals. On further questioning I knew that she was a perpetual car hopper. She spent three hours in front of the TV and four hours in front of the computer. All the time she was gorging on something. How to blame her when the entire country seems to be on an eating spree? It's loneliness you see. I need to be extremely patient with these lonely souls. I want to arouse the will-power lying dormant for ages inside and go on talking to them for hours together. Time consuming, difficult, painstaking but it works, better than medicines. All solutions lie within...'

Mrs. Kundan wipes her face with a paper napkin and switches off the small tape-recorder kept at a corner, 'You start your life anew. The power to redeem is within you. Come out of the ashes of the past. You've the ability to create and you've the ability to demolish. You become the goddess Kali and build the foundation of a new life. The tall and the mighty too will come under your feet.'

The intercom is buzzing. 'Gregory's waiting with his brother for you Mrs. Kundan. Are you going to cancel his appointment for today?' Receptionist at the front desk sounds edgy.

'No. Let him wait for a while Nikkei. Can you make some coffee for him? He likes cappuccino.' There is a solid firmness in Mrs. Kundan's impersonal voice.

Mrs. Kundan comes out with Gayatri and leads her through the huge glass door. She gently taps on Gayatri's shoulder while passing through the half-opened door. 'You're very pretty, intelligent and enormously capable. You can take care of yourself. Next time when you come, we'll talk more. Have a nice day Gayatri.'

The bronze image of goddess Kali has been repeatedly coming to her consciousness. A woman avenged. Gayatri wants to recall that sentence of Mrs. Kundan, 'Creation and destruction are the different facets of the same entity called life.'

She walks fast to reach home. A new spring has come to her steps.

✦ ✦ ✦

3

The slow, distant voice of her brother has been coming to her as if riding on the crest of the wavy, chilled wind blowing all over the place.

A few days back, Anjali's mother went out to dry her freshly-washed-hair in the sun. The elderly lady was shocked to find that the sun was really lukewarm. The golden shine so clearly visible through the huge window-panes of her daughter's home was actually a deception. She had to come indoors with small flakes of ice spread across her hair. 'Sun is so scarce here!' She could not hide her acute disappointment with this insouciant sun.

The elderly couple did not want to come here leaving behind the cozy warmth of their tastefully decorated home in that very beautiful city of Guwahati. But Anjali was insistent. 'You must come. I had my first child all alone and brought him up on my own. It was tough! Particularly those initial months! You don't get any helping hand in this country.... You must help me out this time.'

Her father advised her to come to India and have the child there. Anjali was appalled. 'How can you suggest such a foolish thing? Pregnant ladies from neighboring countries sneak into this country to give birth on American soil and here you are suggesting otherwise when I can lawfully give birth to an American citizen!'

The elderly couple is very lonely here. Anjali's mother is nostalgic about her afternoon gossip-sessions with the neighborhood ladies in her home, her occasional visits to the numerous nephews and nieces and her evening prayer sessions with the local ladies. Here she has been sitting inside a closed house cooped up with her daughter's family. Whenever she opens her door she is greeted by an excruciating loneliness riding piggy-back on an insufferable wintry air.

She has seen the couple living in the nearby brick-tiled house from a distance. They go out in two separate vehicles early morning and come back late evening. She is not aware about the other people living nearby. They are like some invisible inhabitants of an esoteric ghost-town.

Two roly-poly kids of a neighbor came once to pick up their ball which accidentally had rolled into their front porch. Anjali's mother almost rushed out of their house to strike a conversation with the adorable kids with cherubic, doll-like faces. They looked at the strange-looking lady with that tunic-type long-wrapped-up-dress without much of a fuss and sped away as soon as the ball could be picked up from beneath a bush.

'Why don't you call them inside sometime? Such beautiful kids! I want to talk to them...'

'Call them? Have you gone crazy? This is not India. I don't know their parents. Suppose the boys fall down and hurt themselves in my house, I should be prepared to face a law-suit and pay hefty compensation. People here file law-suits at the slightest provocation. The lawyers are the richest professionals here. I know some instances where children filed complaints against parents for trying to discipline them in this country. Can you believe that? So don't talk rubbish...'

Now Baba, Anjali's brother is on the telephone line to wish her for *Uruka*, the community feast etc. prior to Magh Bihu, the post harvest festival celebrated with a lot of feasting in Assam in northeast India. He has been speaking at length about his American experience. 'My new American name is Bob. Hi! This is Bob here. How can I help you?... How do you like my pseudo-American identity dear sis? I have seen most of Eddy Murphy's films, read a lot of books on American culture, watched some real life video films to gain knowledge on America and go on talking to my employers' customers, the entire night, with that fake identity.'

There is a little pause. 'I take home a handsome pay-packet dear and I'm happy about it though I know that what I earn should have rightfully gone to a real Bob in America. But I'm miserable today. The Uruka celebration has been going on all around. We are inside this cage named Call Centre and talking to people. To add to my woes someone on the other side has been trying to nag me. He called me a tramp, a leech and what not.... Hey sis, don't get upset. Occupational hazard! How are our old folks there? Tell them to take care.'

Her mother is upset. 'Why couldn't he talk to me? He must be distressed. We're not there today and he's all alone. But we're going to be with him soon.'

Her mother wanted to tell so many stories to her son. Her excursion to the Hershey Chocolate factory, her forays into the local departmental store, her stroll on the multiple-lanes bridge over the Susquehanna River and the gradual transformation of the mischievous Susquehanna River into a white comatose sheet with the advent of winter and so on.

But Baba has no time for her. Of late, he looks visibly distressed at this routine of day-time sleeping and night-time working. 'What kind of life is this? I can't even talk to my friends. When I'm awake, they are fast asleep and when I'm sleeping, they are thriving...'

Today is Uruka in her own place. Ladies must be churning out all delicacies for their near and dear ones. The neighborhood brats must be on the lookout for things to put in fire in their community kitchen. Scattered firewood, unprotected bamboo fencing, wooden or bamboo gates! Nothing would be spared. This is a socially-approved vandalism for this special night of Uruka. She is worried. Who will look after her beautiful garden with all those blooming flowers tonight?'

She poured her heart out against this alien land to Gayatri that evening when she dropped for the Uruka celebration in Anjali's place. 'Why should someone live in this place when everything is available in our own country? The charm to live among your own people is entirely different. Arup has recently bought this posh car. But who is there to see or appreciate? I'm not going to let Baba set his foot on this country.'

She wants to run away to her home to get rid of this miserable loneliness.

It is snowing hard. Anjali's mother gazes outside intently. The snow-mobile people look like extra-terrestrials from a distance with their white overwhelming dresses. Anjali comes and finds her mother sitting in the living room.

'It's extremely cold outside. It must be cold in our place also. Uruka nights are always very chilly. I wonder if my delicate flowers are still safe or they have been wrecked by those neighboring hooligans! Baba must be in the office, wide awake.'

Her mother has been talking to herself. Anjali does not have the heart now to tell this old lady that Uruka night was already over there and people have been basking under the pale warmth of a winter sun. A new day has arrived in that place.

'Ma, it's too late. Let's go to sleep now.'

The old lady hurries back to her room. In her dream, her home in Guwahati, nestled among hills and overlooking the mighty river Brahmaputra, is going to beckon her for the entire night.

✦

Gayatri has also been trying to make her children understand that it is the Uruka day in her birthplace. A post-harvest festival accompanied by lots of feasting and festivities.

'Streets must be teeming with people today each carrying a large fish with a bagful of vegetables.'

'The feast seems to be similar to our Thanksgiving dinner. I'm going with you to Anjali auntie's place for Uruka feast.'

Katie is euphoric about the proposed dinner at Anjali's house though she identifies herself completely with Thanksgiving as her festival. But Gaurav is clearly apathetic towards this entire hullabaloo about Uruka or the evening dinner. 'I maybe excused Mom. I have to go to Brendan's...'

Gaurav's indifference to his ancestral place is not a new thing. It stemmed during their first and the only visit to India when he was just a three-year old kid. That was his mother's first visit to India after her marriage. Lots of preparations were going on before the trip which included the struggle to get the Indian visas for their two young children from the Indian embassy in Washington. When they arrived at the Indira Gandhi International Airport in New Delhi, Gaurav showed his first signs of uneasiness. He lifted his red-colored Mickey-mouse T-shirt and started scratching his abdominal skin, 'Mummy, India is bad, India is hot.'

Next morning they arrived in Borjhar Airport in Guwahati. An entire battalion of their relatives came there to greet them on their arrival. Gayatri's mother was trying to drag Gaurav to her side and Gaurav was making an equally fierce retaliatory effort to dispel that loving pull.

When the convoy moved, Gaurav covered his little nose with the pallu of his mother's sari. 'Dirty, India is very dirty, yucky, let's go back mummy.' Gayatri was wearing the traditional *mekhela-chadar*, her forehead was smeared with vermillion. Siddhartha wanted her to go that way. A picture-perfect traditional Assamese daughter-in-law!

The pot-holes on the streets of Guwahati were making the car-ride very uncomfortable.

The neighbors and the relatives were gaping appreciatively at her blooming beauty during that trip. 'It's the combined effect of comfort and luxury.' They had all concurred. Gayatri kept quiet. 'When people there'll look at you with envy and awe, don't try to dispel the myths about our so-called fairy tale existence. Rather, make some stories to strengthen that belief.' It was Anjali's command in the departure lounge of the State College Airport in America.

She should not disappoint her dearest friend.

Within a few days of their arrival, Gaurav fell ill. It started with loose motion followed by a queasy stomach. The young doctor in the neighborhood felt that the sudden change of climate was the real culprit.

Too many people were waiting for the doctor in that dingy room of the pharmacy. When her turn came Gayatri had to yank an indisposed Gaurav to the inner chamber where the doctor was sitting.

The doctor gave her a friendly smile. 'Siddhartha's wife! I was his classmate in high school. He was a genius! We could never keep pace with his brilliance. We used to call him Sir Isaac Newton...'

'So many people waiting for one doctor is a rare sight in America. My kids would go only to a physician with whom they have been registered. I do not have the freedom to choose doctors as per my own whims at different times.'

The doctor put the stethoscope on Gaurav's chest, stomach, back and gently tapped his stomach to find out the problem. 'Show me your tongue dear! Haah...haah. Open your mouth like this. You have a white tongue. Why? You should have pink one. Don't worry. This doctor uncle is going to give you sweet tablets. These will chase away your naughty pain. Is it okay?'

Gaurav was stomping his feet like a cantankerous child. The doctor stopped taking further interest in him and got down to the serious business of writing the medicines. 'I'm also planning to go to the USA. I am preparing for the entrance exam.'

'Why do you want to go there? You have built up a reputation here. You are with your own people: father, mother, brother, sister and lots of friends. You have earned enough to have a comfortable existence. And you know, you'll be a non-entity once you land up there.'

She was opening her purse while continuing with her discourse. The young doctor with a boyish grin looked at her and waved his right hand in a strongly dismissive manner as if she was going to do an act of sacrilege. 'No, no. You are the wife of a class-mate. How can I take fee from you?'

The medicines were not very effective.

Gayatri's mother-in-law was convinced that it was a case of evil eye. 'My grandson is so good-looking! He is like a prince! It's natural that people are charmed by the child. But some people have that evil-eye, you know. The result is a bad health...'

Gayatri was appalled at that belief. When she broached the topic to her husband he did not like her quizzical approach. 'Mind radiates energy. It has been proved empirically. If you concentrate, you can move a cupboard from its place. So, looking from that view-point, mother's belief cannot just be dismissed as fertile imagination of a senile brain.'

Siddhartha's stern look was foreboding. She knew that some more scorns were coming her way.

'Even if my mother ends up telling something absurd, her wishes are to be honored....'

The clear emphasis on "My Mother" was discernible to Gayatri's ears.

A lanky, dark-colored, middle-aged woman arrived in their house the next day. She was wearing a bright nylon saree where hues of different colors danced like a roving rainbow. Cheap silver-colored bangles and tattoos of flowers on her both hands added to her bizarre and somewhat baffling look.

She lit a big fire in the backyard and it was diffused after some time. White mustard-seeds were sprinkled over the burning charcoal followed by generous sprinkling of red-chilies. Strangely no aroma from those chilies was wafting in the air. The lady bawled at the top of her voice 'A sure case of evil eye! But it has vanished now. No more illness from this moment onwards.'

Gayatri's mother was equally perturbed about her grandchild. She sent curries made of different medicinal herbs from her kitchen-garden for him so that he might get well soon.

After a fortnight or so the symptoms abated. It might be the fallout of those esoteric rites performed by the lanky lady or it might be the sluggish impact of the different medicines prescribed by the doctor or the slow effect of the time-tested medicinal plants. Whatever be the reason, everyone in the family heaved a sigh of relief at the much-awaited recovery of the child.

This recovery was followed by a frenzied spate of dinner and lunch invitations by the extended family and the friends.

After a few days she was permitted to go to her parents' place for a week. The tiny Assam-type house was standing with a glorious uniqueness in the area among all the high-rise buildings. The sweet fragrance of the jasmine flowers floated to her nostrils and transported her to a nostalgic bygone era of an adorable childhood. She was brought up in this house with an abundance of tenderness, a profusion of warmth and a load of care.

'I want to relax and unwind here. I'm not going out anywhere. And listen, no meat for me in this house. The entire country has been drenched in a deluge of meat there...'

Gayatri was narrating the exhilarating experience of eating beef in a pot-luck dinner in the community-center of the Penn State University. The Mexican research-scholar came and suggested to her exuberantly, 'Try my dish. I have cooked meat in small green tomatoes. It's a Mexican specialty.'

The moment she started gorging on the delicious meat curry, Siddhartha rushed towards her menacingly and ordered her to throw her food. 'Do you know what you are eating?... Beef!'

On the way back home, she was profusely apologetic, 'I really didn't know that it was beef, believe me.'

'See to it that our people back home don't get a whiff of it.' Siddhartha was not in a mood to condone her blasphemous act.

She did not hide it from her mother and that elderly religious-minded lady was laughing her heart out at this inadvertent goof up.

Gayatri's bed was there in the old place: Clean, tidy and spacious, standing there like a virgin princess waiting to be conquered. Even her small room was oozing out tell-tale signs of pampering. 'I didn't allow anyone to use your room. When I look at it I feel you're still here with me.' Her mother's inane attempt at identifying her with an inert object did not bewilder her. She jumped onto her bed and went off to a profoundly peaceful sleep after so many years in the wilderness.

At the time of going back, she clasped her mother's hands and cried her heart out. It was a soundless, motionless sob.

There were lots of words in her unabated flow of tears. 'Why did you banish me to a world where you all are not there?'

At the airport, Gaurav was back to his jovial self. In his naiveté also he could make out that he was going back to his familiar terrain.

India must have left an indelible imprint as that of an alien, cataclysmic land in his mind. Because of Gaurav's prolonged sickness in India, Siddhartha did not dare to take him there in the years to follow though he had that ardent desire to impose India on his son's young, amorphous mind.

Gaurav must still be carrying the image of a dirty, dingy, crowded India with him. He could not get a fresh opportunity to feel the vibrations of a pulsating nation during his growing up years.

On her way to Anjali's house for Uruka dinner tonight, Gayatri drops Gaurav in front of the red-tiled house of Brendan.

There he is, waving at her.

With this waving he is probably bidding adieu in silence to a culture far removed from his comprehension in its myriad, esoteric hues.

✦

Gayatri reaches the doorstep of Dr. Shakuntala Kundan's clinic.

She pushes the wooden entrance door of Mrs. Kundan's clinic. Nikkei is still there. Her warm smile is infectious and powerful. It is heady enough to illuminate her inner self at this moment. She occupies a seat in the sofa in front of Nikkei. One tall, well-built person came inside. He looks remote. 'Hi Greg!' Nikkei's greetings fail to have much impact on his remoteness. Greg? Yes, Gayatri heard his name during her first visit to Mrs. Kundan.

Another stocky person with a kind face comes inside and occupies the swinging chair near her.

'The Iraq war is an unjustified act of aggression by America. What do you think about it?'

Gayatri looks at her neighbor with a perplexing curiosity. Is he playing some tricks on her? She won't let him hoodwink her.

'I'm not an America-born American. I'm from India, settling down in this country.'

'So what? You're a citizen of this world and you've got every right to decide what is good and what is evil for the mankind.' This stranger glares down at her through his broad-rimmed spectacles.

Nikkei's stubborn smile fades slowly. 'He's Rudolf.'

'Why America waged a war against Vietnam? If communism was foisted on some country, then that country should fight back, not America.'

'I'm an ordinary woman. I'm too bogged down with my own small issues.'

'Wrong. You're not aware about the weight of your own mind or your own conscience. This world is not only for George Bush and his cronies. Ordinary people like you and me are affected by the heinous crimes committed by America in different parts of the globe.'

Greg gives out an idiotic smile. Nikkei also looks embarrassedly at the walls around. His smile and her stare convey in unison their helplessness at the situation.

Rudolf comes closer to her and whispers in her ears. 'Do you know because of my outspokenness CIA and FBI are damn scared? They want to exterminate me. George Bush is petrified.

But I'm not worried. Jesus Christ has been guiding me in my mission. I can outwit them with the help of divine forces and with my own intelligence. I've stopped taking nap these days.'

One elderly, frail-looking lady pushes the door and comes inside. 'Oh Rudolf! I was looking for you everywhere and you've come here.'

'I want to talk to Shakhun...I want to tell her about the death threats sent by the CIA.'

'But we didn't take any appointment today. We'll come some other time son.'

'So what Nora? She tells me that I need no appointment. Anytime I can just come. She's my friend. She's also appalled at all the wrong policies of America.'

Mrs. Shakuntala Kundan opens the door of her room with an effusive smile playing on her lips.

'Hi Rudolf! Hi everybody! Good to see you guys.'

'Shakhun, I want to talk to you.' Some kind of desperation is palpable in Rudolf's voice.

'Sure Rudolf. I'd like to talk to you too. Let me first finish it off with Gayatri and your brother Greg. Then we'll go out for lunch. I'm very hungry. A Chinese meal is what I'm looking for. Greg and Nora are joining us if they are free this afternoon. Is it okay with you dear?'

Rudolf nods his head vigorously. He seems to be thrilled at the proposition.

Now Gayatri is sitting in front of Mrs. Kundan.

'You're looking very pretty.'

'Thanks.'

'How've your Effective Communication and Spoken English classes been going on?'

'Yeah, they are going on...'

'Ju...u...st going on! What type of answer is this Gayatri? You should tell me with bubbling confidence that you are striding ahead in your life and others are gaping in amazement at your pace.'

Her eyes are still downcast.

'Look at my eyes. You are fighting a battle to come out from the old mould. The day you are able to look straight at the eyes of another person your metamorphosis into a new person will be complete dear. In our oriental culture it's taught that eye-to-eye contact is a sign of disrespect. In western culture, it's believed that only a sense of guilt prevents eye contact between two individuals. Yesterday a sweet, petite Japanese girl Mikako came to me. She is distraught. Her professor in Sociology asked her – what's wrong with you Mikako? Why can't you raise your eyes and talk to me straight? In her own country she was praised for her humility, for this apparent sheen of femininity and here she has been reproached exactly for this insolence. I told her – go ahead, be a chameleon and merge in this culture.'

Gayatri slowly raises her head. A bright, red mark on the forehead of Mrs. Kundan! The mark of a Hindu married woman! That reminds her of the *Trinetra*, the third eye of the Lord Shiva, the god of destruction. That eye exhorts her to wake up with full vigor.

'This red bindi arouses curiosity in this country.' Mrs. Kundan follows her gaze. 'Once we were traveling and a large car which was coming behind us lost balance. It hit our small, sports car. Nothing happened. But the policeman refused to believe me that everything was fine. He looked at my forehead and told me, 'blood is oozing out from your forehead.' Mrs. Kundan bursts out in a hearty laugh.

Nikkei brings two coffee mugs and places in front of them.

'Thank you Nikkei. You can give one to Greg, one to Nora. Rudolf is not interested in coffee. How to keep him amused? He maybe interested in some spy-related films. Please tell him to find a VCD in the basement hall and entertain himself.'

Nikkei goes away hurriedly. Mrs. Kundan stares blankly at the roof.

'Rudolf is a sweet guy. His father died in Vietnam-war. Mother remarried. His disciplinarian stepfather used to treat him with strictness when he was just a child. He had to find an imaginary enemy for all his troubles during his growing up years. His over-imaginative mind penned one: America! In medical terminology, he has been suffering from an ailment called Delusional Paranoia. What he has been looking for and not getting is love, care and emotional security. He's close to his brother Greg and his stepfather's friend Nora. I'm slowly and gradually taking the place of a friend who's not going to shun him for his outbursts. He can confide in me. Love is such a powerful force that it can change everything.'

Shakuntala Kundan looks distressed and concerned.

'Tell me about you. How're you doing?'

'We've shifted to a smaller house. A one-bedroom apartment. No space even to accommodate the childhood toys of my dear children. I'm doing a lot of odd jobs here and there. I've joined as a cleaning-woman in our community centre and the community gym. On the very first day of my work, when I started wiping the floor with a huge vacuum cleaner, tears almost blurred my vision.'

'You're forced to take the broom for livelihood! I understand your predicament Gayatri! Now tell me, has Siddhartha sent any money for the house or for the children?'

'No.'

'Have you spoken to him on this issue?'

'No. I've spoken only to Vinayak, my lawyer who sent a notice to Siddhartha.'

'How has he reacted to your soliciting legal help?'

'He's extremely angry. He's so angry that he told me on phone not to transgress my limits.'

'Do you remember the moment of Siddhartha's going away from your life?'

'Yes, I remember it vividly. He was enthusiastic over his selection as professor in biotechnology in Chicago University. The moment he was about to get into his vehicle he told me in a soft and almost inaudible voice, 'Nora is also coming. She's joining the same university.' I almost froze there. Like an ice-maiden I waved at him though I knew that I was bidding a good-bye to him from my life.'

Mrs. Kundan draws some meaningless sketches with her on the paper lying in front of her. A veritable clutter of abstruse figures on the visage!

'You know Mrs. Kundan, I have started observing a woman very keenly since the last few days?'

Mrs. Kundan suddenly fixes her snooping gaze on Gayatri.

'The woman is my neighbor. She comes out from a nearby apartment. She's an obese, rotund, podgy woman. I don't know which term may aptly describe her size and shape. Every day she wears the same pair of pant and trouser. Color is faded. She carries a load of pain on her swollen, glum face.'

Gayatri is anxious. Her uneasiness is conspicuous.

'I've developed a curiosity for this queer creature. One day I followed her to the bus and boarded it. I occupied the nearby seat. This has become my daily routine during the last few days. Yesterday I tried to talk to her. I was under the impression that she had been going through a lot of trouble and must be waiting for a sympathetic listener. But the moment I asked her where she was going, she almost screamed out in sheer panic. Her words were not very clear. But she asked me why I was stalking her and what my designs were.'

'From tomorrow onwards you cannot follow this woman and that has made you sad, isn't it? During the last few days all your thoughts have been centered round this woman and in one stroke you are out of this self-created deceptive job. You wanted to escape from your own tribulations.'

Nikkei puts two small Pepsi bottles in front of them. She moves away like a hurricane after accomplishing her job.

'You cannot forget Siddhartha. You lived with him for full fifteen years. He's the father of your two lovely children. But he has gone out of your life, my dear lady! This is the truth. The sooner you accept this bitter truth, the sooner you're going to go ahead with your life.'

Mrs. Kundan puts her right hand on Gayatri's fragile shoulder. 'Please do not go to Vinayak. Compensation from Siddhartha? Could he ever compensate you for your hurt pride and your injured feeling? The answer is a big No. Even then, don't try to build your future on an edifice of anger. When I mentioned the name Nora, a different woman who is Rudolf's stepfather's friend, an elderly person far removed from your life, you seemed to have recoiled in disgust. You need to forgive everyone including Siddhartha and Nora.'

When she is about to step out of Mrs. Kundan's clinic, her eyes met those of Rudolf's brother. He has been sitting in close proximity to that frail, old lady called Nora but his mind seems to have been wandering in a distant horizon. Rudolf is seen nowhere. He must be busy watching a spy film and his qualms and his insecurities must be merrily in sync with what has been going on in a flurry of actions of that make-believe world.

✦ ✦ ✦

4

Effective Communication course has reached its final phase. Gayatri is going to present a discussion on a speech of her choice. Initially she zeroed on Jawaharlal Nehru's famous speech 'Our Tryst with Destiny' delivered in the midnight of India's brush with independence. Then she abandoned the idea. What is the point in discussing Nehru with these students whose vision is totally circumscribed by a monolith called America?

Some of the students bereft of any enthusiasm for an unfamiliar and apparently non-American name would just ask, 'Who's Mr. Nehru? Is he still alive?' Lara Sinclair, in embarrassment, is going to undertake a near-impossible mission of making them comprehend the vast panorama of Jawaharlal Nehru's life. The students will nod their heads forcefully to veil their absolute indifference.

They cannot be blamed either. They have been fed so profusely with the notion of American greatness since their childhood that an outside world becomes almost invisible in their mindscape. Tales about three hundred years of glorious existence of their motherland and heroic deeds of George Washington, Abraham Lincoln, Thomas Jefferson,

Robert Lee and the likes have been implanted so firmly in the impressionable minds that they start peering at the world from their divine existence. They develop a natural apathy or suspicion towards anything not grown in America. Not Invented Here or NIH is the phrase coined by some people to describe this American indifference for ideas taking shape elsewhere other than in America.

After she came out of her cloistered life last year, Gayatri met a few Americans who never felt the urge to go out and see the world. What is there to see somewhere else? We are in the most beautiful and noblest country of the world. They reasoned. Even a highly esteemed bioscientist like Nora once told her, 'Look Gayatri, I'm an American citizen and by virtue of that I've become a global citizen too. How can I remain unruffled by so much poverty and darkness afflicting the other spheres of my dear little globe?'

The vanity of the Civilization's Child was very much apparent in this suave lady's voice.

Nora was shattered when she saw preponderance of poverty in the vicinity of the Taj Mahal, the podium of love. It was narrated by Siddhartha to her in one of those days when they were together. Nora was a college student. Her taxi was stopped on the way by a beggar-woman who was carrying a frail child. The woman was starving. The child was crying in hunger. Nora could not sleep for days together after this incident.

Was Nora that emotional? A woman, who could fritter away several million dollars in the name of cloning rather than in assuaging human misery, could really shed tears at the plight of the browbeaten? Had she been so dim-witted not to appreciate the simple logic that even a fraction of the mind-boggling amount spent in her mindless race with the Creator was more than enough to chase a curse like poverty away from the streets of Agra?

Nora Roberts! World famous bioscientist, Siddhartha's companion! She wants to forget everything about Nora. A temporary amnesia should obliterate the bitter memories.

Gayatri was a very ordinary woman busy in her mundane life. Her brush with American life was confined to her interaction with the sales-woman at the shopping mall or her occasional interface with highly sophisticated person like Nora. Even in that situation also she sometime tends to feel that most of the Americans go to the under-privileged countries not with a desire to unify their spirit with the soul of that country but to shore up their already heightened self-image in the midst of a swirling sea of miseries. So much poverty! So much dust! Such rampant despair! It is our duty to save the civilization of the world!

With this attitude in mind most of the Americans supported the American invasion of Iraq a decade and a half back for the defense of Kuwait when a great majority of them were not even aware whether Kuwait was in Asia, Africa or Antarctica.

The Vietnam War was not an act of aggression but an act of war to defend civilization!

Saddam Hussein is a barbaric despot and deserves to be reproved! The war against Iraq has proved to be costly in terms of American lives. The fall out is a public outcry. But Public opinion in America tilted against mayhem in Vietnam or Iraq not because of its unethical dimensions but because of so many Americans losing their lives and limbs in those pointless conflicts or the home economy suffering immensely in these wars.

The American story is itself a story of might triumphing over reason. It was the land of the Native Americans and they were marginalized completely in their own land by the marauding Europeans through use of vicious forces. Discovery of America was credited to Columbus, a sea-bandit and Columbus Day was observed with a lot of fanfare on 2nd Monday of October every year.

The Native Americans have now raised a voice of protest. They have scoffed down with zeal the very idea of a discovery of their homeland credited to a seafaring brigand, 'What's there to discover? A landmass called America has already been there on the global map. Columbus just landed up there when he started a voyage in quest of a flourishing country called India. He didn't create a new land nor did he find out a virgin area. When he set his foot on this country it has already been pulsating with life. He tried to throttle that life with his saga of carnage. Why should there be homage for a felon like Columbus?'

Because of these protests Columbus is no longer projected as the national icon by the country. But that does not pale into insignificance the tales of tortures perpetrated by the invading gun-wielding people on the Native Americans to establish their rule of might. There were brutal stories of infecting an unsuspecting mass of people, the Native Americans, with small pox virus and wiping out a vast majority of them through these vicious means.

The same nation is now trying to assume the role of a conscious-keeper for the entire humanity and shows signs of restlessness at human rights violation elsewhere.

No, there is no point in talking about brilliant oriental speakers like Dr. Radhakrishnan or Jawaharlal Nehru in front of this megalomaniac American crowd.

She suddenly realizes with deepening horror that she is also paranoid about America like Rudolf and she needs to forsake it on her way to a better life.

Gayatri is in look out for a better paying job and for that she is to strive desperately for a good grade in Effective Communication. Enthusiastic participation from her course-mates may not be forthcoming if Nehru's speech is thrown open to them for a meaningful debate. And Lara Sinclair will have good reason to believe that Gayatri's analysis has failed to evoke any perceptible curiosity in the class. She cannot afford to play a gamble with her career or for that matter with her life at this crucial juncture. A column-writer's post has fallen vacant recently in the local paper. An American degree may bolster her chances of landing up that job. Mrs. Kundan has only informed her about that vacancy and has been encouraging her to apply. 'Apply for that job. You are cut out for it. I am confident.'

You are cut out for it! Such beautiful words!

If Siddhartha had told her once! Only once!

A video film is going to be shown to the class now. 'How to Flirt!' The caption is amusing. As soon as this film-show is over she will have to tell the name of the personality whose speech she is supposed to dissect in all its dimensions in the next class. She has to think real hard.

The video-film is progressing. A thin, middle-aged brunette dressed precariously in a midriff-baring shirt and tight jean slowly proceeds towards an elderly, bald person with sharp features inside the book store. She let a fat, bound book to fall with a thud on the floor. She is attracted to this man and this is her way of conveying that message. The man instantly looks at the book and then he glances at her with a kind smile. She returns that smile with an embarrassing grin. He goes away slowly in the other direction. 'No, Priscilla has failed to hold his attention. She was not confident and that was obvious in her body-language. Confidence is the key to success in any such ventures.' A grave male voice in the background has been giving away observations like an erudite scholar preaching discourse on metaphysical matters.

The next scene! Clara and her colleague Ray. Clara has invited Ray for lunch in a restaurant. Ray has accepted with a smile. So far it has been progressing well. The camera zooms on Clara. There is longing in Ray's eyes. Suddenly Clara scratches her head. Then she starts to tug on the hemline of her not-too-long skirt. The look of desire in Ray's eyes has been taken over by a cold irritability. 'Oh shit! It's over. Who is going to desire a woman who scratches her head on the first date?' It is another male voice, garbed in total disappointment, from the background. Then the same voice has gone on elaborating the retinue of desirable qualities a person looks for in his partner. No one wants to discuss Japanese attack on Pearl Harbor or G8 summit on a first date. Man prefers a dumb, frivolous woman as his partner who can giggle at the slightest provocation. 'Clara, the girl from Memphis has lost out badly...'

Girl from Memphis! Memphis? There is a chord somewhere. Yes, she got it. Eureka!

Lara Sinclair stands toweringly in front of her desk. 'Have you made up your mind Gayatri?'

She nods her head. She has made up her mind. She no longer treads on an undecided territory. 'I Have A Dream.' She announced. The entire class looks at her. Lara raises her right hand and with a rhythmic motion of her raised hand she speaks out in a musical tone, 'Martin Luther King. Okay guys, we are listening to Gayatri in the next class...'

✦

'I Have A Dream' speech fired the imaginations of one million African-American people who congregated in Washington on a sweltering summer day of 1963. With fluttered hearts and buoyed hopes they dreamt of equality and liberty.

But bombs exploded in a number of cities as counter reaction to this non-violent uprising and many people lost their lives.

Martha Harris, a colleague of Siddhartha, was a frequent visitor to their house because of her love for spicy Indian food. She was very critical about the imperceptible but very solid racial segregation in American society. 'White racial group like Ku Klux Klan still has a sizeable following. How many mixed couples have you seen in the last few years of your stay here? Love usually doesn't blossom between the African-Americans and the Whites. There is always an invisible wall between the two.'

Gayatri was barred from using the words like Black or Negro by Siddhartha even before they landed up in America, 'These are considered offensive. They're now referred to as African Americans.'

Martha's diatribes against the white people irritated Siddhartha very much. 'Martha could accomplish so much only through the affirmative action.... A war was fought just for the cause of giving them equality. Who espoused their cause? Who fought for them? White-Americans! But this ungrateful lot is not content.'

When Gayatri was a young girl, her father read out a portion of that famous book 'The Adventures of Huckleberry Fin' to her. The suffering of Jim, the Black companion of the main protagonist Huck-Fin, at the hands of the White people, filled her heart with compassion for that vulnerable boy. 'Tom Uncle's Cabin' which acted as a catalyst against racialism in America also made her shed tears at the plight of the Black people.

The compassion and the feelings, implanted in her mind by her father when she was a young girl, have been flowing in her psyche unabated. She protested, so many times, against Siddhartha's spiteful comments, 'They didn't come to America on their own. They were chained and shipped to an unknown land to work as slaves. Don't you think that they should be suitably compensated later for this grave injustice meted out in the past?'

She also shared her anguish over casteism and resultant untouchability prevailing in the Indian Hindu society with Martha. '...When we were in elementary school a young, jovial man came to sell snacks to the school children. Most of the children refused to buy from him. Why? Someone spread the news that he was born in the sweeper-caste. Children shied away. In my grandmother's place, there were separate sets of crockery for the use of the so-called lower-caste people...'

Martha was like a family friend and would drop in without any prior announcement. She was full of life and used to emblazon the atmosphere with her gleeful recounting of events. She hardly went to visit her people in Philadelphia. 'I've only one brother. He's an alcoholic. My own people laugh at me for emulating the refined behavior of the White people!'

Siddhartha also concurred, 'Most of the Black people talk very loudly and most of them use obscene words on slightest provocation. They don't want to slog like their White counterparts. That has ensured their permanent place in the cycle of poverty.'

A few days back an African American professor of Brown University wrote a book against Affirmative Action. His contention was that the Affirmative Action had actually crippled this vast majority of people. 'When the pressure to perform is not there the motivation to excel also withers away.' He spoke of the only African American girl in his class who never bothered to finish her assignments on time. When asked, her convenient excuse was death of some family members. 'At that rate her granny from maternal side died four times in the year and her mom died twice. She is from a well-to-do family. I'm there as her professor. Where's the question of discrimination in her case...?'

The book 'Some thoughts on Positive Discrimination' created a stir in the Brown University campus at that point of time.

Her decision to talk on the great legend Martin Luther King and his celebrated speech brought back many memories, both bitter and sweet, which were lying inert in her mindscape for long.

A few years back Gayatri and her family traveled by the Amtrak train between Pittsburg and Philadelphia. There was a shoot-out incident, the day before, on that train. One beautiful lady just whipped out her pistol and fired in the air without provocation. The train was full of security people that day. One police officer came to Gayatri and politely demanded to check the contents. He was profusely apologetic. When done, he thanked her for the cooperation. Then the commotion started. An African American lady in her black leather coat and pants started screaming in a shrill voice, 'What do you think? Just because I'm black, you're going to frisk me? This is racism!' The police officer quietly went away to the other direction.

Siddhartha's bias against the African-Americans was so strong that he scoffed at Gayatri's excited admiration for the magical skills of Michael Jordan or for the splendid showmanship of Oprah Winfrey. 'They're good only in two things, music and games. The white people have engaged them in these two pursuits. They bring the maximum number of medals for the country during Olympic.'

There was no trace of respect in Siddhartha's voice.

The day was 13th January, the birthday of Martin Luther King. Martha was clearly excited. 'We've organized Miss Dark-skinned Pennsylvania contest today. The beauty-pageant was a huge success. In my inaugural address, I told the gathering that beauty is not synonymous with fair-complexion. The way the whites despise our dark color, we too are not impressed by their not-too-excitable pale skin.'

Gayatri knew Martha was in dialogue with herself; she was deliberating with her own stubborn beliefs.

'But I received a Hate Mail today in my mail-box. The anonymous writer has threatened me that he's going to finish me off for my tirade against the White people.' Gayatri could hear a sigh of grief-laden despair in Martha's faint voice. 'We're going to organize protest....'

But what was amazing for Gayatri was that the new African immigrants have been barred from showing solidarity with the cause. 'They're gold-diggers. They've never faced slavery and all the cruelties associated with slavery. They've trooped in at a time when everything seems to be fine. How can we, the baseball-loving African Americans, identify ourselves with the cricket-loving new immigrants from Zimbabwe just because we share the same skin color?'

Martha's annoyance with these new entrants from the African continent is a fresh input for Gayatri's carefully built-up archive on this riddle called America.

Martha has been keeping in touch with Gayatri even after Siddhartha's sudden flight from the scene. Her occasional phone-calls in the lonely, desolate evenings are always very refreshing. 'You're young and pretty. Why don't you find out someone else? Look at me. I've lot of lovers. But no plan for settling down with a particular guy...!'

One evening she dropped in their place. 'I want spicy Indian food. Biriyani and Chicken Tikka.' Her demand was strident, somewhat more than vociferous. And that is Martha. She would bring verve wherever she goes.

The close-up of Rev. Peter Johnson's face on the TV screen! The much revered Rev. Peter Johnson! Martha's idol and almost a divine figure for a huge chunk of people.

He was not in his usual poised self. His demeanor was that of a person who lost everything. Relationship with a young girl and fathering a child from that relationship was indefensible for a moralist like him whose virulent condemnation of

Clinton's action was aired with much bonhomie days earlier. Gayatri saw him several times on TV during Clinton-Monica Lewinsky episode sharing screen space with a number of other unabashed Clinton-baiters on this issue. Another gossip of Peter Johnson's swindling of federal money given for church activities in the African-American dominated areas also vied for space in the media. Gayatri was familiar with this name.

'Why so much noise over Peter Johnson? Just because his skin color isn't white, he has been hounded! See Gye, others do worse things and they merrily escape.'

'Mr. Johnson hasn't done a decent thing either....' Gayatri was agitated but calm.

She is going to inform Martha about her plan to talk about Martin Luther King. Martha is surely going to be thrilled and might give her some tips to make the discussions livelier.

On the appointed day, Gayatri initiates her discussion on 'I Have a Dream' speech. The social scenario of the 60s, with feminism-Hippism kind of things in tow, becomes the vast landscape under whose canopy this speech is discussed.

During the last journey of that apostle of peace and equality, his wife and four little children were dazed with grief but showed no apparent signs of it. Gayatri is in tears while describing the last journey of Martin Luther King. Suddenly so much grief and misery have been competing for an outlet that they almost catch her off-balance during the deliberations!

Discussions and the commentaries are lively! The entire class is involved in this saga of heroism and sacrifice! All the white students condemn a monster called racism of the 60s and dwells upon the significance of the speech in the context of the present day America which stands for international harmony. Outpouring of emotions from the anchor enhances its dramatic exquisiteness.

Lara Sinclair seems to be overjoyed. Lucia, the brightest girl in the class, is going to sum up. Lara wants it that way. 'America has become a great Melting Pot of the world now with diverse communities proclaiming unique togetherness. If Martin Luther King was brought back to the world today, he would be overwhelmed by the expanse of our mental horizon at this point of human history. The Great America is on her way to extend this therapeutic vision to an entire world vivisected by sectarian considerations. Our friend Gayatri whom we affectionately call Gye was great as an initiator of the discussions. Her attempt at integrating the speech with the path-breaking events of the turbulent decade was superb. She deserves congratulations.'

There is continual thumping of desks and she feels overjoyed.

✦

Two strange but disparate events occurred at the same time. Mamata, a friend committed suicide and Gayatri got "A" grade in Effective Communication course.

Manish is shattered; his stupefied gaze at the gyrating world outside appositely conveys the wreckage inside. How it has all happened? It was a normal autumn morning. Mamata, his wife was watching the colorful leaves of the oak tree in front of the house, totally enthralled. How could one tree carry so many different colors on it? Before withering away in the chilling winter, the trees probably wanted to show their fiery passion in a poignant autumn. 'It's a deceiving act, you know

Manish! To bloom before you go.' Mamata's monologues were heard.

'I've given up the idea of becoming a medical practitioner. Why not try some other avenues? So many opportunities are there waiting to be picked up...' Mamata's words were laden with hopes. She had been trying so hard to pass the qualifying examination for the medical practitioners during the last three years, but success was eluding her. Her childhood friend and husband Manish had passed in the first attempt and he was a busy registered practitioner.

Manish was happy. His happiness doubled when he saw a beautifully-dressed Mamata waving him from the front-yard of the Immigration and Naturalization Office building after he dropped her there on his way to the hospital.

'I didn't know that it was the last time I could see my wife.' Manish is inconsolable.

Mamata was putting all her bodily force on the massive glass-door but it refused to budge from its place. Then it opened on its own and one official sitting in one of the plastic chairs pointed his fingers at the word AUTOMATIC, written in red color in bold letters on the glass door, with a disdainful smile. His customary 'How can I help you?' query was also very scornful. 'If you want to experience another facet of American civility, come to this office. We're treated like beggars who've come for alms here.' Mamata's hurt pride was revealed through her faint sobbing in the phone when she called up Manish.

'I've got H2 Visa. My husband's a professional. What should I do to get work-permit? Should I apply for Social Security first?'

This thin man with an elongated face looked at her again with utter contempt. 'Social Security? Are you a retiree?' His small eyes were sneering at her.

'No, I mean the social security number.'

The man was not making any real attempt to enlighten her about all the regulations for getting a social security number. He just gave her a form and told her to fill it up in due course attaching the essential documents. At the time of her departure, Mamata was weeping like a small girl while narrating all these to Manish on phone. 'What was the point in coming to a foreign land and getting all these humiliations? I could have worked in a small Medical Dispensary in my home country and lived with my pride intact.'

Gayatri has understood the trauma of Mamata. She also feels for this little boy sitting downcast in front of her at the moment. She is not finding any words to soothe his wrecked feeling. But silence has its own weight too which becomes too heavy in certain situations. She must keep up some pretences of conversation. 'I also applied for a work-permit after Siddhartha was gone.' Manish slowly raises his head and looks at her with his swelling, red eyes. Her pain and his pain must meet at a point. 'The angular distance between the face and the head in the passport-sized photograph in the application for work permit should be 30 degrees. My first application was rejected on that ground. After I became a student it was issued without much fuss. I saw rudeness all around at that time....'

Her sigh is audible.

'In our country, hordes of astrologers, palmists, soothsayers, friends, gossipy family members play a part in retrieving your bruised heart in some way or the other. Here, you don't get any outlet to bare your mind and soul.... She has been depressed. But I could never imagine that she'd take her own life...'

Manish weeps like a child in distress. Gayatri leaves in a huff so that he can be with himself.

She applied for the job of managing the women page of the local daily 'State College Time' and got it.

'One look at you and I knew that I had got the right person. My choice has always been right.' Greg Amherst's words have touched Gayatri. So much trust on an ordinary woman like her! She must not fail him. Greg whom she met briefly in Mrs. Kundan's clinic didn't display any flicker of recognition during their meeting in his office.

She rushes to Mrs. Kundan. Mrs. Kundan is ecstatic. 'Didn't I tell you earlier that life sometime emerges out of ruin also? Human mind and Noah's Arch have some uncanny similarities. Both relentlessly carry seeds of new creation in the face of acute destruction. Your life's going to take a turn for the better.'

She tells Mrs. Kundan about so many other things in her flawed Hindi! 'After we came to this small town as a newly-married couple, we used to go very frequently to a solitary place between Springtown Park and Kellydon Lake. It's a beautiful place with the abundant nature in full glory. We used to sit on the stone-bench placed at the undulating ground between the lake and the park and Siddhartha would plant kisses all over me. The coy Indian woman inside me would come out sometime, at such moments, to make me conscious about that very public display of emotion, usually forbidden in our country. One summer evening, when a cool breeze from the otherwise placid lake was whistling past the trapped, grim warmth of the park, our bodies became one on the soft, green, grass-carpet under the watchful eyes of a demure moon.'

Her eyes meet Mrs. Kundan's eyes. Mrs. Kundan's deadpan face is inscrutable. 'I went to the same spot yesterday. The ground was full of leaves of all colors, a testimony to a colorful autumn. The cool breeze from the lake was still blowing. Everything has been the same excepting the fact that Siddhartha was no longer there in the frame. A suppressed cry came out from me. One couple who were snuggling to each other behind the bush sped away in panic. The pale moon was staring at me from the lake. She remained a speechless witness to my intermittent howling. When my sobbing was over, I felt so much lighter. The weight called Siddhartha vanished to a very large extent from the edge of my mind at that very moment. Things have been happening at fast pace during the last few days. My e-mail conveyed the good news of my getting an A grade. Then this job in my kitty now.'

Mrs. Kundan slowly gets up from the chair and pats her right shoulder with lot of affection. 'I understand that our relationship should have been purely professional. You were in a mess and you paid me to get some professional help for coming out of that jumble. Where's the place for emotion here? But life's equations maybe at variance with the mathematical ones. I've met many people in this profession who come here for specialized support but later on develop so much attachment with me that they sometime propose to spend their life with me. Strange, isn't it? As a psychotherapist, I draw the line between emotion and reality in such cases. But with you it's so different. You no longer need my assistance is a good news. I might see less of you is a bad news. I'm both happy and sad.'

While opening the door for her, Mrs. Kundan clasps her hands and tells her, 'You can come here anytime. My doors are always open for you.'

It is a new life for Gayatri. Since the last one week she has started jogging and joined a yoga class. Sara, the thin, young girl gave a short, crisp lecture on yoga for the beginners. 'Yoga means union. Blending of mind and body and unification of man and God! The health of the hardware called Body is determined by the software called Mind. Through yoga your soul is elevated to a higher level and you are connected to the universal soul.'

Sara paused for a while. She might now talk about Beatlemania and George Harrison's role in popularizing yoga in the 60s. The four Beatles came in contact with Maharshi Mahesh Yogi and they camped in his ashram along with Mia Farrow. Their fascination for the yoga made the West sit up and take notice of this oriental fitness mantra though these youth icons of the 60s fell out with Mahesh Yogi amidst allegations of the yogi eyeing their girlfriends and resources. John Lennon even went to the extent of composing a song lampooning the yogi, 'Sexy Sadie, what've you done! You've made a fool of everyone.' But the lightning speed of yoga in the West as a means of physical and emotional well-being could not be arrested after this impressive opening.

It seemed Sara had got no time to delve into such long and somewhat needless deliberations.

Today she has already started the breathing exercises. Gayatri has to learn and be fit enough to fight her new battle.

'Inhale...slo-o-o-w-ly...and exha-a-ale. Please close your eyes. The air's going inside you and embracing your entire being. Impurities are coming out through your breath....'

A cool breeze has been blowing in that autumnal evening. The light jacket is not enough of a protection to ward off cold. But Gayatri is not perturbed. She is in a mood to fly with that animated breeze. On reaching her apartment she checks her mail-box. There are two mails from India. The rest are very colorful discount coupons. She switches on the heating arrangement inside the house and comfortably perches herself on the sofa. The first mail is from her mother. The not-so-legible handwriting of her mother has its own language, the language of unalloyed love. 'People have come to know about my son-in-law's issue. So many of us are there these days! I've dismissed it as a story.... Anjali's mother has comeback. She has spoken so much about that beautiful country that all of us feel like going there. She enjoyed her stay in that lovely place...'

The other mail is from her brother-in-law, 'Could you find out why our brother got annoyed with you and left you in a haste...?'

Now she is going to open the large, red envelope. 'If you are lucky, you may get a hundred-dollar bill inside.' Lots of offers are there – buy two pizzas in Pizza Hut and you will get one pizza free...buy two cassettes and you will get 10% discount on the third cassette...25% discount on the entry-fee of the Mio Zio Disco....

There is no hundred-dollar bill inside. Katie has also been looking expectantly at the envelope.

'We might get next time.' Katie's voice vibrates with hope.

'If not next time, we might get some other time.'

Gayatri joins her daughter in this trance of exhilaration, in this saga of hope and dream.

Dreams and hope should never go away from life.

✦ ✦ ✦

5

It was such an exhilarating feeling! Gayatri has just finished her job of acting as an intermediary between a mentally challenged Indian origin child's parents and some voluntary charitable groups which have come forward to help the child. The elementary school where her children Gaurav and Katie began their education was the initiator in organizing help for the child and the principal requested Gayatri's help in smooth flow of views from one side to the other. The parents, particularly the mother, though not being recent migrants had difficulty in communicating with the would-be-benefactors in American English and Gayatri could bridge the gap effortlessly between these two worlds.

She feels immensely grateful to Anjali, Dr. Kundan and Lara Sinclair at the moment for pushing her this far and also to the school for reposing so much trust on her. This is the same school where she spent quite a bit of time of her life on different occasions as parent of two young, restive kids.

Gaurav's first day of school was marked by a get-together of students, their parents and the teachers. A kind of eclectic bonhomie was apparent in the air. 'We need volunteers from parents to come for an hour on a particular day of the week and help us in the class.'

The principal's request was greeted with round of applause. The Principal, a kind rotund lady was visibly pleased. She lowered her voice a little and went on, 'We're particularly fortunate in the State College. It's a multicultural community and parents have come from diverse cultural background. Our students may see the world through the prism of your eyes.'

Further clapping followed her speech.

Gayatri joined the school as a parent volunteer. Those days were sweet, innocent ones. She tried to bring some semblance of orderliness to the class by commanding in her broken English and curiosity for this exotic language was more than enough to keep these little ones still for a few initial moments. However, that did not prevent them from bouncing back with a lot more vigor later.

One day the class teacher Mrs. Morgan told Gayatri to speak something about India and her native place.

She was making a valiant attempt at drawing the sketch of a one-horned Assam rhino and it was turning out to be the picture of a completely different non-existent animal. The kids, being convinced that what was drawn on the Board was the replica of an unheard of animal called rhino, were drawing their own venial adaptation of that alien species.

'Garry's mom, where's your home?' Tess, the doll like little girl in the class, was looking at her and the rhino with amazement.

Gayatri rushed to the atlas that was hanging on the wall and rotated her index finger very gently over a tiny landscape.

'What else is there in your place?' Bernard, as usual, was very inquisitive.

'A huge animal called elephant, a fierce animal called tiger, innumerable birds, lots of green and lots and lots of people. If you open a window of your house there you will see a huge procession of people all the time.'

They were looking at her bewildered. Their innocent eyes were emitting exhilaration.

'We have a place in our homeland where we get the maximum rainfall in the world.' Gayatri's finger was trying to locate Cherrapunji and Mausinram in the map. She knew it to be an impossible task but was pretending to be doing it.

'Do you get bored in so much rain?'

Mrs. Morgan was not happy with Jesse for such a question. 'Do you get bored with snowfall Jesse?'

'Nooo...' The kids said in unison.

'Why?'

'We can go for skating...we can make snowmen...we can throw snowballs at one another...we can wear red jackets...' There was so much enthusiasm!

'Rain is also very beautiful. The sky gets covered with cloud. These naughty clouds fall as rain in different patterns. Children can make paper-boats and the paper-boats go and go up to the sea. Rivers become full and colorful fish float on them. Colorful rainbows form after that.' Mrs. Morgan's picturesque description of a vibrant rainfall had a poetic flavor to create an aura about an ordinary happening.

'India, my country, is a huge country. But it is smaller than America. It is full of people. Do you know how Columbus discovered America? Columbus was actually looking for India. You know India was full of jewels at that time? It had nice-looking prince and princesses and very big palaces. But he lost his way in the sea and arrived in a land that was later on named as America. There was no big road or big house in America at that time. Poor Columbus! He named all the people in America as Indians. Till these days native people are sometime called American Indians.'

The small children with angel-like faces were listening to Gary's mom with rapt attention. A new land, new stories!

'There were many hermits, the people living in forest or in the hills praying and thinking in India long, long years back. They found out so many things. They didn't have any machine but they knew all about the stars in the sky. They also knew that the earth moves around the sun...Tess, suppose you are given one chocolate and you have eaten that chocolate immediately. You are left with how many chocolates?'

Tess was little bit bewildered. 'None...'

'Yes, none. What number is that one, two or...?'

'Zero, Garry's mom...'

'Correct, it is zero. Those hermits, praying monks and thinking people in India found out about this number at that time. Mathematics, the sums you do with Mrs. Morgan, developed only after that. India is not a very rich country these days, but it's still a very interesting country. How many of you would like to go there?'

Graham raised his hand and all the kids, as if on a cue, raised their hands in unison.

'Good, I'll take all of you to that country one day when you grow up.'

She put her index finger on Assam and started 'Whatever is eaten in this place or whatever is worn here is not eaten or worn in this other place.' Her finger had swiftly moved to another place on the west side of India's map and was resting there when she was making the second part of her statement. Then her finger made another downward sloping movement towards southern tip. 'The people here do not understand the languages of the other two places and they eat different food. Even they look different.'

Mrs. Morgan's face lit brightly. She was going inside a new world. She joined the group of listeners.

'India is such a diverse country. But there is some inherent strength in that society. Democracy has been going on and there was never an attempt to topple a government.'

Gayatri made this concluding statement for the consumption of an adult listener like Mrs. Morgan. Democracy or toppling of Government really had no meaning for these very young children whose world revolved round snowman, burgers or an exotic fairy tale realm of prince or princesses.

Mrs. Morgan was nodding her head excitedly.

'Sorry Mrs. Morgan. I'm not fluent in English. I can't express all my thoughts in this language.'

'Why should you be sorry? You have at least made an effort to speak an alien language and that's incredible. Look at me. I do not know any language other than English.'

Mrs. Morgan's sincerity was obvious. She spoke from her heart.

'Can I show my country Mrs. Morgan?' It was Krista. But she was not waiting for permission and immediately sat down on the floor to find and show her own country on the map. Her face was glowing in anticipation.

'We came from that place to America by a very weak wooden boat. It was such a long trip. In another boat our uncle and his family also came. But they got drowned on the way....'

Mrs. Morgan and Gayatri looked intently at the map. Some tiny red landmasses were floating in a huge pool of blue water. Cuba. The Bay of Mexico was separating them from America. Only one sea was standing between two profoundly conflicting systems.

'Please show one of your folk dances.' Mrs. Morgan wanted to ease the situation. Gayatri also wanted to come out of the palpable tension.

How could she bring herself to swing her body in front of so many onlookers on that day is still a mystery to her! In no time she found herself to be surrounded by all the tiny-tots who joined in that brouhaha of song and dance. Mrs. Morgan's enthusiasm was in stiff competition with her own very plump body when she was swiveling her fat waist in that scenario of merry-making.

'This is Bihu dance, our own folk dance. This is a dance of love in the lap of nature.' Gayatri tried to explain but felt terribly guilty at the same time that a very beautiful, rhythmic dance of her area has been spoilt by her inept handling in front of a foreign audience.

But the children savored her coconut laddoo. 'Garry's mom, your coconut cake is very tasty.' Graham was looking really happy. 'Please tell my mom to make ones like these.' He came slowly towards her and asked her in a hushed tone, 'Can you give me another piece?'

Gayatri gave him her own piece. He ran away. Mrs. Morgan was not amused.

'Graham, come here.'

Graham looked back. 'Why didn't you thank Garry's mom?'

Next day the school bag of Gaurav was full to the brim with multi-colored 'Thank You' cards. Drawing-papers were made into rectangular cards with pictures of trees or houses or cakes. 'Thank you for your talks. We knew so much about India.' Another child wrote, 'Your coconut cake so tasty. Thank you.' Another one wrote: 'Your dance was very good. Can that song be sung with a guitar?' All the innocent writings on the cards were amusingly full of spelling mistakes.

A huge and elaborate thank you card from Mrs. Morgan.

After two years her daughter Katyayani went to the same school and Gayatri became Katie's mom this time. She repeated all those old stories with the same passion.

Drew, the naughty boy in the class, was putting his little palms on hers and asking, 'Katie's mom, why your color is so different from that of mine? Yours is mud color.'

Mrs. Morgan was aghast. 'Drew, didn't I tell you that you were not supposed to ask question on somebody's color or god?'

Gayatri was trying to put Mrs. Morgan at ease. 'They're small children and very pure. They want to know the world. Let them be innocent kids.'

The quietest boy in the class Niew was scribbling something with his illegible handwriting. 'Your Dad might be upset if he finds that you are writing something not very nice.'

Niew did not lose his composure. 'My Dad doesn't stay with us and I hate him.'

An interesting episode which happened during that period often comes to her mind to provide a comic relief at forlorn times when she was down with the pain of rejection and bogged down under so many responsibilities. One day Katie came back home with the information that a pest was found crawling on the floor of the classroom. She opened her exercise book and showed her mom a drawing of that insect. Gayatri looked at the drawing intently for some time and on an impulse drew another of the same kind that looked more stable with a firm outline.

'Yes, mummy, this is the insect. How could you draw it so well? You didn't even see it...' Katie's eyes were sparkling in amazement at this artwork indulged in by her mother who otherwise never showed any proclivity for any kind of fine art.

'I've seen so many of them during my school and college days that we literally grew up with them. All girls in school had them in abundance in their long unkempt hair. I also had a plentiful of them. In college I washed my hair with a shampoo that promised a lice-free head. It was effective. But many girls at that stage also had lot of lice.'

Katie did not believe her. Her very beautiful mother with a long, luxuriant and jet-black hair could not afford to have this vicious insect at any point of time in life. She gaped in sheer disbelief at her mother.

'Tomorrow the school nurse is going to see our hair under a bright light in the school medicine room. If she finds someone with this pest, that student will be thrown out of school. Mrs. Morgan told that this is a very dangerous insect and spreads very fast...'

Gayatri's heart skipped a beat. If Katie was found with lice, then what was going to happen? 'No Beta, this is not dangerous. They live on blood sucked from the scalp. If it was so dangerous, then half of my school and college mates in India in those days would have perished by this time....'

Next day it was her turn to go to the school as parent-volunteer. She looked with a little bit of trepidation at the children taken out in groups to the medicine room for a thorough screening under the glare of a miniature arch light. After some time they all trooped in after this apparently grueling but somewhat comical exercise. Katie was in smiles all over, 'She couldn't find this on me.'

Mrs. Morgan also seemed to have visibly relaxed. 'Not found on any of my children. This pest must have come from somewhere else.'

Classes started with the usual earnestness with Mrs. Morgan talking on issues like the westward journey of the people and the Cowboys fighting the Red Indians at that time. Gayatri also sat at one corner with the kids around on the carpet listening intently on these topics of American History. Suddenly her eyes got transfixed on a surreptitiously moving object on the straight but rusted-looking hair of Gargi, one of the girls of Indian origin. It was a louse, a big, fat one having almost a free run over this child's young head. Gayatri sighed in relief when the bell rang and the children screamed and ran out to play in the open.

Days were passing. Every morning her kids would board the school bus in front of their house and every afternoon they were dropped at the same spot. Parents could never see the books that were taught in the class. Gayatri had lots of grievances. Teaching was limited to additions and subtractions. In case of other subjects even if they wrote something with indecipherable syllables, the class teacher would mark 'excellent' and send back the copy home. It was but natural that she was fuming in disgust.

When it was mentioned to the teachers, they were not apologetic, 'They're too young...they should learn from nature around.... We should teach them to be confident to face life...'

Gayatri's mind has suddenly been taken over by a deep sense of gratitude for this school. This feeling has overwhelmingly spread to the new homeland too and to so many other things connected with it, some way or the other.

✦

Greg has been sitting in front of the computer, his fingers crisscrossing the keyboard in rhythmic motion. He is fully engrossed in the instrument at this moment as is evident from the near-numinous look in his eyes.

Greg is a handsome man with tall, slender body and an inscrutable face. When he is involved in work, he looks more enigmatic. Natalie, Gayatri's colleague, has been scribbling something on her notebook on a nearby desk. Her frothy, translucent look swathed in a voluptuous body seems to be in dissonance with the pensive gawk of Greg at his machine.

Greg looks at Gayatri, face is still inscrutable, 'I've got two complaints against you Gye. First, you have come today wearing a saree.'

Gayatri is annoyed at this unwanted encroachment on her personal life. This is her choice. He has got no business to object.

'This is a unique dress. So feminine yet so gorgeous! The look of a woman is completely transformed by this pretty outfit.'

'Then where's your irritation?' She has almost screamed out in a fit of annoyance. Her reaction must have immensely surprised her boss.

'I'm worried about your safety.' His voice is calm, but some amount of edginess is built into it. 'The twin-towers of American vanity were raged to the ground by a few lunatic rascals.... After that Black Tuesday, the one thing that has gone away conspicuously, in this great nation, is tolerance.'

Greg looks distraught. His fingers make a swift vertical movement through his thick, golden hair.

'A closed society can't go forward. It is just another name for suffocation.'

The other two persons in the room have allowed Greg to go on with his monologues. Sometime it's better that way.

'The other day an Indian Sikh has been butchered just because he had a beard similar to that crazy Osama. In the same logic some thoughtless people might go after you also. This alien identification mark, the saree, should be discarded for the time being.'

Since the last few days most of the ethnic minority groups have switched over to western outfits. Manish's mother who has come from India to be with her distressed son came to Gayatri's house last evening in a loose shirt and a baggy trouser. The elderly lady who had always draped herself in saree in India had to drone a dress she never dreamt of wearing in her lifetime. Her awkwardness in this situation was discernible even to ordinary eyes when she was trying to pull up the slippery trouser above the waist level and at the same time complaining against the weird dress and the weird country where her daughter-in-law lost her life.

When Gayatri first came to this country, she was amazed to see people wearing some bizarre hair-style, hair-color, different kinds of tattoos, and rings all over the face. Siddhartha was furious, 'Don't look at others as if they're some zoo species. It's not a done thing in this country.'

The same country has become obsessed with abandoning the varieties. The much adored concept of Pluralism has become a suspect.

'Don't worry. This is a short-lived occurrence. This feeling of mutual distrust is going away soon.' Greg's soothing voice is more than reassuring.

'Coffee? Black?'

She nods her head. 'Without sugar please!'

'But there is another and more serious complaint against you.' Greg rolls his eyeballs in mock anger. 'Did you call up the McEwen family?'

'Yeah.'

'A male voice told you that his husband was not at home and you immediately put down the phone.'

She is not going to deny it.

'They feel that you were very rude...'

'I was. In fact I was so flabbergasted that...'

'This is a free society. Individual choices are respected here. Elvin who is the wife in this relationship is unhappy at your impudence. I've explained about your culture, your conservative upbringing and somehow managed to calm him down.'

She was planning to write a piece on aversion of some American couples against having kids. She picked up some numbers at random and dialed one number. A male voice was on the other side. She explained her project. 'We'd like to talk to you, a fascinating subject.' The person on the other side was eager to cooperate. 'When my husband comes back....'

'I'm so sorry Greg. Sometime I behave so impulsively.'

'It's okay. This is still an unfamiliar terrain, an alien land for you. You'll adjust soon. The Gays are a sensitive bunch of people. These days they're very influential also. The US Army that has always been flying the flag of discipline had to take a neutral posture as far as Gay's entry to the force is concerned. Don't

Ask, Don't Tell, in short DADT is the strategy. But many change-mongers are clamoring for change in this dubious strategy. They're asking for some openness in the armed forces also.'

'You know Greg, we had two class-mates in college. Two pretty, fashionable young women! Girls were talking about their unusual intimacy in whispering tones. One of them came back from her in-laws place after marriage. The grapevine was that she refused to sleep with her husband. At that time only I heard a new word Lesbianism and took the dictionary to a corner to find out its true meaning. The entire operation of looking at the word was done in such a hush-hush manner that no one in my household was aware that I was adding a forbidden word to my vocabulary. It was then a taboo to talk about homosexuality.... My cousin went to an Engineering college in a far-off place. He was a handsome boy with a fragile look. Within a few days he came back from that college with a shattered look. His mother, my great aunt, was telling the relatives that two big, bad boys were on the top of him, going almost to the point of smoldering him to death...'

Gayatri makes a journey to her past which is so intricately woven and knitted with the present.

When she arrives home Manish's number is there on her answering-machine. She must talk to him. 'Gayatri *ba*, I've been released today only.'

'Released? From where?'

'From police custody. You didn't know about it? My mother created such a fuss that anyone and everyone who matter has come to know about the big story. My dear mother felt that her little boy should be saved from this calamity at any cost. She went crazy.'

The natural ebullience in his voice is still intact. He does not seem to be disconcerted about his arrest at all. An attempt to laugh in an ironical situation!

'Are you not keen to know why I was arrested?'

'Yes. Why?'

'Thanks to Osama Bin Laden. I called up my gas company to complain about an inflated gas bill. At the other end, the customer relation person asked my name and consumer number. I told coolly...M.K. Das, M for Mullah, K for Kosovo and D for Destruction. The lady snapped the line. After some time some cops came here in a siren-blaring car. The lady in the Gas Company got so scared that she immediately informed cops about sneaking of a dreaded terrorist who might be a partner in crime with Osama or Mullah Omar...Oh God! What fertile imagination! I could come out of this big mess somehow this time. My employer also came to my rescue.'

Manish's laughter has been floating in the waves and hurting her ears.

'Don't laugh dear. These are all very serious things. People have gone mad out of panic and you want to fiddle with their frayed emotion at this hour? Stupidity! Please do not play with fire Manish. Not at this time.'

'Don't grudge my laughter now. I was crying like a small child in the police vehicle. Remembered my dead wife Mamata and other people back India. It could have been an awfully bad case for me. But it's a new lease of life, ah! I am inhaling this new freedom that could have gone out of my grip. Let me now laugh Gayatri ba, let me take pleasure in my own imprudence.'

The television is on. Giuliani is on the television screen. The city of the skyscrapers, the Big Apple, linked to the rest of the country through Brooklyn Bridge must emotionally be assuaged so that the city can build a bridge of love to the world though carrying in its womb two gutted towers of hate. Giuliani, the Mayor has been speaking from his heart. Residents of New York are swayed by his message of peace and togetherness.

Till a few days back, the name Giuliani was an anathema for the New Yorkers for his infidelity. His failing health assailed by a prostate cancer attack was almost driving him out of public life. But he has come back to the public mind in a big way during this earth-shattering crisis. He has been standing in a bruised city as a pillar of might.

A vast area of Afghanistan has been raged to the ground in American bomb-blasts. Torabora's landscape has been changed beyond recognition. A vast majority of Americans have gone into a neurotic depression triggered by the shadows of war, death, terror and destruction; hatred with its clawed fangs sapping the life out of a thriving humanity.

Natali reads aloud all the war news to her newsroom colleagues, her voice swelling, heaving and surging at the turn of events in the far off Afghanistan, the Black Tuesday hovering over. She stands up suddenly with a jerk. 'Let's enjoy life. Let's make efforts to come out of this gloom. Some lunatic people can't do this to us.'

There is no stopping now. She is on her wheels ready to whir past anything. When she comes back in an hour's time her hands are full with packets of all shapes and sizes. 'I bought a whole lot of stuff, mostly useless. Fashionable clothes, fancy jewelries, shoes, purses and music CDs. Let's freak out, let's fall in love and let's splurge.'

In the evening the spring in her movement while leaving the cozy but drab office is quite apparent; the swing is still on when an elderly pot-bellied man almost drags her to his waiting car, blaring of loud music from the speeding vehicle seems to be in sync with the foaming camaraderie between two people who have been fighting hard to keep within their grasp the lithe grace of youthful exuberance.

The Americans always sing the songs of life. Their liturgical journey in Mayflower from England to America and further dicey expeditions to the interiors and down south in the seventeenth century under the undaunted spirit of the fledging pioneers goes to prove this point. There were the wild, mysterious animals, a rasping landscape, harsh climate and also the Red Indians to contend with on the way; handmade horse-carts along with axes or crude firearms seemed to be poor bedfellows to fight the perils. But their unflagging courage was doing it all for them.

This spirit is still alive. The mighty people have just received a blow. But like the proverbial phoenix bird they are soon going to rise above the ashes of death to sing again the song of life.

Gayatri, apparently an ordinary Indian woman who can fecklessly be clubbed with any other Indian woman of her age in a crowd in a foreign shore and who has, of late, been waging a war in the difficult terrain of her own inner self against all odds like the Pioneers in her adopted Home, is in a mood to sing paean to the never dying American spirit at this moment.

✦

The masks of ghosts, demons, vampires and other perplexing creatures of different shapes and sizes have been adorning the walls of the shops, sometime these contumacious creatures merrily occupying places in some beautiful shelves and gorging on a delectable meal of human bones and black earth washed in a soup of hot, green, bubbling water.

Halloween. 31st October. Preparation is afoot to celebrate that zestful festival with passion.

'The origin of this festival is not known. The purpose behind it also couldn't be understood. But who bothers? A fun-filled day. We all look forward to it.' Natalie is casual about it.

Gayatri has read somewhere that probably the Native Americans, like most of the primitive people, used grisly figures to shoo away the evil spirits in their simple belief that evil can only enervate evil and the White Americans, being buoyed by the innumerable possibilities of enjoyment, lapped up these extrinsic customs of using grotesque figures, figurines and masks for a particular day for deriving some innocent fun.

She shared her purely academic knowledge with Natalie. 'In far off India and that too in my part of the country, we have a similar festival called *Mahoho* festival to shoo away the mosquitoes and other wicked characters. The boys of the neighboring villages would come to the towns to ask for tips wearing different kinds of masks and rotating their wooden sticks exultantly in the air, their lips would belch out some peculiar song on the occasion *'...O Hari, mohoho! Mah khedbar takon lo. Mahe bole morloo re, takon pura khailo re...'*

...Let us take a stick to kill the mosquitoes. The mosquitoes would scream in pain when the full blows of stick comes on them...

Natalie freaked out on the song by gurgling out the strange words in her gruff voice to the accompaniment of her gyrating body. Natalie is always a beguiling phenomenon for Gayatri. A woman without any close friend or kid, without any permanent love interest but still following ungrudgingly her gushing enthusiasm for all things mundane in life!

Gayatri has come out with Natalie to buy two masks for her children and also two suitable dresses for them. Katie, an eternal dreamer, wants to be a beautiful fairy with helical wings and Gaurav, with his penchant for anything esoteric, wants to be a heady knight of the middle age with a shockingly incongruous flowing black robe.

It is also the time to pluck all those fat pumpkins lying higgledy-piggledy in the vast expanse of farmlands of autumnal America. Gayatri has already got a huge pumpkin from the organic market to keep it in the sun. When it will be totally drained of juice, the interiors will be cleaned; a human face will be carved out and by putting a small bulb inside, a Jack-O-Lantern will be ready to be placed outside her small apartment to radiate a faint light in an otherwise dark evening. Masked children wili come in hordes with begging-bowls to ask for treats of chocolates and candies. They are not to be turned away on this special 'Trick or Treat' day. Earlier times trick by the kids to embarrass the elders was allowed on refusal of goodies. 'Once we plucked flowers in one of the houses for their refusal to give us candies. My, my, the lady was almost in tears! On another occasion, our pranksters threw a ball at a window. Such great fun! But those days are gone. Such pranks are no longer allowed.' Natalie giggles.

Gayatri has made some mental plan to make coconut laddoos for the children this Halloween. She might generously supplement it by banana cakes to keep the swarming children of the neighborhood happy.

'Hi Gye! Looking great!' It's Linda. Her joy at meeting Gayatri is too obvious.

'Meet Kevin. My boyfriend.' Kevin is a young man, as if an actor in a pantomime, with a look of crass stupidity flowing through his dehydrated smiles. Linda must have left the other boyfriend. Gayatri's eyes leave those of Kevin and she tries to look at the exquisite costumes in the nearby shop.

'What're you going to wear on Halloween?'

'Me?' It's her turn to be stunned.

'You must be looking forward to give all of us a surprise! We understand that and won't put pressure on you to part with your secret.' Linda's twinkling eyes jostle for words. 'But we don't want to be secretive. I'm going to be a witch and this sweet, little Kevin is to be a demon. A huge unused house with splotches all around and a sprawling, unkempt garden has been there in our vicinity for quite long. I went to the owner and offered to hire it for a few days. He has agreed. The house is going to be decorated with cobwebs, giant-sized spiders, vultures, vampires – all artificial and I'm going to sit snugly among all those sinister-looking objects. You know what, I'm going to gorge on human bones, skulls, flesh, all artificial, to the blaring of loud music. There'll be an entry-fee of ten dollars. Isn't that all sounding interesting Gye?'

'Oh! I can barely hold my excitement Linda. Such an original idea! I'm sure people will enjoy it.' Gayatri takes care to conceal her contempt at this juvenile behavior of an elderly woman.

'This money is going for charity. It will go for meeting the expenses of some of the elderly patients in the community hospital. Healthcare has become so expensive of late.'

Suddenly Linda looks very pristine and beautiful, almost like a fairy.

'Hey Gye, look at that pink frock. Isn't that wonderful?'

Gayatri comes out, a little bit jerkily, of the stupor Linda has uncannily thrown her in and cranes her neck to look at the delicate dress hung prominently on one corner of the nearby shop at Natalie's prodding.

'Your daughter will be looking cuddlesome in this pretty dress.' The sales-woman seems to be immensely happy. The touch of the soft fabric produces a squashy feel in Gayatri's mind too, almost nudging her to merge her inner self in an overwhelming spiritual bliss; the delight of the sales-woman further adding to that ecstasy.

Siddhartha is far away from her surge of thoughts now though Nora's controversial sound bites on cloning on the television channels and the newspapers sometime transport him back in her mind. Nora has been speaking from the same platform as Massimo Moratti in the 'National Academy of Science' meet held in Washington these days and unveiling her plans of creating human-clones. Two hundred women are ready to conceive human-embryos for the purpose of cloning. 'The first half of twenty first century will be a story of human cloning.' Nora has screamed from that podium and media chaffed and clawed their way for more potions. The critics are not silent either. Dolly, born out of old Polly, was not young biologically and as expected swirled under that curse of the old age, Arthritis. Dolly ultimately had to embrace a cruel, untimely and painful death as anticipated. It is not proper to attempt to usurp the powers of the great Creator. Any such misadventure at arrogation might create more Dollys and the result would be a gigantic chaos leading to disappearance of all traces of life from this planet. The critics have been reasoning with equal vehemence.

Siddhartha must be there, lolling around his lady love and be smitten by her racy dream of creating a brave new alien world. Katie, her own young daughter, looks heavenwards and wants to don the attire of a beautiful fairy. Her son, running after that eternal quest for mystic strength, is taking the robe of a medieval English knight.

A wave of sympathy for all of them sweeps through her entire being.

'After so many days of gloom, I can see joy all around. America has learnt to smile after that stupid attack on this peaceful country. You know, many youngsters want to dress up like Bin Laden this Halloween. Bin Laden has been bracketed with ghosts or evildoers in their minds. This is a good sign.' The sales-woman's gaze is fixed on the motley crowd of fun-loving people moseying along the square outside.

On the Halloween morning, a colorful parade with legions of frenzied people on open, hoodless cars, wearing all types of masks, would go around the town; equally multihued onlookers would look at the lurid procession with wonder and young and old alike would pick up toffees or chocolates thrown from the procession in the spirit of that wild bonhomie.

Gayatri has received a mail from her mother this afternoon. 'I'm amazed that you are driving your own vehicle. But for God's sake, don't ever offer me a ride there. I've got no desire to leave this world so soon.' Her mother, that frail woman of steel, is obviously very happy at her coming out of that orifice of despair weaved by a real life drama of infidelity and rejection.

Siddhartha's brother is more patronizing. 'Don't worry bou, we're going to make our Dada see reason and come back to you soon...'

Her own brother wrote, 'People are more concerned about falling of Twin Towers in America than the real problems affecting our own country. So many people have been massacred in terrorist violence, so many others lost lives in state-sponsored counter-terrorism during the last few years in this part of the country! But no one is bothered as if life is more precious there than in their own homeland. I'm shocked.'

Then suddenly she hears that faint scream coming from the other side of her bedroom wall and a bizarre sensation flickers through her mind almost coaxing her to rush towards that door.

A young Chinese man in his 30s opens the door. He seems to be not amused at this intrusion of a stranger. 'No, everything is fine with us.... Oh, those sounds? My wife...not well...headache... nothing to worry.'

'But she cried two or three days back also!'

The young man pauses for a while as if trying to recollect something slipping away from ambit of his procrastinating memory.

'Oh, on that day? One of her close relatives died in Shanghai.'

'Do her relatives die very often? Or else she must be suffering from frequent bouts of migraine. I can hear her wails most of the nights from across the wall.'

He looks at her, bewildered. She must act really fast. She forces herself in, through the half-open door, to land her in the scene of imbroglio to the consternation of all the villains in this sordid drama which apparently includes the triad, the young man, an elderly woman (must be his mother, it did not require much ingenuity in thought to come to that conclusion) and a frail, very fair, pretty woman, must be the sufferer (again a foregone conclusion) The elderly woman is dry-skinned, scrawny with a venomous look mainly directed at the young woman but now poised to overwhelm the new, unwelcome entrant, her purple-colored pajama in collaboration with her polka-dotted shirt of the same color adds to her dangerously poignant allure.

The young woman rushes towards Gayatri and clutches her hands as if she is some kind of a messiah coming from nowhere to rescue her from the filthy hands of these cruel perpetrators. Words come out from her mouth, words which are otherwise unfathomable to Gayatri, but touch her heart with their melancholic chord. An alien language singing the saga of misery!

The young woman puts her T-shirt up to show the bruises all over her soft and supple skin, her slender index finger is very much focused on the man and the old woman.

Gayatri drags the young woman to the corner of the room. Now it is the turn of her solicitous fingers to do the talking volubly, by zigzag movement on the numbers 9-1-1, magic of that number was explained with a flourish through sign language. A savior would arrive on the scene if she dares to put her finger on these three digits one after another, Gayatri elucidates and young woman, not in the know of things in this new world, seems to understand it all.

The husband is visibly frightened at that moment. Gayatri stands in front of him, towering over his small physique by her own tiny body and shakes him out of his stupor, 'Listen Mr...next time if I hear any goddamn sound in this house I'm not going to be nice, I'm straightaway rushing to the cop and you'll be flown, all at the expense of the state, out of the country, the very next morning...'

'I've selected a new topic for my Sunday column.' Gayatri announces rather grimly in their Monday meeting for topic-selection, 'Plight of Asian women at the hands of their cruel in-laws.'

It is her turn to talk glibly on the strange turn of events in her neighborhood and people are engrossed in the editorial board, a small cohesive group of Greg, Natalie, herself and two young staffers. Her emotive depiction of the family, the putrid mother-son duo, an embattled young, vulnerable woman has been gripping enough to keep everyone glued to their chairs. 'Virtually a captive woman! She doesn't understand the language of the land, doesn't have an idea about the law of the country and doesn't know where to look for in case of trouble. What a pitiable state!'

Gayatri is now confined to the world of pain of a woman with whom she shares a common spectrum of rejection.

+

Her ravenous eyes cavort around the beautiful building of the apostolic Capitol Hill lapping up everything from ice-filled white lake to the consuming structure of American pride, memories cascading at a fast pace.

That was also the Christmas time and this lake was also pristine white. 'Oops! It's going to be a white Christmas.' Siddhartha was not sharing his wife's zest for everything so abundantly white at that moment, his surly look was telling it all. Some men and women were trying to tread through the dangerously slippery pathway created by the masked ice water on lake surface; their wobbliness was all too obvious in that moon-lit night making them all look like some quivering surreal objects in the backdrop of a thickly tasseled snow hanging everywhere in scads.

A young girl in white fur-coat and white cap was waltzing like a fairy in that wiggly line of wild people. And whoops! She was sliding down fast through the fractured crust of the white surface of the lake and in a minute's time she was gone!

A girl in white lost her life in white! Gayatri still shudders at the thought of that perishing of a fragile life at the hands of an apparently adorable nature on that fateful night.

That was not the only trip that they made to Washington as a family. When the children were little bigger they went to Washington, the city of museums, the second time during one of their much-desired vacations. Gaurav was petrified at the skeletal remains of a dinosaur fretted so painstakingly at Natural History Museum to resemble the human vision of this exotic but extinct animal. He squealed in joy at the audacious space odyssey of Apollo11; two human beings could actually go and land on that tiny ball of silver was a matter of wonder for him. 'How could it bear the weight of two big people, mummy? Had it fallen off, these two uncles would've also been badly hurt!'

Gayatri had to make some real effort to dissuade Siddhartha from starting his glitzy intellectual discourse on force of gravity, distance of moon from earth, the size of moon and so on and so forth. 'They're just kids and let them be kids for the time being. Let the moon be just a little-brittle silvery play-ball for them.' Siddhartha relented to this gentle persuasion of his wife that time, not getting wantonly bristled at her pedestrian attitude towards things so important in life. Rather he kept his wariness under wrap and went on to pinch his son's ears playfully with an impish grin, pointing his index finger at the personal items used by the astronauts on display in one corner of the museum, 'Look, Neil Armstrong also used Colgate toothpaste on Apollo11 like you do every morning for brushing his teeth. But he doesn't cry like you do when mummy puts that semi-liquid white on your brush.'

Whenever they came to Washington, they used to go to the Sesapic Bay to buy fresh sea-fish, serried in rows, from the sea-vessels stationed at the shore, tantalizing smell of freshly caught fish wafted through the air reminding Gayatri of the crowded fish market on the bank of the river Brahmaputra in her birth place and this longing for a place far-off from her grasp usually left her in tatters.

This time the desire to go to the seashore for that nostalgic homecoming smell drifting mostly from the piled up shoal of fish is no longer there. Those shingles of reminiscences of a make-believe homeward journey have lost their ways in her life.

She is currently interacting with the members of Saakshi, a voluntary women group to share their concern for the plight of Indian-origin women in America at the hands of their cruel in-laws.

'I work for a small newspaper of a little American town. I want to tell the people of my town about me, about us. They will listen only when we're opening up. They'll feel for us and this feeling might, in some way, lessen our anguish...'

Fear still oozes out from the soft, pretty face of Kamlesh as a reminiscence of her brutal past. Just after her marriage, her highly qualified husband said forebodingly, 'You didn't bring enough.' Her mother-in-law chipped in with equal ferocity, almost went to the extent of muttering imprecations, 'It seems you wanted to get away cheap. You bitch!'

Then began a saga of torture for this young, vulnerable, small town girl from Punjab in India whose American dream got shattered at the hands of that simmering combination of her husband and demonic in-laws! She ran away to another town and there she met a member of Saakshi who helped her to set up an Indian grocery store.

Vinita is an extremely good-looking, smart, highly educated woman married to an equally handsome, accomplished, educated guy holding a highly-paid job. He was merrily carrying on an extra-marital affair with a neighbor, a Delhi-bred Indian, a loquacious character with a lot of accent. Vinita was trussed like a caged prisoner in a small room. Whenever someone called up, she had to narrate make-believe stories of her happiness under full glare of her hawk-eyed husband. But one day her sister from Canada flew in to give her a surprise. Her banging on the door did not produce any result. She was about to leave the front porch when she heard a feeble sound, a kind of groan and she saw a face peering through a murky darkness from one of the tiny windows covered with tainted glass. Vinita was rescued from that human hell then and there.

'I'm back to a normal life. But my lively smile has gone out of my jaded life forever.' Vinita's voice is soaked in grief.

Gayatri quickly wipes her face by a paper napkin, her own weapon of camouflaging herself, her turmoil, her vulnerability at this elegiac moment, when all the stares are glued to her look.

While coming back, Katie seems to be thoroughly perplexed at this gargantuan downpour of emotions from grown-up people; abuse or beating etc. are words still alien to her concept of a world redolent with joy and beauty. The hard reality of going away of their father from their orbit of life was unable to transform her rosy, innocent vision of life into a mawkish one.

'Why were they crying?'

'You'll understand it later.' Katie would take time even to comprehend her mother's cryptic reply churned out quickly to fend off her curiosity.

How she should start her write-up on this crucible of blending, hatred, pain and anguish of women of a particular culture in the backdrop of a western milieu? An Asian woman in this land is to cruise through her life all alone. Relatives or families are far away, beyond the vast expanse of land and ocean. Friendship or bonding with the outside world, when she has been confined in her grotty little shelter most of the time, is out of question. There is no perceptible difference between her indiscernible neighbor-next-door and someone in far-off Africa. A towering nothingness lolls around her and devours her.

But there is ray of hope there too. She can immerse herself in this society like a nameless, faceless immigrant responsible only to her own being once she comes out of her lair of sinned existence.

Gayatri is going to start her write-up soon.

✦

Julia, the huge woman in her forties is howling like a small child at the recollection of all the pains and horrors she had to undergo at the hands of her tormentors. Gayatri wonders how a woman with a mammoth size like Julia could be subjected to so much brutality when she seems to be capable of retaliating like a fierce tigress.

'Look, all these marks are burnt marks from the electric iron. All over my body!'

Marks of different colors – pink, mauve and violet – wove a design over her pale skin like a colorful spider's web.

Greg has persuaded her to come to this place, to this forum, where problems of American women were supposed to be deliberated. She is to hear, see, ponder and write on this issue too in the aftermath of her highly acclaimed write up on the plight of Asian origin women in America. Their paper has sponsored the discussion and this local bookstore has provided a cozy and convenient space inside which is generally used for book-reading purpose.

'Why do you assume that things like harassment or oppression happen only with women of Asian origin? Nearly three million American females are subjected to different kinds of cruelties....'

Greg in his mild persuasive way has been trying to make her see the other world.

How could she believe such a phenomenon when most of those astoundingly erect, fiercely beautiful and awesome ladies move about with sweeping confidence and electrifying speed? When they go for a leisurely stroll too, they generally give the impression that they are going to catch the next flight in the airport with their hurried pace. Once, when she was just a new arrival in the university, Gayatri even tried to catch up, just for fun, with two young girls who were going ahead of her in the campus, fully absorbed in their world, unaware about this impromptu competition silently staged by a total stranger.

After some time she found herself to be virtually running and even when those young graduate students were going in their normal speed in that cold afternoon either to the café or any such destination, they disappeared out of her sight very soon. Gayatri was embarrassingly left to grasp for her breath.

And now she is a witness to this apparently unbelievable but true story of torture on some such strong, stout and immensely confident women!

Stephanie has been narrating her tale of never ceasing woes. 'He, my husband, used to put his loaded revolver on one side of my body and on the other side he would go on flogging or canning. A slight show of resistance would have triggered the revolver or that was what I was made to believe then...'

Stephanie cries inconsolably! Gayatri feels like comforting her and take her in her arms to reassure that not everything has been lost.

Natalie has just brought a cup of hot, steaming coffee for Gayatri as if to rejuvenate the sagging spirit of her friend in this distressingly hermetic ambience. How refreshed Gayatri has suddenly felt after the first sip!

She had come to this bookstore so many times earlier in her life to be with all those mystifying, leather-bound books. She would order for a cup of coffee and sits there for hours in the company of all those adorable books. It was strange, paradoxical situation. She used to hate books and anything remotely connected with them at another part of her life in India and here she tried frenetically to bridge the void in her life by weaving a bond with the same books.

What was really a source of amazement for her was the nature of this bookstore which was more akin to a public library where a reader can pick up a book, shuffle through it for hours together and go away even without buying. There were times when she saw people, particularly Indians buying a book and coming back after some time to tell that it was not the same book he or she wanted. The counter clerk with his deadpan face used to accept the argument without a question and return the money. She was so embarrassed at this behavior of some of her countrymen that when she met Siddhartha in the evening she would narrate such shameful acts and she was doubly shocked when Siddhartha would laugh his heart out: So far the White Men exploited us; now, it is our turn to exploit them.

On most of those occasions she would look at him with lot of consternations and Siddhartha would go away without even bothering to give credence to her hurt or shocked feeling.

'...Do you remember last time when we went for a trip in the countryside and there was a small temporary shop for selling red tomatoes on a deserted road? We looked but couldn't find a single soul there. Just the red, juicy tomatoes were piled up neatly on the table, several brown paper bags lying side by side with a jar where few dollar notes and some small changes were vying for space. A small weighing scale along with a price list was also found nearby.'

Siddhartha had to pause and listen to her carefully worded elaboration with indifference; his indignation was concealed under that veil of apathy.

'We left two dollars in the jar and bought two pounds of tomatoes. Before we left we saw a faint figure at a distance in front of a house far away. We waved and yelled that we had taken two dollars worth of tomatoes. He waved back and nodded his head in approval.... Can you imagine such a thing in India? If anything was left unprotected like this in our country there, people would just take the things away without bothering to pay.'

It was probably a deliberate attempt on her part to prick the inflated ego of her husband by telling something nasty about the Indians on his face though she knew that it was rather a sweeping statement about the simple and gullible country-folks of rural India who had to earn her verbal wrath only because of a bloated Siddhartha. While pointing an accusing finger indiscriminately at all Indians, she could hardly erase the intractable memory of that poor rickshaw-puller who came back to return her purse when she had left that purse on the rickshaw one day. She was petrified when she realized her grave mistake of losing the hard-earned money bequeathed by her husband during that India trip. But that night a frail person with an apparently worn-out look knocked on her front door, fear seemed to have lurked behind his gentle eyes. After reposing that distended purse clumsily in her unsuspecting hands he went away hurriedly like a shadowy phantom fast evaporating into an eerie darkness. Such deeply embedded memories were popping up in quick succession at that time of her unduly implicating an entire nation of people for the mean acts of a few.

This incessant cycle of Gayatri's grumbling and Siddhartha getting vitriolic pleasure at the mean acts of some of the people from his birthplace was going on for some time till he left her life unannounced in one fine morning. From that moment onwards these small betrayals of trust by some petty people at a bookstore started to look like insignificant happening compared to the magnitude of massive perfidy unleashed by her closest person on her trusting soul.

When the women who were talking one after another on the issues of atrocity or neglect were finished, the Sheriff of the town stands up and talks, '...One recent study shows that incidents like wife-beating etc. happen mainly during winter when both husband and wife had to stay indoors most of the free time. Winter is a very long spell of time and it's very severe in most parts. Couples would naturally be irritated with each other soon. It may lead to verbal duel which may in turn lead to physical abuse....'

Mr. Bill Forrester, the indomitable sheriff of the State College looks sad.

'Both of us, I mean me and my ex-wife used to work in two different organizations. We would come back late after our busy work schedules. In one of those hectic days I came home to find that the youngest son was howling and my wife was screaming at him. I was so aghast at this entire crying-screaming scenario that I gave a tight slap to my dear wife. She took the kids, packed her things and stormed out of the house. I thought it was just a momentary reaction. She would come back. After all, she was my wife and she had to come back. But things did not happen that way. She filed for a divorce and I didn't contest. Let her go. Who cares...?'

The pause taken by this custodian of law seems to be too protracted; his brooding gaze is fixed upwards.

'...But it was followed by a bitter custody battle for the children. Till the Court decided, the children were sent to Remand Home. The eldest one was in his teens at that time. He took to drugs there. The other two followed suit. All my three handsome young sons are addicted to drugs and all three of them are now in jails.'

Bill Forrester looks really crest-fallen at this moment. Gayatri had to go to this man quite frequently in the past few years for professional reasons and every time she found him to be a joyous person with an avalanche of energy. There was not even a single occasion when she could find an iota of sadness in his face or in his demeanor. The Americans are excellent actors!

She has come to this conclusion. When they are at work, they can so conveniently camouflage their emotions or their private sorrows!

It is another matter that they may let their guards off on social issues when a large number of people are affected like the widespread display of grief in the aftermath of 9/11.

America is still a fascinating country for Gayatri who, after living here for full two decades, is still trying to grapple with this country's unique ways of coping with life. Here she is in a position to take a pause, witness all passing events like a dispassionate observer and reflect and go for introspection on everything, tiny or big, ranging from social behavior to individual fad.

Whenever she talks of India, her mind flies back to her initial days in America, the days when she used to clutch on to her memories of India to tide over a roller coaster ride in an alien terrain. Her busy life with two small children and an intellectual husband was heavy with wrapped up feeling of loneliness. During those days she would wander around aimlessly with her kids in the shopping malls to snuff out that overwhelming feeling of being left out from the life of Siddhartha.

During one of those days when Gaurav was rushing inside the shopping mall excitedly, an old lady quipped with an apparent humor, 'Don't you love your son?' It was Gayatri's turn to be surprised. 'Why are you asking that?'

'Don't leave your son unescorted inside these places dear...' There was a very beautiful smile on her pretty, kind face.... 'So many people come to these places...you see, some of them maybe mad. They may look apparently decent but maybe vicious inside. Anything might happen here...'

She looked at Gayatri's stunned, inquisitive face and she told very soothingly, 'No, not all people. Very few of them. But they are there.'

Martha concurred with that lady in the shopping mall when Gayatri spoke to her the next day: Yeah, some apparently decent people maybe psychopaths. There maybe some pedophiles lurking also.... Loneliness in our society, you see, is the root cause. You should be careful in busy, public places about your children....'

That fear rattled her so much that it became an all-consuming panic in her and it has made her to keep track of her children even to this date, even when they seemed to have grown up sufficiently to assume control of their lives. Sometime she would try to talk to her son when he was playing football in the field or to her daughter when she was busy in her after-school projects in the community centre of her neighborhood.

Gayatri is going to buy a chocolate-box for Katie today on her way back home along with a lot of other things for decorating their Christmas tree. Katie already has a crooked premolar loose tooth and any time it might fall off; that fallen tooth will be kept under her pillow before she'd go for sleep. This was done when she was a little child and her milk teeth were going away one after another. Though she has now grown up, her faith in the tooth-fairy is still intact. Who can prevent the tooth-fairy to buy a beautiful gift for the girl whose tooth has fallen off? That is the belief of this society and her pre-teen daughter who has been brought up in the beliefs of this society would surely expect that the enigmatic tooth-fairy would come surreptitiously this time too to bestow an exotic gift on her when she would be engrossed in a never-ending sweet dream during the night.

Let her, her young daughter, a bundle of joy and an innocent soul, live in a make-believe world for some time till harsh realities shake her out of that reverie!

Tomorrow morning when Katie would get up, the first thing that she would find is the chocolate box near her pillow and she would explode in sheer joy.

Her fallen tooth would be taken stealthily by her mother and thrown to the rooftop with the hope that her daughter would have a tooth: tiny, sparkling and sharp, like that of an eternally elusive mouse.

This is the belief of the society where Katie's mother was born.

Tomorrow morning when Katie would be wide awake and Gayatri's act of throwing up the tooth is over, two different beliefs of two diverse societies would merge.

✦ ✦ ✦

6

Siddhartha has been sitting on the sofa, his stilted gaze being fixed on the flower-vase on the glass-top table.

'I've read your write-ups. Somewhere...'

Gayatri is not in a mood to be modest or to cower in the face of a gristly arrogance that might surface at any time pervading this initial coat of feigned refinement.

'Our paper has a tie-up with some other national newspapers. Half of the money for such write-ups goes to the paper and the rest comes to me. I think I'm not doing too badly....'

Siddhartha nods his head, somewhat stingily.

Siddhartha has come. It will be more apt to tell that Nora has left. The highly peripatetic icon of science has left for a deserted island named Firego near Antarctica in South Sea to pursue her protean research on human cloning. Since Firego does not fall in any country's territory, no man-made law touches this island. She has set up her laboratory on a burly ship on the beetling coast of south sea in that island. This time her companion is Massimo Moratti, the Italian bioscientist on cloning, who harks back at anyone daring to snigger at their not too halcyon dream of producing human clones. His wrath has not even spared the venerable Pope for criticizing their hedonistic effort of attempting to usurp the exclusive domain of the Maker through this abstruse research.

The acrimonious verbal duel carried in dizzying pace between Nora-Moratti duo and Christian clergy has managed to snatch a prominent place in all the prestigious dailies of the country.

Siddhartha's sulking silence for some inexplicable reason is reflected in his brooding, conical face. His intemperance is obvious in his squirmy body-language.

'This has always been a sleepy town. Everything is in a state of being static...almost stagnant.'

'No, Siddhartha, there are lots of changes here too. This residential complex was not there at that time. The very big Beaver Stadium with a seating capacity for two million spectators was also not there. You took us out for the Sunday football matches to a rickety stadium nearby then...'

She could feel the perplexed glances of her husband pouring ceaselessly on her frail frame.

Siddhartha must be told without insinuation how his action threw their lives into haywire and how their jumbled lives had to be brought under a semblance of orderliness by a lot of strenuous, interlacing actions.

Siddhartha has put down his coffee mug on the table silently. The person who always displays so much flair in dealing with the mundane objects like this inanimate, brittle coffee mug has lost all his flamboyance while fiddling around with the bigger spectrum of life.

'Gaurav and Katyani must have grown up.'

'They have. So many changes have come to their lives too. That day someone called up Gaurav. I picked up the phone.... A girl's voice.... Hi! I want to talk to Garry...she was confiding about their plan to go out that evening with her date, my son. Gaurav went out to spend an evening with his girlfriend, a 13 year old girl. A very ordinary event in the life of a teenager here. The Indian value-system within me was ridiculing the mother in me – what you are up to? How could you allow your son to spend an evening with his girlfriend? What a shame...!'

Gayatri is in front of Siddhartha, sitting on another sofa, her long, black, wavy hair going on a razzle in the open, untied state, and her slim, beautiful body is covered ravenously by a flowing kurti-type-top in conjunction with a loose pant.

'I hope you're keeping him under check?'

Siddhartha, who was so used to getting unconditional obedience from his minions, is certainly unhappy now with this swift tide of events.

She knows him too well by this time, after his long, stimulating absence.

'No. I've only put some restrictions in place. He's supposed to reach home before 12. I spoke to him at length about AIDS and advised him to use condom. I do not see any logic in imposing Indian value-system on our American children.'

'But they're Indians...'

His sharp voice coupled with the restlessness of his body is intended to send a shiver down the spine of a rebel.

'They're not Indians, they're Americans. I spent many a sleepless nights pondering over the dilemma of imposing alien values on our children. In one of those sleepless nights, I realized that I should accept the truth of our children being *pucca* Americans. Look at our own hypocrisy. We're telling them...extract all the good things from this place, enjoy your existence here but keep your loyalty to a place which has got nothing to do with your survival.... Why should they accept such a contradiction?'

Siddhartha's sickly pallor and his voluble eyes clearly condemn his wife's mindless actions.

'If they follow American lifestyle fully, they're going to be doomed.'

'No, they're not going to be doomed. Rather they're going to develop resilience against so many odds. You left all of us for your lover in a typical American way and they accepted it stoically as a fait accompli like most of the American children do. It's not that they didn't want your presence. Gaurav wanted you as his partner in the football field and Katie wanted you to indulge her in the ice cream parlor. For the first time in their life they came face to face with want and scarcity. For the first time they saw their home-bound, lazy mother going out in the street in search of a few dollars. But just because they're Americans they could accept so many changes in their life, all at the same time. Their dad has gone away with another woman. It's not a very big thing. Jessie's father has also gone away with another woman, Tony's father too left them. Their American thought-process has been helping them to cope with their trauma and loss.'

Siddhartha tries to light his cigarette, but, probably, on an after-thought puts the snazzy lighter back in his pocket. A fag in a closed room might rustle up his wife's disapproval and he cannot simply afford this kind of sacrilege at this moment.

'Yeah.... Things would have been different if I was around.' The usual splenetic splutters of his voice have gone. He sounds grave and rueful.

'Things would have been different in so many other ways Siddhartha. Our Gaurav would have gone for a *mundan* ceremony like a true *dwija* and with a cute, clean-shaven head he would have roamed around in style. Katie would have gobbled up all the ice cream cones in the ice cream parlor in the town. And my life would have remained confined in the making of your favorite fish-curry. I've never thought about so many different scenarios in the backdrop of you not leaving the family. I simply had no time for luxury of day-dreaming.'

She has told too many things and she is not going to hold her injured feelings in leash. She is not going to let her pride lacerated again by a mangled arrogance.

'My views about life have gone a sea-change Siddhartha. Do you like to hear what all I have gone through during the last three years...? Neil and Rebecca! A nice couple! They looked for a baby-sitter and I joined there. Both of them would go out early morning and I would look after the baby in their absence. A beautiful, bonny baby who won't give trouble and continue to sleep and play most of the day! I had enough free time. So I volunteered to do some extra work like cleaning the dishes, making the beds, doing the laundry for a little hike in pay. They agreed readily. Like a typical American family, they wasted a lot. They would bring a large Domino pizza, eat a fraction of it and leave the rest for dumping in the waste-bin. While cleaning, instead of throwing this leftover food, I used to eat them regularly. I was very hungry at that time and didn't think much about eating food meant only to go down the drain. But at the month-end, Neil just gave me my pay-cheque and told me to budge off in a very polite manner. His wife Rebecca was profusely apologetic.... Your care and concern for the baby was so much obvious in the hidden camera. Even Neil had to acknowledge it. But Neil is a stickler for rules. He didn't take it kindly to your eating those leftover things. That was not a part of our deal with you. I didn't mind. But Neil is adamant.... Look at my plight Siddhartha! I had to be chucked out for eating throwaway food. Such a humiliation! But I had to go through all these.'

Siddhartha looks at the floor, eyes downcast, his pedantic expression is hard to fathom. She did not tell stilted bedtime stories to this arrogant man. These are poignant, sniveling tales of a woman who could rise above her helplessness only after a searing trial.

'Then I worked in the McDonald during the night shift. You get more money when you work in those ungodly hours when normal people go off to sleep and night birds roam around in the streets. One night while coming back from my work on a foggy, snow-laden night, a mobile police van stopped near me and a police officer asked me if I was in the lookout for some escort service. A young girl was raped a few days back on a lonely street in this small university township. An unheard-of-incident in the history of this sleepy town! Police have become more alert after this unsavory episode. They have arranged for escort service for any working woman who has to go and come alone during night time for their job. I told him that I was not interested in any kind of security. I further told him that I had developed abhorrence for utopian words like safety or security. I looked for security in my marriage. I tried to feel that security in the warmth of my kitchen fire. All those make-believe senses of security evaporated in just one air-trip of my husband to Chicago. Safety, security and the likes are some magical words devised to con gullible people like me. Huh! The cop kept on staring at me for some time and then sped away without telling anything more.'

Siddhartha is still not looking at Gayatri. His eyes make cyclical movement at different angles of the tastefully decorated room adorned with all kinds of tiny mementos gathered during his prolonged absence.

'Look at the irony in my life. At one point of time I considered the words as the greatest pain on this beautiful earth and the exams as the worst form of curse. Now I earn my bread by selling those words and get a kick out of it. I've geared myself to face all kinds of changes that might crop up at any point of time. My daughter Katie might come to me one day and tell that she is pregnant. In this country you get a lot of unwed teenage mothers. One day Gaurav might also be caught while sniffing cocaine or any such stuff. These are the worst probable scenarios but they are not impossible either. In the same way many good things might happen in our life and we must accept them all in the same equanimity. Life doesn't move on a straight track. I have come to terms with that truth.'

Siddhartha stands up with a quick jerk and slews past his wife towards the wall. His posterior is visible. 'We might bring all our lives back to track. We might try.'

'You were the leading light in our life. You lost control and sped away. All of us also lost our orbits and created our own small individual universe. You cannot drag us away from our territory now. It's too late Siddhartha. Like the mythological Rama, you were going away in search of an elusive, mesmerizing *maya-mriga*, the magical deer as bright as the golden sun. You were so involved in that chasing that you could not even draw any *Lakshmana Rekha*, the protection line, for me and my children. We were left to fend for ourselves and we survived.... You came back very late.'

She drops Siddhartha in front of his hotel. Before getting down he puts his right hand on her left shoulder, his face is wreathed in a scornful look.

'I'm worried about my children. This permissiveness should not go too far.'

'When your own action was not in harmony with the values you espoused, how can you take responsibilities for the future actions of some other people? They might be your children, but they're not you.'

Siddhartha puts his left hand also on her shoulder. She could feel the burden of that poignant moment.

'It's cumbersome to get a divorce in a Hindu marriage.' The tone is menacing again.

'A Hindu marriage is a union of souls, a sacrament. It's not supposed to be an agreement. But if one partner goes away, the tie is gone forever. It cannot be held together in the name of religion, tradition or society. Our marriage is over Siddhartha. We might stay together for the sake of our children. But when there's no trust, no respect, where's the basic bond for this union? Our kids would stop respecting us if we do something like that. Law is not going to be an impediment in the path of this divorce. Go to Alabama and declare that we are not together for two months. A quick divorce will follow.'

Siddhartha leaps back to the front lobby of the hotel with such alacrity that Gayatri could not even say bye to him.

As soon as she enters the house Gaurav too rushes in with a football in his hand. She is amazed at this inexplicable love of Gaurav for a comatose winter.

He must have seen his father entering the house. Probably he must have felt more affinity towards his skittish ball in this stifling winter than for his father who has been elusive in his life for the last three years. Whatever be the reason, he decided not to barge in.

'Dad came.' It is an arid statement.

'What did you say?' The statement is followed swiftly by a question.

'What did you want me to say?'

Gaurav has already perched himself on the cushioned chair. He looks totally lost, almost crestfallen.

'I've told him that there isn't much space for him in this house.'

She could hear the overexcited sound of her own breathing as if it has hatched a diabolical scheme to disarray her whole being.

'You did the right thing. There is no space for him here.'

Gaurav stands up and his sinewy strides towards his room leaves behind a trail of blazing memories of the past, a past which can never be buried but can never be resurrected either.

Her attention is suddenly caught by the heavenly sight outside her house on the snow-covered lawn. The sight of the three wise men staring ardently at the baby Jesus lying at the lap of Mother Mary in a pastoral ambience, the mesmeric star in the background weaving a tale for the coming millenniums!

All those tastefully crafted figures in white wool made by Katie with the passion and zeal of a consummate artist are ensconced on a sea of a silvery snow in their garden under the glazed stare of a colorful Christmas tree in an evening crackled with the anticipation of a White Christmas. A light and snow show erected with celestial grace in her foyer by her own child in commemoration of an event presumed to have happened long time back!

A heap of Christmas gifts for all members of the family would be accumulating under this decorated Christmas tree soon.

Gayatri can feel a massive pile of void in the midst of this ocean of joy and opulence. She couldn't find any other way to welcome Siddhartha other than bidding him a sweltering send-off. How could she accept his audacity of expediently coming and going as if she was a patch of listless weeds to be conveniently trampled, discarded or arraigned at his own sweet will? Though it is a fact that they lived for more than a decade together and weaved a trying dream of being in sync with each other, it is also an equally momentous truth that they have drifted apart.

Siddhartha should understand that the petite and apparently straggly woman who came to his life with the promise to cook fish-curry all throughout her life within the stifling confinement of a house is no longer alive. She is gone along with a load of warm memories to the grave.

✦

It is a huge two-storied, red-brick-tiled house with all the spaciousness and ornamentation of a usual American home, the backyard going torrentially towards an edgy combination of dense forest and a slanting hill and signaling a limitless expanse of an existence perilously close to a void.

That's what Gayatri likes to think philosophically about her new acquisition.

Her two grown-up children need space. Even she looks for space these days after her day-long toil.

She fell in love with the area, green and barren, and a sketch of her new home got fructified in her imagination like a beautiful work of art. Two separate rooms for her two children and a room exclusively for her. They never got a nursery and they spent their childhood nights with their parents in the same bedroom. The tiny body of the baby Gaurav was a cause of immense concern for Gayatri during night time. A small oscillation here and there by the mother might trample his teeny, almost boneless body. This stalking fear of discovering a trodden baby in the wee hours next morning kept her wide awake many a night. That was the Indian way of bringing up a baby, a fidgety mother and an equally hyper baby demanding its share of feed, the nursery concept was not fitting into their convoluted existence.

Inspite of all those complications Gayatri was never comfortable with the idea of a nursery which seemed to act as a chasm between the child and the mother, as if a borderless overwhelming affinity had been circumscribed by some artificial walls. '...A nursery is a brutal way of separating two inseparable entities.' Greg is astounded at her outcry on an issue over which no American would ever shed any word of disparagement or advice. It is as overpowering an icon as the statue of liberty or as old as the cult of freedom in his society.

In his country space sometime assumes more vociferous dimensions than an ordinary human-being endowed with very ordinary human sensibilities.

There are a number of invitees for the house-warming party – Greg, Natalie, Anjali, Arup, their children in tow, Ashifa bau, Ahmed dada, Manish, Dr. Shakuntala Kundan, her affable husband and her beautiful young daughter, Martha, John, Kenny, their cute young son David and Lara Sinclair. The priest Sudarshan with his tall, aristocratic look and deep, thrusting voice is the defining cynosure; his chanting of the hymns in the ritual of the Vishnu Yagna with all those mystifying Sanskrit words is just too beguiling to be ignored. He has been taking care to see that the fire which was lit to offer obeisance to Lord Vishnu is doused immediately so that the fire alarm does not go off.

Natalie is spellbound with priest Sudarshan's scholarly discourse on Lord Vishnu, the preserver in Hindu pantheon and whose bountiful blessings are being invited to be showered on the new entrants in the cloistered ambience of the house; bad vibrations have already been bustled off by him from the vicinity through his divinely ordained hymns. Natalie has suddenly transformed into a solemn person. 'We also go to the church on such occasions to seek His blessings.'

Sensing Natalie's interest in the rituals, priest Sudarshan tries to elaborate. 'We have three primary Gods in Hindu pantheon: Brahma, Vishnu and Shiva: Brahma, the creator was forgotten the moment he created this beautiful universe from a small mass of matter. Vishnu as the preserver receives our attention and Shiva as the destroyer gets the maximum pampering in the form of innumerable temples being dedicated to Him. Anyone having a nuisance value should be accorded the prime slot.... It's natural, I guess...'

'As human race we're all paranoid about our extinction from the face of earth. We, the Christians created a fable called the Noah's Ark in the Bible to get over that fear...,' Natalie quipped to the discourse of priest Sudarshan.

'Nataraja, the Dancing Shiva with His cosmic dance is sometime identified with the perpetually expanding universe. In that sense, the destroyer and the creator are united in one single entity...'

'Oh, He's very cute. That dancing half-naked God! Gye often uses a word which I like very much: *bindaas*, carefree. When I first saw that statue of the dancing God in a museum in Washington I uttered the word bindaas on an impulse. One Indian man was standing near me and he belched out a hearty laugh....'

Natalie could not stop laughing at this recollection.

The red roses and the yellow dandelion flowers are lying in perfect harmony in the crystal flower-vase on the glass-top oval-shaped dining table. An inimitable gift from Natalie! It is Natalie's way of chorusing 'All the Best' to her dear friend on a unique occasion. Hot dogs, chicken burgers, Indian delicacies like biriyani, butter chicken masala, paneer malai kofta, *payasam* etc encircle like pendants in a necklace around the flower-vase, huge bottles of Pepsi and Tropicana juices cleaving at one corner. Bowls of crispy snacks are strategically positioned on every available location so that the guests, particularly the children, can entertain themselves whenever they feel a pang of hunger.

Anjali is on a new high today. Resplendent in a *muga*-silk saree, she seems to have been enjoying the ambience right from the word Go. She sings a Bihu song and the rest of the people dance to its peppy tune. Martha's African folk-song is equally perky and the crowd continues gyrations. Gaurav plays a Beyonce number and this small group of people has gone berserk. The mood becomes somber when Kenny's song as a prayer to the Virgin Mary is sung; Gaurav joins her with his Guitar and all-pervading calm dawns on all of them with that blissful rendering. The crowd continues to be swayed blithely in that bonhomie for quite some time even when music has ceased to flow.

Then the group proceeds to see the rooms. They are amazed at the new idea of converting the usually dank basement to a library and also the computer sitting beguilingly at one corner.

'Congratulations Gayatri. We salute your fighting spirit. Our best wishes are with you.' Ahmed dada's right palm is on her head as a sign of blessing.

'That lanky man is in love with you. He has been looking at you through those Smirnoff-laced droopy eyes.' Anjali has always been proud of her insight and this time too her words spew confidence.

'Oh God! Stop all this nonsense. He's my boss, the editor of my paper and he doesn't touch alcohol. Poor thing! His brother is in a hospital for getting treated for psychiatric ailment and from what I could gather from grapevine in the office, his wife left him a year back because of his obsessive concern for his ailing brother. Love? Ha! It has gone out of my life forever.'

'Gone out? Has it ever dared to make an entry in your life? You were made to marry a person and you made an effort to like him. The effort failed miserably.' The usual smug smile of

Anjali played on her face on such moments of brutal frankness is noticeably missed this time.

Gayatri left an invitation in the answering-machine of Siddhartha for this house-warming party. A space which his two children are going to inhabit needs his blessings in profusion.

She met Siddhartha last month in New Jersey where Assamese crowd celebrated bihu, their post-harvest festival. He was at a distance avoiding mordant glances and sly innuendoes. '...This is the man who once propagated the so-called Indian values with a crusading zeal and then ran away from his family to be with his lover...ha. Only to be unceremoniously dumped.... Oh, oh, such an insult on his manhood! Serves him right! Conceited man...!'

The man with narcissistic arrogance must have felt being persecuted by words never uttered, insinuations never made.

When people came to America 30 or 40 years back from a country like India, the otherwise gaunt shore-line between these two cultures was almost invisible. Where was the Indian face on the street? Where was the Indian store? And the ubiquitous telephone? America might have been bursting at her seam with these speaking-machines, but it was a different scenario in India where a telephone was only a rarity or at best a luxury. Internet, the razzamatazz of communication revolution, was not even conceived. These pot-pourri of causes conspired to increase physical distance between the birth-place and the adopted homeland. For those stranded people, there was no other choice than to blend well with the milieu of the country of their adoption.

But for some of the relatively new immigrants, it has become fairly easy to make a pretension of staying apart from the mainstream. This vociferous minority argue, 'We have come to America to get a comfortable life. We're not Americans. It's a purely a professional marriage, a marriage of convenience....'

Siddhartha was the leader of this mutineer brigade with his consummate skill in speaking and arguing.

Siddhartha once sent an extremely vituperative e-mail to Sukumar Bezbarua, president of the Assam Association and a respectable person in the community, accusing him of grooming his son in the American way of life... 'Your son cannot speak, read or write Assamese. Do you have the moral right to hold the exalted chair of the Head of a cultural organization of this community when you do not have any respect for its cultural ethos?'

Sukumar Bezbarua was visibly hurt at the imprudence of such a young man and he quit immediately.

The spicy news of Siddhartha's running away with a white-woman was bound to raise titters.

That was the last time Gayatri had a glimpse of Siddhartha. Though she managed to sneak into his elusiveness for a few solitary moments to strike some mundane conversation, she could not penetrate that thick rampart of wounded pride. She is not happy at the fall of a self-proclaimed titan like Siddhartha and this involuntary voyage through that memory trail always leaves her somewhat distressed.

She also couldn't erase from her memory that sharp nasal voice of the anchor of the bihu function who was announcing the items in her bizarre Assamese. Words seemed to have juggled with one another to sound as weird as possible while coming out from her thick-fat-pouted lips. '*Eya Amar* Ananya. Ananya Thakuria. *Borgeet gabo*. Our Ananya will sing a devotional song. Give her a big hand.'

No raucous clapping could be heard. The girl in her teen called Ananya was trying to hold the attention of her audience with her rendition of this devotional song on that make-shift stage inside the chapel. But the supposed-to-be-captivated audience there was exchanging information among themselves on so many things, spanning across two continents, from Minnesota to Washington and then hitch-hiking through Delhi to Guwahati...Rubul got green-card? So early...? Has anyone among us lost job? No, not here, who knows what's happening there in the Silicon Valley! Don't worry. All those who had come earlier with BBA or MCA degrees from all those shady colleges have lost jobs. Yes, those with Java language types.... Ah! Your mekhela-chadar! Beautiful color! From Sualkuchi?... Oi Birina! If you go home next month, I am going to send a face-crème for my Ma...Kanika Bora's son is getting married? Assamese girl from Guwahati? Very lucky to have such a son who agreed to get a bride from India and that too from Assam. That Smita girl got married to a white man.... Who Smita? Arre, you don't know her? Borkotoky's daughter! They were living together before marriage. Yuck.... Hey! you must come to our *Satyanarayan* puja. In the South-Indian temple nearby. Cost? Not going to be much. They have a fixed rate. Hundred dollars. No further headache...

Ananya's song was over. The anchor-lady with her tacky visage and a wiggling body was coming forward to make another of her announcements, 'Felicitation to Gayatri Borthakur for her brilliant write-ups.' Suddenly people were stealing furtive glances at Siddhartha who was perching himself casually atop an ornately curved wooden table behind the last row with the dangling feet swaying aimlessly and avoiding all those cacophonous stares. But he was ravenously following his wife when she was on the podium to receive the traditional mode of felicitation there, a coiled *gamocha* hung elegantly round her slender neck and a bouquet of bright chrysanthemum flowers put in the fetters of her strong grip, the raucous applause was also fiddling with that moment of joy. For her, it was a moment oscillating between a piercing pain and an intense ecstasy.

Standing in the midst of all this merry-making on the occasion of the house-warming party at this instant, she has still been vacillating between smudges of pain and the soughs of pleasure. So many things have been lost and so many things have been added.

It is life.

It is life: varied, volatile and impetuous like that of an excruciatingly capricious person.

Gaurav is keyed up at this moment. He is going to join a serpentine queue of ecstatic teenagers who are all excited to have a peek at the first show of a Harry Potter film. Katie is engrossed playing with a tennis ball inside the living room, her swinging body tries to keep pace with her vacillating pellets of thoughts where she must have been imagining herself as Harry's very special friend Hermione Granger and conjuring up different piquant tricks in her own mental plane.

Gayatri tries to play the role of both mother and the absentee father, sometime she becomes a story-teller, sometime a guide in their frenzied path to a startling adulthood, in an another time she just becomes a fun-filled companion. She wants to be there with them all the time, the canopy of her enduring and endearing presence is offered to facilitate their entry in a mystifying future.

She feels the profound weight on her shoulders but this schlepping is pleasure-fretted, inviting and wonderful. When she looks at their gullible faces, she feels that she must go on. They are just too beautiful and need her now in their orbit of life. She is their pillar of strength and she cannot let them down.

Last evening while coming down from her office in the fourth floor of Gateway Building, she met two young women inside the lift. One of them was heavily pregnant. Suddenly the pregnant lady put her hands on her big belly and exclaimed to her friend in a voice which was unmistakably drenched in delight, 'Look, she's squirming inside. Naughty child! Why should she think that she can play kick-boxing inside her mother's womb?'

Gayatri also felt like participating in this slap-happy conversation, 'Your first child?'

'No. My fourth. That's why...she cannot brow-beat me....' The young mother giggled at her own wit. The twinkles of joy were still lingering on her pretty face when she left the lift along with her companion to dissipate among a milling crowd of evening grazers. Her happiness was so contagious that Gayatri just squeezed Natalie's hand in an inexplicable joy.

'They are the new baby-boomers.' Natalie's wavering eyes were following the fast disappearing figure of the would-be-mother. 'American economy boomed during Clinton. People became more confident and more babies were brought in. There's gloom in the economy now but the earlier trend of baby-rearing has largely been going on.' Natalie was trying to explain this gargantuan appetite for babies in the present-day American society. She appeared to be grave; her usual impishness was missing. It was always so whenever she talked something serious.

This time too she looked reflective.

'It's not only the economy. There is this religious aspect also. The number of devout Christians has been surging...I mean the Catholics.... Abortion is a total no, no to them. Even birth-control is abhorred. Birth-control is killing life even before its arrival.' Natalie's elaboration on this topic went on. As a new entrant in the American mainstream, Gayatri could no longer afford to remain indifferent to the happenings here and Natalie was the recent passport for her entry in this enigmatic world.

'Birth means creation, birth means life. When the young American soldiers returned from the war-ravaged Vietnam, they were tired and shattered. They saw death from a very close angle. Poor boys! They were quite distressed about it. Death was always so frightening! Most of them got married immediately and went on a baby-rearing spree as if that was the way death could be challenged. The same thing happened after the Second World War too. The soldiers who came back after the War were quick to settle down and rear children. This baby-rearing generation from 1946 to 1964 was nick-named as the baby-boomers. Good jargon yeah, good one!'

Natalie's enchanted face suddenly erupted with a sharp but engrossing glitter not usually seen in her frivolous euphoric demeanor, 'Hey, I want to adopt a baby. I am serious. I mean it dear, I mean it.'

'Go ahead. I'm with you. I've also fallen for this nation-wide sweet-craze for babies. In India, there are too many people. That's probably the reason why life is not valued there. You're rarely going to get a woman who will pat her yet-to-be-born fourth child so lovingly....'

Natalie's eyes were moist. Crazy woman! Such small things would move her to tears.

'In India, birth of a girl-child is loathed and some of them do not even get to see the rays of sun. They are killed in the womb. If they are fortunate enough to escape death then, they might be finished in their marital homes. You may ask why! For the unpardonable crime of not bringing enough dowry. This is happening even in the developed parts of India, even among the super-duper rich. Among some communities in northern India, men are left without brides. There is simply no living girl. They have all been murdered....'

Natalie was looking intently at her. Story of an unfamiliar world had been unfolding in front of her eyes.

That accidental meeting with a giggling would-be-mother was bringing forth a whole rush of emotions to Gayatri. She wanted to recollect all those fragments of adorable time when she accompanied the kids to the Christmas-tree-decoration competition in the Bryce-Jordan Recreation Hall or to look for the elusive eggs colored briskly by the little ones and hid craftily between the bushes to be found out during the Easter celebrations in the Coledon Park. She has always been an active partner in their process of growing up in a land where childhood is cherished.

Their recent fun-filled trip to the Disney world in Orlando was also full of so many cherished moments. Ah! A world of fantasy where old and young alike can revel.

This trip to Disney world was a gift to the lovable children from their dear mother and Gayatri felt a sense of total involvement during the jaunt. She felt fulfiled and remembered Dr. Shakuntala Kundan, Anjali, Lara Sinclair, Kenny and all other people who were there during her difficult cruise through a delicate phase of her life. An overwhelming feeling of gratitude for America was also engulfing her for the strong, wide, indelible space provided by this country to a pair of quivering, alien and terrified feet scouting for just an alley at a distressing time.

She narrated her myriad emotions wavering between pleasure and bewilderment to Natalie when this memorable trip to Disney world was over. The pangs of pain for Siddhartha not being there with the family were lying inert at her heart but a carpet of joy for her ability to transport her children along with their imagination to a magical world entirely on her own had also been overwhelming.

'It happens. Each painful incident is followed by a desire for stability, peace and happiness. People try to forget the aching past....'

Natalie's gaze was fixed on the illuminating computer-screen, her right hand index finger was making a semi-cyclical, melodic movement, but her usual evanescent mind seemed to be working overdrive that moment. 'After the Vietnam War, the baby-boomers besieged this place with their little ones. And after the Bin Laden episode, there has been a sudden spurt in the number of church-goers in this country. A tiny book called The Prayer of Jabez immediately became the new best seller for the country. Imagine a record 3.5 million copies were sold within three months!'

'Who is Jabez?'

'The 35th son of Judas. He was just mentioned casually in the Bible. Of course, he was more respected than most of his siblings. But he had a favorite prayer which finds a mention in the Bible.... O' God, bless me and increase my kingdom!...Bruce Wilkinson, a priest from Atlanta wrote an analytical book, The Prayer of Jabez on this simple appeal of a God-fearing person. Most of our Christian scriptures are telling us what not to do. Humility in front of God has been stressed again and again. In contrast, Jabez is more positive and more demanding. He is asking God to bless him, help him and increase his kingdom of thought. This is a more upbeat prayer, not a passive desire of a depressed person.'

Natalie's thought at that moment seemed to be in harmony with that cheery entreaty. She wanted to go out and look for joy in the midst of ruin like the rest of her irrepressible countrymen.

Gayatri also wants to be a part of that buoyant mood. Siddhartha's going away was as catastrophic for her life as the 9/11 has been for this great country. An insane person with a burst of vitriolic froth saw to it that two pillars of American pride had gone down the rubbles and so also a lot of innocent, unsuspecting lives. A cheerful, friendly country was suddenly taken over by an overwhelming feeling of grief, fury and antagonism. The day Siddhartha announced his decision to go away to Chicago taking Nora in tow it was a terrible blow to her innocent, hassle-free, virgin self. Her life crumbled like those two collapsed towers and thousands of innocent entities like trust, love, self-belief, poise, notion of security etc. perished in an instant.

America, a massive country, has devised her own mechanism to fight back against gloom and also to rail back on the path of sense. A demon called fear should not trample her convivial spirit forever. Sometime a baby-boom might do the trick; sometime the challenging prayer of a hitherto inconsequential entity might tilt the balance. Gayatri, an ordinary woman, has also been trying in her own small ways to defy shocking odds and change the course of her beleaguered life by rallying whatever skills and means she has at her pint-sized kitty. An internecine feud between the precarious past and an assured present has been going on and the present must lie in her poised grip. 'O God, bless me and increase my kingdom...'

Her whispering prayer which has escaped with vehemence is now a part of the limitless expanse of the universe.

✦ ✦ ✦

7

'You're going to write a book? On American life? Great. But why on America? I don't want to sound cynical. American life is insipid. Our birth-place has got so much to offer in terms of varieties....'

Manish's exuberance is frizzling and Gayatri is awash by that genuine flow of bubbling enthusiasm coming forth from someone who himself is steeped in an abyss of despair.

Her mother is aghast on phone, 'You want to be a writer? It cannot be a full time vocation. You'll starve. Do you remember my uncle, Mohan daiti, that wrecked old man, who wrote a book and sold off everything, including his plot of land, to get it published? No one bought his book. People used to run away as soon as he was sighted lest he would try to sell it. He used to carry a pile of his books on the back of his ramshackle bicycle....'

Even before Manish's suggestion was forthcoming she wanted to write something keeping India in the backdrop; rustling up imagination in a familiar terrain where she had sprouted long time back among her near and dear ones, is not as difficult as conjuring up a reverie in an alien land where she has still been groping to find a toehold like a wobbly toddler.

Then she was contemplating, like a meditative sage trying to find the apotheosis of life, about the journey she would have to make in her yet-to-be-conceived book. Where she should start? She asked herself, but couldn't find a gratifying answer. Her quivering walk, from her home, on the winding pathway through the *samsan*, the Hindu crematorium where dead-bodies were consigned to leaping flames, to the faraway High school was never an interesting event though the faces of those somber looking young men, with the mourning attires of dhoti, the loin cloth on the lower parts of their bodies with the upper parts remaining uncovered looking intently at the last remains of their father, still haunt her. They were absolutely shattered and engrossed totally in the soot and grime of their grief. On an impulse she just veered towards them. 'Why did he give away that house to her? We didn't know about her game-plan. She was looking after our father in his last days with that intention. She maybe our own sister, but...'

The young, innocent soul of her cowered inside in an intense agony, but pain had to first emasculate the bubbling despair growing there unwittingly like a flashing sword out to slay her effervescent hope.

Or else should she write about that frail, handsome boy who proposed a life of togetherness with her by pushing a blue-color envelope hastily in her hand? A curved, decorative, deep-blue I Love You was popping out from a blue paper and staring brashly at her prissy face.

A litany of new anecdotes of her growing up years might be coming up and an interesting story might be unfolding on the moraine of an off-shore land. Who knows her lackluster initial years in America might also spawn a wonder!

Those years in America when she craved for noise and chaos! Then one day that hassle-free life ended abruptly and Siddhartha went away in a huff. A new life of struggle and conflict began and a delicate balancing act was required between the crazed frontiers of mind, body and time. Should she write about her marching footfalls on the heaving streets of State College on her way to the McDonald and back, cruising past an ocean of white snow on a velvety night? Or about that sordid tale of pizza-eating in Neil and Rebecca's house and her inglorious exit? Or should she write about a food experiment in the Penn State University in the Department of Food and Nutrition for a paltry sum of fifty dollars?

The notification was published in the local paper, 'If you are a woman of normal health and in the age group of 30-40 years, you may join this food experiment conducted by the Food and Nutrition Department of the Penn State. For full three days, you are going to take breakfast, lunch and supper in our laboratory. Your behavior, attitude etc. will be studied in the context of your food preference and health. For such cooperation, you will be paid fifty dollars.'

It was the period when she was in a state of intense penury, work-permit was still not forthcoming and reservoir of saving was fast drying up. Her bruised ego was not allowing her to go to Siddhartha with a begging bowl.

'I'm a healthy woman of Asian origin with 110 lbs weight, 160 cms height and I want to join this experiment.'

She was accepted on telephone itself and asked to report the next Wednesday. On that particular day, she was ushered into a cubicle by a very cute, lively girl with a cherubic face and Gayatri was amazed to see a heap of foodstuff like cake, cheese cake, white bread, brown bread, cheddar cheese, cottage cheese, cheese without fat, butter, calorie-less butter, grilled chicken, fried chicken, lots of green salads, one pitcher of black coffee with sugar and crème in separate containers, all arranged delicately on a wooden table with a cherry-red glass-top.

Too much food, a huge heap of food with Himalayan proportion, her famished, tired body was tempted to gobble up everything. But her tongue, used to relish spicy Indian food, was finding all these typical American food very bland. During lunch, the same kind of food was served, spaghetti was the only addition. And again similar tasteless fare during dinner with a cabbage soup! By the third day, she was almost choking. After every meal, she would just go to the washbasin and throw up. She knew she was being observed through secret camera placed there. On the last day after the last meal, she had to fill up a questionnaire about her feeling, her mental and physical health, food preference etc. The lively girl was little bit sad. 'You don't enjoy your food. You're tense and depressed. You want to throw up....'

She wanted to tell that it was the piled up flavorless food which even her near-empty stomach had refused to take in. But she kept quiet and waited with bated breath for the fifty dollars.

The girl paused for a while, 'There is a little problem here. You don't seem to have a work-permit. As per American law, we can't pay even a cent to a person without work-permit.'

Gayatri was shattered. How could she tell this young girl that only for those fifty dollars she had agreed to sit like a guinea-pig in a food-laboratory and eat all those insipid food?

'We're so sorry. But if you agree, we can find a way out. We've an arrangement with the Giant Supermarket for buying our weekly provision of food-items. If I buy food-items from that store for you worth fifty dollar will it be okay?' She wanted to jump like a small girl and exclaim in a full throated voice, 'Okay.... Okay.... Okayyy.... Why I was doing all these? To feed my children.' But fortunately those shoddy outpouring of emotions was not forthcoming. On the other hand, she managed to keep her cool and told in a dignified voice, 'That's fine. Thank you.'

Provision of food for a week! Not bad. Lentils were available only at the Indian stores. But that was a small price to be paid. Chicken curry would do.

This was a class meant to study the effect of food on human psychology in the context of several new generation diseases like Bulimia, Anorexia etc. and here was she, an India-born housewife on the American soil, subjecting herself to an experiment for the sake of her kitchen-fire going.

This should hold the interest of her American readers if she includes this in her proposed book.

She was fired from Neil and Rebecca's house for the offence of eating their excess food which would have otherwise gone to the garbage-bin. She can write flamboyantly on that also. She had to go to Lara's class to learn American English. That ceaseless flow of words without visible punctuation was to be grasped for her continued existence in this society and bubbly Lara with her multicultural class of American-born students gave a new orientation to an abandoned existence and conspired to boost her abbreviated ego. And how can she omit her numerous visits to Dr. Shakuntala Kundan and quaffing

Dr. Kundan's advice like a passionate adherent in that time of loneliness?

She shuddered at the thought of consulting a psychiatrist when excruciating depression was devouring her with all its fangs and she was just sinking and sinking in that abyss. 'I'm not mad. Why should I go to a psychiatrist?' She thought. In Gayatri's birthplace, people who have evidently become insane would be forced to go to a mad-man's doctor. Her maternal uncle who was virulently violent had to be taken to a mad-man's doctor as a last resort and that was the spiciest news among the people around providing fodder for the neighborhood gossip. Uncle's daughter's engagement to a college lecturer had to be called off because the groom's parents' stubborn refusal to get their son married to a mad-man's daughter.

But she was in a different country when she decided to go to a psychiatrist and in this country going to a counselor or a psychologist or a psychoanalyst was as mundane as going to the library or the movie-hall. The day she put Gaurav in school, one mother was telling the class-teacher that her son might like to go to the restroom frequently and his imploring to frequent the restroom should be totally ignored as advised by his counselor. A four-year old boy and counseling! What an irony! Have the parents gone mad? Her very Indian mind was horrified at this bizarre juxtaposition.

She can write her feelings about the entire episode of a small child being dragged to the dopey world of a psychiatrist, that psychiatrist's didactic reading of things about childhood which were otherwise so normal in childhood in another culture and her own planet going disarray in the wake of her decision to go to one of them later on. Americans might gape at the Indian society for their lack of riches or for all the superstitious beliefs but Indians might look at Americans with the same scorn for small, little things like an innocent childhood prank being subjected to scrutiny of an imperious psychiatrist or a counselor.

Her lonely home-coming during fog-filled nights through the deserted streets of State College, after her work as a waitress in McDonald, might also form a small part in her writing. One night a cop stopped her and wanted to safely walk her back home.

During those late-night lonely walk back home, memories of a far-away but sweet past kept coming back to her to give her company. It was mandatory for the girls in her parental house to reach home before dusk. One day she was late in returning home from her friend's place, all the college gossips woven and spun around a select few were keeping them captivated and time just flew away without them being aware of it. When she reached home she could meet both her parents in the front porch with scads of trepidation writ on their faces. 'It's so unsafe for unmarried girls to roam around after dark.... When you're married, then there will be a husband to protect and look after. Till that time, no more such foolhardy late-evening adventures....' Her father roared in anger.

Tears were trickling down her mother's eyes. Those were the tears of relief at her safe return.

And here she was, all alone, treading a path strewn with loneliness. A swaying blizzard filled with snow was blurring her vision and the cops offering her those romantic connotation like safety and protection. She had to laugh it away.

In one of the college dormitories five girls were sleeping peacefully over a carpet. One of the girls just felt a touch, hard and painful. Another girl screamed. The stranger violated all the five girls with his strokes or kisses under the cover of darkness. The intruder, a Chinese postgraduate student who was arrested later on, narrated his stories of woes. Too much academic pressures in the form of project, dissertation, participation in the class lectures, assimilation of what was going on in the class, were all affecting him and there were no stress-busters in an alien atmosphere in the form of relatives or friends to hang around. He lost mental equilibrium at one point of time and derived a vicarious pleasure in touching the soft spots of sleeping American girl students. It was his way of taking retribution on a system which was on the verge of purging someone who had come all the way from a far-off land in pursuit of a great American Dream.

In oriental countries like India, China, Korea etc. sweet childhood is lost under the back-breaking, disconsolate pressure of a weighty school-bag. Adolescence is also gone at the onslaught of a burgeoning curriculum. On the contrary, here childhood is cherished and adolescence is pampered but beyond that education becomes an onerous business. You do or otherwise you perish. A doctoral research must lead to something new or fundamental.

In her writing she is not going to consign the Chinese boy to the leaping flames of outright condemnation in spite of his abominable act. A sea of compassion will flow throughout that narration on an otherwise grotesque story. Will American readers be able to accept such a view-point which might be far removed from their own way of looking at things? She does not know.

She has already bared her mind, her apprehensions, and tribulations to Greg about the proposed book which should encompass a vast space and time with author playing the role of an active anchor.

Greg was an attentive listener. He was convinced that there had been enough materials in her kitty to weave magic, to sprout wings for going skywards. 'But I suggest that you may write on America and on an American family which migrated long time back from Europe.... I'm eager to see such a family through your eyes.'

'American family? I do not have a firsthand knowledge on a typical American family of European origin and their aspirations. In fact, my ideas are very vague and colored....'

'You may try. I'm going to talk about my life. You're going to listen and then decide...'

Greg's belief in her has become her might. She has decided to go through 'a riveting journey' with him to comprehend this beautiful country with all her myriad hues.

But she is not going to bare her mind to Manish at this moment. When she is fully ready to capture some captivating moments of American history and American life, maybe in its miniscule fragments, she might tell it all to him. His innocent enthusiasm might still be there with her in that exciting journey through this exotic continent.

✦

'My great grandfather Ronald was fond of adventures. Though America was keeping herself isolated from the First World War in her desire to pursue the agenda of development Ronald just left his homeland to join British force and fought in a place called Tsingtao in China against the German East Asia Squadron. The Germans were in occupation of that beautiful seaport since

1898. During First World War, a vast contingent of German naval forces was based there and they conducted operations throughout the Pacific. But the British launched a relatively minor attack on that port to free it from German occupation and they were largely successful. My great granddad was a part of that British attacking force. He came back to tell the manifold stories of his adventures in an exotic Asian country to an amazed crowd of onlookers at Tionesta.... The girls in China so beautiful, so inviting, so full of life that it is just impossible to resist them. I made some of them pregnant. I killed so many German soldiers that I was asked to command a full battalion.... Most of the shoppers at the Maple's shop were awestruck. My great grandmother Emily who was engaged to be married to Ronald was green with jealousy for all those pretty Chinese girls whom her lover had bedded. Her impending marriage had been hot news for quite some time in that small town and she couldn't afford to break off that engagement for the fear of getting a bad name. Who would have married a girl who broke off an engagement for a supposedly masculine act committed on an enemy people?'

Gayatri is stunned. Is Greg talking of America? Her thoughts unveil a thin thread of cohesion between an early 20th century America and late 20th century India where the life of an individual was consummated by the liking or disliking of an intangible but an all-pervasive society. This gripping society is lost forever in the tangled mess of a fast forward motion both in America and also in urban India....

'Maple's shop was the only shop in that small town where town-folks flocked to buy the provisions and also to get the latest tit-bits about the other people. The day Ronald and

Emily got married in the local chapel, all the bouquets and all the chocolates in Maple's shop were just flying off the shelves.'

'Emily must have been very happy. Poor Emily! She was so worried.'

'Yeah, poor Emily. It was a story of life-long suffering. It was the Great Depression! Things were not sold, not even the maize and wheat of her rich farm-land. Shops, mills, offices were competing with one another to put their shutters down. A dismal state...!'

Greg looks exhausted, worn-out. His mind is there in the past now and the gloomy stories of the Great Depression must have flowed back to cause him consternation.

'Till that time capitalism had too much faith on itself. It was bloated with self-pride for its supposed inherent capacity to mend any ill and bounce back on the path of recovery without any magical hand. Where was that inherent strength when thousands of helpless unemployed thronged the streets of America? The most powerful government in the world just looked on.'

Gayatri's mind, always colored by the romantic beats of Keats' or Wordsworth's poems and the pictures of a multihued Western Autumn interspersed with lovely Daffodils, cannot simply fathom this curious scenario of unsold things or begrudging unemployment making a hay in the American life in a time not far removed from her own time.

'Then came the New Deal policy, based on Keynesian economics, applied on American economy as a balm by President Roosevelt and there was transformation. It worked wonders. State intervened with pumping of money. The economy revived.'

'The gloomy days of Depression were over and Emily must have had lived happily ever after with Ronald.'

'Real-life stories are never like those happy-ending tales Gye. Not even with real prince and princesses. Look at poor princess Diana of our times and her travails.... There was no end to Emily's grief as well. Her only child William lost his life in the second-world-war. She must have gone to her grave with a feeling of that crushing loss.'

A woman in a different time and space but still hovering over them in a thread of unremitting memory!

'America had already established herself as the greatest force in the world till the outbreak of second world war. She could no longer afford to remain indifferent to the happenings in the world. Hitler was crossing all limits and his alley Japan dared to launch an attack on America in Pearl Harbor.'

'Your America destroyed two mega cities of Japan by dropping atom bombs over them. Too many lives perished.'

'I admit that it was an inhuman act on the part of America. But what could she do? Why Japan should launch an attack on a neutral country without any provocation? Japan needed to be taught a lesson.'

'It was not retribution Greg, it was an experiment. That was carried out not on the real villain of peace, Hitler's Germany, but on a tiny Asian country. It was easier to conduct such a gruesome test on a brown Asiatic population rather than on a white one....'

'We started with Emily and ended up in Hiroshima and Nagasaki. We have strayed Gye.'

She has probably taken a puerile pleasure in his embarrassment.

Gayatri wants to scribble down all the details, even the insignificant ones, about the life of Ronald and Emily in a small, sleepy town in America. She has already jotted down the awfully busy life of Ronald in that idyllic town on his return from his hectic trip in the war-ravaged Asia. Ronald had hunted down a huge boar in preparation for the coming winter, salted the meat to be put into the cellar so that the family could have ample supply of meat during the hibernated period of a sprawling winter.

All these preparations were going on in anticipation of his imminent marriage with Emily, his heartthrob, whose beauty and irresistibly innocent charm had made him to rush home from that anodyne battle-field in Asia. He was making an alluring house from the wood chopped off from an oak tree of the Allegheny forest, a painstaking effort steeped in an encircling hope of a life with Emily. He used to laugh without betraying any outward sign of a smirk at the brooding face of this innocent girl for her hurt feeling displayed inexorably but wordlessly for the waywardness of her man in an alien land. He was not going to reveal that he was miles away from the girls in Qingdao as the British soldiers there were strictly forbidden from even looking at the girls, not to speak of touching or being very cozy with them.

He was happy that he was back to his dear Emily and to the virgin wild of Alleghany forest. He was in love with the untamed jungle and could recount each and every tree in his immediate neighborhood.

During their walks through the forest and the foothills of the surrounding mountains, at a much later time, Ronald was always pointing out to his granddaughter Ethel, his bundle of limitless joy, at the small openings here and there in that dense forest through which some rays of sun were stealthily penetrating. 'There stood a crab-look-alike tree years back. It's gone forever.... And here, another small, fat tree, the branches looked like a porcupine, was standing. It had a white, tasteless, watery fruit which we used to eat in the afternoons. We, the kids, fought over them....'

Ronald's granddaughter, the little Ethel's sojourn with the forest started with her grandfather like this and the convivial forest which had always been in a state of flux had almost become her mother for sometime till she met someone special in a mystifying circumstances.

Gray-color twilight has been gradually falling all over and electric bulbs of different hues try to dare that assuming darkness with their equally bouncy playfulness. Tionesta, Emily, Ronald, Maple and Great Depression: she wandered through all of them, a fuzzy world outside her time and space but she consumed them with grace and ease. Now she feels jaded, drained out.

Siddhartha sent a notice for divorce and she signed on the dotted line this morning.

Anjali also rang up in the morning to call out all the names of people, whom she knew and who lost their jobs. Ananta's friend Deepak was summoned to his boss's cabin yesterday. 'You've been doing a good job. We're happy with you.' A congratulatory message from such a hard-to please, stingy boss! A rare feat! A euphoric Deepak immediately started contemplating about the next thing to come. A rise in pay or a rank! Or maybe a one-time bonus!

'Our company lost heavily in the share market. We're going to off-load some of our people. Unfortunately the list includes your name also...we're going to miss a good worker like you... If the company again starts to do well, we might recall you. Now you may take two-months' pay and push off.... Bye...have a good day.'

There was no sign of remorse or vacillation in his face or words.

'A slump is going on in the American economy. Some people are going to lose jobs.' Anjali informed her about these latest goings-on matter-of-factly. A downward slide is there in American economy, Recession in Economic jargon. Greg was talking of Depression and Anjali spoke of Recession. What a strange co-incidence!

When she heats up the chowmein in the microwave during her lunch-break Ashifa bou calls her up and passes on the good news of daughter Shahiba's school graduation being over.

'Such great news.' She almost screams out in sheer delight.

'We're organizing a party next Sunday in our Baltimore house. This maybe our last party together. Shahiba will go out to the big, bad, social world of America and might be lost there forever, for all of us.'

Ashifa bou's voice chokes with an intense emotion.

She does not want to tell Ashifa bou that it is unethical to apply Indian value-system to an America-born young-adult. She restrains herself to give a long-distance telephonic discourse to a harassed Ashifa bou gripped by an overwhelming fear.

The Dutta family of Washington brought a child to their home from an orphanage in India after all their efforts to conceive biologically failed. The affectionate couple brought her up with endless love. She was their dream child, a little princess, an exquisite fairy and there was an incessant pouring of hope and adoration over that blessed kid.

When she started living with her German boyfriend in his apartment since last year, it was not only her parents but the entire Assamese community had been livid.... How could she do that? Brought up from nowhere and that is how she wants to pay her parents back...?

Whenever Gayatri tells her Indian friends that she is never bothered about Gaurav going out with his girlfriends in the evening, Gaurav is an American and he'll follow American social ethos, their faces writhe in total disapproval.

Greg's ancestors came to America from Germany in the nineteenth century. Does that country still shake him emotionally or it has gone far away from his orbit of thought? She has not dared to raise this futile question, pointlessly absurd at this point of time.

But while coming back from a long story-telling session with Greg, that question has started piercing her bit by bit, raising a quagmire of wayward emotions. Her small parental Assam-type cottage atop a green hill where she spent her entire loving childhood, the rhythmic sound of a hilly spring creating music in a venerable silence like a wild, dancing village belle going on a waltz in the lap of nature near that cottage which became a part of her growing up process, her apartment in the State College in America where she started a humdrum life with the father of her two children where hope was the only elixir, her two grown-up children with their idiosyncrasies associated with a normal adolescence in a disoriented but highly advanced western society: all these are gradually devoured by that overpowering emotion.

She could clearly see and feel a crying Ashifa bou in all those fragmented pictures.

✦

William had to slog for twelve hours a day in a synthetic-fuel producing factory in Berga, a tiny, kidney-bean shaped place in East Germany where nature has always been complacently bountiful. But the menacing shadows of death were also lurking somewhere behind that deceptive beauty. It could easily be sniffed in the air during those difficult days of world history when people talked of race or lineage or perfidy and snuffed out life as if it was the most heroic job to be done at the moment. After the War of Bulge in Poland in December, 1944, almost one-thousand American soldiers were captured by the Germans and herded as prisoners of war to Berga factory.

William, son of Ronald and Emily, was a twenty-year-old boy at that time, who was bubbling with energy and life and a mystifying innocence was also bursting forth at the seams as happened with most of the boys of his age.

'German blood flowing through your veins and still you want to fight against us! Shame on you! You're worse than a Jew, a traitor having no right to live.' Strong words of condemnation were pouring forth from the Nazi soldiers.

All these esoteric talks of fatherland, the land of the Fuehrer, Aryan superiority etc. were incomprehensible to William who was brought up in the vast, green countryside of America and his dreams or thoughts only centered round that virgin, copious greenness. He was unaware about existence of another world beyond that realm, a world of the past which did not even inhabit his memory-lane.

There was a discernible tenor of apology in Greg's voice.

'The burden of his forefathers was not passed down to him. That was the most sensible thing to have been done with someone as young as William. I'm trying to adopt the same strategy with my children too. Why to burden them with thoughts about India? There're are enough people there to take care of things.' Gayatri chipped in.

'But you can't really disown that weight. The boundary line between the two times maybe blurred but never actually goes away. That maybe resurrected any time and a stubborn time in the past about which you may not even be aware might just stare at your face. That was the case with the Jews and that was the case with our poor William. Someone just put a bayonet on his back and said...you were a German and you betrayed our cause....'

The Nazis had a policy to kill people with too much work and too little food. One piece of dry bread, one small bowl of tasteless soup, one tiny bed for two of them, defecation and urination through one small hole on the floor and twelve hours of ceaseless work inside a dusty tunnel, William had to go through all these motions.

Then the typhoid infection was the last straw. There was no medicine, no doctor. A betrayer, a quisling did not deserve to be treated like a human being. Even occasional slapping or spanking was also going on during his illness. Death was inevitable. Ronald and Emily received the shocking news from someone who managed to slip away from the camp under the cover of darkness. They cried so much that there were really no further tears to shed for them.

Even Pamela, the young girl in Tionesta who was visibly pregnant, became unusually quiet after this sad news spread like wild fire in the small town. What an ignominy it was! An unwed mother was totally unacceptable for this archaic town. Emily decided to honor her dead son's love by accepting Pamela in the family. How could she discard someone who was carrying a part of William inside her?

Gayatri's mind is in doldrums over Berga and poor William who reminds her to her own Gaurav, Garry to his American friends. If one day someone raises a finger on Garry for something happening in far-off inscrutable India, how is he going to respond? Has she prepared her son to face such a contingency? No, not so far. A Berga in a different form might recur anywhere, in anyone's life....

Siddhartha always strived to make them Indians and she, as the mother, wanted to make them Americans with an equal vengeance. She wanted to undo the past. But past is never dead, it is dynamic and might catch up at any time.

'I abhor war. Look at the two World Wars, Vietnam War and now this insensible Iraq War! So many people got killed and maimed. My grandfather William lost his life in Berga, my Dad lost his life in Vietnam and my brother has become a lunatic. His sense of this irreparable loss has translated itself into a bizarre anti-Americanism. Effect of a war only...!'

The Jews became an object of a collective ire of a society bereft of pride and steeping in a kind of acerbic, systematic deprivation imposed by something as monumentally illogical as the Treaty of Versailles. The fuming society looked at the indifference with which the trading community was carrying on their usual business, the apparent indifference was identified with insolence, prosperity with treachery and an abscess-like object of common hatred was weaved. The architects of the Versailles' Treaty were sitting far away ensconced in their own comfort zones, not reachable either by hatred or by anger. But fury had a borderless dimension which might go anywhere, anytime and shake off anyone, even the most complacent ones. The result was a fireball spanning across continents, touching lives everywhere, decimating trust, annihilating love and destroying a much-vouched-for myth that sun was not setting on the horizon of certain empires.

'That was a dark period, a depressing time in human history. At such time if someone pointed out a finger at you and told that you were the root cause of all their troubles, it'd simply be lapped up. Hitler was only doing that. That insane man was too shrewd to turn a personal hatred into a collective bitterness.'

Hitler and the Jews. An abominable story to be tethered in public memory for years together; a blot in the face of an otherwise triumphant humanity!

'This holocaust was so horrible. I lost my mental equilibrium for a few days when I first saw the photograph of a young pregnant woman. Two Nazi soldiers were standing nearby, hands of one soldier were on her protruding belly, and fear was there all over her face. In the next photograph, it was her still body, eyes shut with belly split wide open and a dead baby lying by its mother's side. Oh God! What a sight it was...'

Fear oozes out from her face at the thought of humanity being butchered by some insane people in not-too-distant past.

'You know Greg, it's mandatory for all Israeli children to go to the Holocaust Museum in Tel Aviv. This is a state policy.

Israelis are not supposed to forget this terrible cruelty which happened in the past. They're to carry this wound forever with them to go ahead. I wonder what impact it'd have on young minds when a matured mind like mine could not take it too long....'

The composed look which Greg was wearing so gallantly a few minutes earlier is no longer there.

'The Jews always look back to the sordid events of their past. That's their tradition. Have you heard about Passover festival? It celebrates their freedom from slavery in Egypt three thousand years back. They were engaged in pyramid-building activities, a back-breaking toil, but released as God took pity and interceded on their behalf to the Pharaoh. It's a Biblical story.'

Greg pauses for a while.

'Do you care for a cup of coffee?'

He seems to be not interested.

'The freed Jews crossed the Nile River to go towards Europe. During that difficult voyage, they had to control their hunger with yeast-less flattened bread. Flattened dry bread, sweet spinach, bitter gourd and roasted lamb meat are provided in the Passover feast. The sweet spinach speaks about the sweet taste of liberty while the bitter gourd reminds them of the bitter memories of slavery. When they can remember slavery in Egypt, how'll they forget a recent episode like Holocaust?'

'Please tell me about Pamela and Emily....'

'I met Victor, my grandpa's friend, who could escape from Berga's concentration camp, some years back when he was almost on the last league of his life's journey.... My grandfather was in his death-bed at Berga. He held Victor's hands and appealed to him: Will you marry Pamela if you go back alive from this place? For the sake of our love-child growing inside her womb.... Victor agreed to fulfill his dear friend's last wish. But a surprise was awaiting him in Tionesta. Pamela thanked him profusely for offering his hands to her in marriage but she declined that offer, 'Why should I need a name for my child? He's William's child and I'm going to bring him to this world.'

Gayatri's staggering brain waves at the turn of events in a small town in America in the early 40s is obvious from her amazed look. William, one of the would-be-characters in her book, was worried about the fate of their love-child and also wanted to protect the name of his lover from the curse of an unwed motherhood, a thing far removed from the realm of imagination of the present day temporal America.

'Pamela died in child-birth.'

She was awakened by a rude jolt by this heartless announcement!

'My mother Ethel came to this world as an orphan.'

When the hungry child looked for her mother with her deafening cry, the mother had been long buried deep inside the earth. But there was no dearth of love for her. Her grandparents Emily and Ronald took her in their loving arms and an armor of fortified affection around her was built. Emily also did not survive very long. Ethel was the child of the nature. She bonded well with the dark, deep but somewhat elegiac Alleghany forest and the dancing, wild Alleghany River.

How is Gayatri going to describe Ethel in her book? A girl with a long curving frock, a tiny pony-tail moving up and down with her frantic pace! What should be the color of her frock? Pink would blend well with her pink complexion.

Or else a blue dress would also go down nicely with the blooming gentian flowers of the mountainside. When Gayatri was a kid, she was gifted a blue frock by her father and she used to roam around in the grassland near her grandparents' home in upper Assam in that new dress hopping over wild bushes or negotiating with truncated trees and sniffing the damp fragrance of a summer afternoon mixed with a putrid smell of grazing cows, her swinging ponytail competing with her swaying footfalls in pace. Ethel near Alleghany River has become Gayatri near Brahmaputra River in the far-off India, the two frail figures merging with each other making their contours almost invisible.

This morning Gaurav told her very candidly that he was keen on music and might take up music, his current passion, as a career. The lackluster classroom lectures were never his cup of tea. The school-report-card was also echoing the same view: he left most of the school assignments incomplete; very poor in math; an avid footballer and a very good musician...

Siddhartha also called her up this morning in the office. Their first interaction after their divorce. 'I'm not happy with Gaurav. He has done too poorly in math. I don't know what's wrong with him!'

'He doesn't like mathematics. He isn't interested in academics. He's crazy for music. He has got a flair for it. Let him carve out a life for himself Siddhartha. Let us get rid of that Indian mentality of earning a university degree, joining as an executive in an office with a desk job or as a reputed academician in a university and bringing in a fat salary with an assured life.'

Katie and Gaurav are kids from a broken home. But Gayatri has never implanted seeds of hatred or bitterness in their young, impressionable minds against their estranged father; his arrogance has been portrayed as his little foibles. She has been trying to weave a tale of love and trust around them so that when they look at the world through the prism of their home, only rainbows rush in and other positive events of life follow this vivid color spectrum.

What Gaurav is doing now, at this moment? He must be with his guitar playing some rehashed country songs as he usually does at this time. During weekends he is in a buoyant mood and goes for new, peppy songs. David maybe with him teaching him all those beautiful, melodious songs of the Amish community when they take out their cows for grazing and sing in the lap of a lyrical, lurid nature or all those spiritual songs called the Loblied sung in the church as a tribute to God.

David has become a rebel in his atypical way by choosing to become a doctor in a community where, in their zeal to preserve purity of life, use of electricity is shunned, a formal education is barred and horse-cart or bullock-cart takes the pride of usual mode of transport. He felt that this austere way of life of his community was rather arcane and he felt an urge to get out.

The Amish community boycotted David. 'You've discarded our society and we've also banned you from our community.' The Amish elders declared prudishly.

'I'm proud of my heritage. It's my life's mission to popularize Amish music through length and breadth of America. The Amish society may disown me but I'm one of them and continue to be one of them.' David told Gaurav and his classmates when he came to talk about Amish music and Amish way of life to the High School students in their school. Being an avid music lover Gaurav immediately struck a friendship with David: his musical talent was instantly recognized by David and an incredible camaraderie based on an undeniable mutual love for music has been formed between these two strangers.

With David, the rebel, Gaurav is going to sing the song of a bubbling life.

✦ ✦ ✦

8

'My mother Ethel joined the job of a forest Guard in the small forest town of Rockwood overlooking the Allegheny River, not very far from her hometown of Tionesta.'

The dark, brooding Allegheny river and the deep, impenetrable Allegheny forest held a very special place in her forlorn, orphaned childhood when her grandfather Ronald would take her for a stroll over West Hickory Bridge, the mystical, ancient bridge of the late 1800s and the she would gape at the original piers and abutments that were still supporting the amazing bridge with bated breath.

Greg has been trying to project Allegheny forest and the river as the two living, vibrant identities in Ethel's life infusing a kind of warmth in her otherwise desolate existence.

Ethel would go through impenetrable patches of forest in the Potter County dotted with giant trees like sycamore, silver maple, white pine, shagbark hickory and green ash through foot and keeping watchful eyes on varieties of wildlife like kingbirds, wrens, warblers, leopards, deer, bears and Bald eagles nesting areas. Sometime she would go rafting through the river between Kinzua dam and Tionesta and taking a break over any of the seven islands – Crull's, Thompson's, R Thompson's, Courson, King, Baker and No-Name that dot the river line like marbled statuettes guarding over a fragile landscape.

Her attentive stares were always on the lookout for something stirring.

Bald Eagle, American symbol of pride had to be conserved against extinction. It had already become endangered due to indiscriminate use of pesticides or haphazard felling by bullets. As a child Ethel used to look at this huge, exotic, brown and white bird with awe when it would just swoop down the wild current of Allegheny to catch its prey which might be a salmon or a tuna. Perching itself on the leafy branches away from prying eyes it would demolish the prey with the consummate skill of a trained hunter. As a forest Guard it was her mission to prevent its killing at the hands of stray hunters.

When oil was first discovered in Pennsylvania in 1859 it changed the world. Oil City founded in 1791 became a thriving city with a booming oil business. But pollution destroyed some of the natural habitats of the Bald Eagle in the forest areas throughout the river-way between Franklin and Pittsburg. However, Allegheny islands Wilderness was still offering virgin, green and sparklingly unsoiled areas for proliferation of this wild species and young Ethel was particularly felt inspired to go all out to keep her vigil for its conservation.

Ethel was going at a fast pace, the black T-shirt and the trouser was hugging her curvaceous body and a steady stream of body-fluid was draining her completely in that summer heat. Her indifference to her own discomfort was all too visible when her cold, devoted stares were straining to find out pug-marks of some wild animals or sudden noisy, frightful flight of a bird from a tree-trunk nearby. Her eyes were brightening up with any new discovery. Pug-marks of a leopard family! Their arrival was a welcome sign. From there, the tract had joined a winding pathway through a hill covered with chickweed, moss-covered rocks and a row of white-pine trees.

Tionesta was not very far, on the other side of the hill. Last time when she went there Agnes, Maple's daughter was thrilled, 'Ah! Your skin has become so shiny and evenly tanned. We're all trying to get a tan like yours, but it's not coming.'

'Most of the time I am inside a forest.'

That Ethel was working as a Forest guard in Rockwood was spreading from Maple's shop to other people of Tionesta in no time. Ethel was not supposed to tell other people about her vocation individually. One word to Agnes was doing the trick and the small town was abuzz with all gossips about her life in a log-house in Rockwood and her numerous jaunts inside the forest was a very good topic for speculation.

Her not-too-incredible parentage, lonely adolescence and dejected youth were all dragging her in the ambit of pitiful town-gossips. 'Poor thing!' became the common refrain, 'What else can she do!' they would say in a reflective mood.

'When I hear these stories I'm transported back to a small town in India where personal lives of people become topic for intense scrutiny. It's unthinkable in present day America. So many changes have come to America in a span of just fifty or sixty years. Unbelievable.'

'All these changes came after the Vietnam war. Maple's shop or any other family-based shop just vanished from the shore when the giant, monolithic structures like the Wal-Mart,

K-Mart, Giant, and Uni-Mart etc. came in a huff and occupied spaces around the towns and cities. They offered everything under the same roof in a highly reduced rate. The small family-based shops were the life-line of a town aligned intrinsically with the laughter and tears of their inhabitants. People could buy, pause, relax and exchange feelings. A huge structure like the Wal-Mart spreading from Boston to California had no time for people of Tionesta or Georgetown or Franklin. Their pain or pleasure had no relevance for these profit-driven machines. Can you imagine a situation when you are talking about you or your neighbors to a harassed counter-clerk of Wal-Mart in State College? Maple or Agnes had all the time on earth to listen to all neighborhood gossips and then pass on them to the next customer. That era had simply vanished from America with coming of Wal-Mart.'

'Hi guys. I have made coffee for both of you. I got some brownies also.' Natalie always brings something to eat or drink at this time. It is a welcome break for all of them.

'Greg's mom was a Forest Guard. I'm listening to her life story.'

'Must be very interesting! I'd have loved to hear. But my page on town events is still not complete. I must hurry.'

Natalie pushes the chair and stands up to go. Suddenly she puts her hands round Gayatri's neck very indulgently and tells her in a low, hushed, lingering tone, 'I've got some opera tickets for all of you. For this evening. Your children may like it. And Greg! You should also come. Today, let's take a break and go.'

Gayatri has always seen some kind of altruism in Natalie's attitude. She has bought the tickets and she has wanted that all of them should come and enjoy including Gayatri's children. It is such a rare gesture in this highly individualistic society!

Ethel was negotiating her ways through the chick-weed canopy, her pace had to slow down to find a pathway and balance her advancing body on rocky surfaces camouflaged skillfully by the white flowers of the chick-weed cover. Last night's heavy rainfall had made the area damp and dangerously slippery; the scorching sun had miserably failed to have any visible impact on this chimerical sogginess. Her log-house in Rockwood was almost quivering at the onslaught of the lashing storm when she was trying to get some sleep after gulping down the heated canned bean.

While she was walking she could see a huge bald eagle flying away in speed towards the nearby river. She knew that a colony of bald eagles was coming up there away from snooping stares and she must see to it that they thrive in that new habitat.

Suddenly she felt too tired and sat down instantaneously on a protruding rock and she went on sitting there like a zombie when a pitch dark night and a whirring sound of a storm at a distance woke her up from her stupor. She had to run back to her refuge, the feeble log-house which was quite far from her present spot, through a precipitous path down the mountainside, to have a sheltered but a lonely night...

In the evening the entire group is going for the opera. Enough of Ethel, her numerous strolls inside Alleghany Wild and her brooding fear for safety of a colony of Bald Eagles in a dark, storm-lashed forest!

Gayatri is thrilled about Gaurav and Katie joining her for the show.

Opera Falstaff: composer Giuseppe Verdi. The icon of Italian opera. Fallasta, a man with a huge belly and who was so proud of the gargantuan proportion of his own belly was chasing beautiful women. All these pretty women ganged up against risible Fallasta and taught him a lesson by calling him to Winedor Forest and some people masquerading as ghosts ran after his life.

It is reiterated again and again in the opera that the World is a Joke and the Life is a Folly.

Gaurav has been enjoying the musical wide-eyed, his otherwise placid demeanor is engulfed by a wild excitement not usually seen in him. He is well ensconced in the rippling effect of the musical ocean created around him. He is mesmerized by Nannata, one of the leading singers of the opera whose ritzy rendering of the songs is lapped up by him.

Natalie also bubbles with joy; her luminous eyes, titillating with the all-pervading jubilation, could be seen clearly in the nebulously-lit opera hall.

Natalie, Gaurav and Katie, all have been teeming with joy at the grand show in the opera hall and Gayatri wishes them to be frozen in this moment of abundant gaiety.

✦

'Hey Greg, why did you run away from the opera house that evening without telling any one of us?'

Natalie yells at Greg as if she has been seething in anger at his rudeness of getting away but that veneer of a mock anger fast disappears after the first bout of screaming.

Gaurav also noticed his sudden flight from the hall. 'Why did he leave in a huff? Is he not interested in opera?' Gayatri had to remain silent. She has never bothered to find out what was transpiring in the mind of that excellent story-teller; his crafty detachment from the plane of his footfalls was as mystifying as her own bewildering aloofness from his waves of thought.

'She was sitting in the first row along with her boyfriend.'

'Your ex-wife?'

Greg nods his head in approval, eyes lowered, and a sheet of disconsolate sadness almost blanketing his face.

'Please grow up Greg. You're no longer her husband. Let her live life as she pleases and you too live life accordingly. Now tell me, where's your girlfriend these days. You were going steady for some time with her. Right?'

Why is Natalie trying to spill the beans in public? But Greg who is otherwise so reticent seems to be not bothered this time.

'Oh! That one! She went away with a group, to Honduras....'

'Why are you sad?'

'Who is sad? In fact, it's a huge relief. One day when I came back home a little early, the entire group was there in my place, in a state of drug-induced trance. I asked her to leave immediately....'

There is a little pause with interplay of both anxious and cathartic feeling on his face 'I went for the Elisa test after her exit from here. It was a terrible period. The life was hanging on a thread between two possibilities: death or life. When clean chit was given after test result, I howled like a small baby, what a big relief it was!'

Gayatri struggles to understand the story of a man who is fiercely in love with his ex-wife but lives with another woman without any involvement of heart just for the sake of a biological companionship.

Being a woman from not a very thriving part of India she can feel and share a common chord with Ethel or Emily but most of the time she seems to be at a supercilious distance from the world of Natalie or Greg.

She understands the murmurings of whisper floating in the air of Tionesta about Ethel, a young orphaned girl who was moving in a carefree manner in the dense jungles of Alleghany in her mission to protect bald eagles. Whenever she recollects the last episode of Ethel's life in the lilting, earthy and rustic Allegheny as elaborated by Greg through his pedantic exposition, she feels connected to her in some way or the other.

...One morning that girl was going on a different exercise. A particular space was fenced off to protect the luxurious acacia trees from the leaf-eating herbivores like the deer or the wild cattle with the hope that in the absence of these predators the trees would blossom. But the protected trees were actually withering. It was not puzzling to the young girl who understood the rhythm of the throbbing nature better than a Botanist. When she was a small child she would go to bed only when the acacia tree in their backyard folded its leaves in the night: Why should I sleep now when our tree has not started her prayer? She used to tell entreatingly to her indulgent grandfather and he would invariably wait for the tree to say its prayer.

But some conservationists conceived the idea of protecting the acacias from the tree-grazing predators by keeping them at a place away from the herbivores in the heart of Alleghany forest and she had to bring that idea to life and to keep a watch. Right from the beginning she was aware of futility of such a project where the intricate relationships among fragile web of life were seemingly ignored for a more simplistic view of a two-species mutualism.

She was going sluggishly towards the dying trees. A stranger was there too looking at the trees and looking at her in turns. 'Huh! What a sight! Loneliness isn't doing any good to the trees.'

His mocking smile was spreading across his face and towards his sparkling eyes. He was a young man in his late 20s with unkempt hair, rugged exterior; a rifle was dangling casually from his arms and an amused smile was playing on his lips all along.

'...The ants which were finding shelter on the trees' thorns and sipping on their nectar were a grateful lot. They would swarm out ferociously, ready to bite, when a tree was disturbed by a grazing animal. But somehow the trees seemed to sense that no one was munching on their leaves and after a year or so apparently decided to reduce their investment in ants by not producing so many roomy thorns or so much tasty nectar....'

Ethel found this man, a strange man indeed in a lonely forest, as someone who could be trusted with her deep secrets. He was seemingly interested to know what was going on here, in this huge landscape, in the lives of roving and inert objects. His face was exuding a torrential flow of innocent sincerity and she could feel those vibes around.

'But the hungry ants also retaliated, lassitude was one, it eventually encouraged wood-boring beetles to invade the trees. Soon their tunnels left the trees sickly, dying or dead. You can see them in front of your eyes, those shriveling trees. The language of our nature is not that simple; it is deceptively complex.'

He listened intently though his gaze was fixed on her watery, hazel eyes.

Ethel gaped at his gun, 'You aren't going to hunt anything here.' There was a tone of apprehension in her voice beleaguered by so many conflicting emotions of trust, fear, a little bit of pull for this stranger's interest for the wild and his rugged handsomeness. 'In fact there's nothing here to hunt.' She was worried for the bald eagles and other members of her precious jungle family and a stranger with a firing-machine was a real danger to the song of life hummed melodiously by the forest since ages.

He narrowed his eyes and looked at her as if he was savoring an appetizing thing. 'I don't believe that there are not many things to hunt here.' She could feel a kind of numbness engulfing her at that moment. 'I work for the US Army. We're here to complete the Kinzua Dam along with our Engineers. A difficult job, I say.'

'My mother never told me much about our father excepting that first chance encounter. He had to leave one day for the Vietnam War which was raging through Vietnam at that time and he must have died there.'

A sigh has just come out of Greg's mouth.

The longing to see, feel, inhale an entity called father must have been gnawing at him since his childhood though his words uttered like sweet whispers are not going to bare those impregnated emotions.

'He used to write letters to my mom in the initial phase of his going there and my mother was looking forward to that perennial flow of mails. Then, one day, that flow just stopped. He vanished in the wilderness. There was no trace of him and US Army was clueless.'

Gayatri decides to keep quiet. The American sitting in front of her has been carrying in his veins many untold stories about annihilation: it maybe Holocaust in Berga or the First World War or the not-too-old Vietnam War.

'The war was going on in Mekong Delta area. That was a new moon night with a thick blanket of darkness pouring over a war-ravaged zone. Have you heard the name of Paul McCarthy, the famous Senator who talks and writes a lot against human rights violation anywhere in the globe?'

'I'm his big fan. He can speak on any topic. And the way he speaks, so unassuming yet so profound! A lovable old man, like an affectionate grandpa.'

Greg watches her gusto with indifference, his eyes are on her face but mind seems to be playing a different game altogether of phrasing or rehearsing sentences for his lone, entrancing audience of a frail woman. 'He was the commander of my dad's group. That dark, stilted night in Mekong Delta Mr. McCarthy had devised a noble idea about fighting a war against the enemy. His enemies were some weak, hapless residents of that area who were simply dragged out from their worn out huts, stripped of their clothes and were ordered to stand in a row in tattered clothes. Even the old and the infirm, women and children were not spared from that humiliation. These unarmed people were killed by a volley of shots fired from the commando's guns. Mr. McCarthy was the first to fire the shots. He just screamed at his team of seven commandos: Kill them. We have been here in this goddamn country infested with germs or mosquitoes for these stupid people who are fighting a war by listening to a fool called Ho Tsi Minh. They should all be killed. Interestingly there was no protest from the group members. My Dad was appalled. He wrote to our Mom about this despicable incident in details. Probably he protested to Mr. McCarthy and probably Mr. McCarthy was not taking kindly to Dad's protest. Dad wrote to Mom: That night some young boys could escape under the cover of darkness carrying with them a load of hatred against the Americans. They're going to swell the rank of the red communists.... That was the last letter of my father. No one heard anything from him or anything about him after that... Mr. McCarthy, the villain of the Vietnam war, whose hands were despoiled by spilled blood of hundreds of innocent men and women, came back to his homeland as a hero to get a rousing welcome. The truth was known only to a few which included my mother. All of them kept quiet. His teammates were with him in that heinous crime. So they had to keep mum. My mother was probably too scared to raise her voice at that time.'

'Where's the letter Greg?'

'I don't know. My mother never showed it to us. In all probabilities she must have been scared. Public opinion was so strong in favor of all these so-called heroes of Vietnam War that she didn't dare to raise her voice. No one would have believed her at that point of time. After sometime, Paul McCarthy became too powerful a man to be attacked. She wanted a hassle-free life for her sons.'

'Let's find it out.' There is a kind of resolute determination in her crisp voice which Greg also probably couldn't afford to miss.

'It's not there. She must have destroyed it or else she must have passed it on to one of her trusted friends.'

'Is your brother...I think he is called Rudolf...aware about this letter and the incident in the Mekong Delta?'

'Yes, he's very much aware. That has made him a sworn enemy of America. In his highly tangled mind he imagined America as a devilish thing out to destroy everything that personified good. Mr. McCarthy and America merged together in his psyche to form an evil thing. His emotional problem started with that. Of course there were some other factors also in his childhood affecting him in his later life...'

Gayatri is in a mood to run away from this nauseating macrocosm of war, be it Vietnam War or a maddening war of emotions at this moment and trundle herself off to the Beaver Stadium where a football match is to start off shortly. She looks through the window to find a riot of colors bristling down below as men and women in bright attires going at a fast pace towards the stadium along with cars of different shapes and sizes shoving past the serpentine road towards the game venue.

A football match is going to be played in the newly renovated Beaver Stadium between Wisconsin and Penn State. People from the nearby areas have also flocked to have a glimpse of the fight between these two giants looking forward to cheer the Penn State team on their home turf.

In one of those days when Siddhartha was around and a football match was played between Penn State and Virginia State University, Siddhartha was accosted by a rustic looking white person while he was coming back from his laboratory. 'You bloody Indians. You come and take away all our jobs.' His vicious looking red eyes were on Siddhartha's face and his large hands were on his shoulders, smell of alcohol was hurting his nostrils. Siddhartha froze for a moment in panic; but the frail wife of that man came to his rescue.

'What're you doing George? Leave him.'

The faint voice of that puny woman did the magic. The massive body of the man just slumped as if in anticipation of some kind of retribution, his hands making a jerking backward movement; there was hardly any resistance when his wife dragged him from there to a recreation vehicle parked nearby. She flashed an apologetic smile at Siddhartha. 'He isn't well.'

'He was from nearby rural area, must be some factory worker or a maintenance staff of a public utility. Like our own downtrodden people he was also suffering from the phobia of outsiders snatching away everything. The conservative Republicans manage to get majority in these areas only because of this underlying anger.' Siddhartha narrated this disgusting incident to his wife giving his interpretation of the situation.

Suddenly his face was lit up in anticipation of something, 'But migrants have become such a big force here that no one...not even the big political parties or strategists can ill afford to ignore us.' Siddhartha who was always so cut up about migration of Bangladeshis to his home state Assam was too euphoric about his own strength as a migrant in this country.

Human migration is as natural a process as the motion of the universe. When everything in the universe is in a state of flux, how can there be a static scenario in case of human beings? Hordes of Mexicans entered through the southern states of America during the last several decades and this influx has been going on unabated. Yes, they've become a powerful force these days. They've become so potent a force that George Bush rushed to Mexico and then to the nation of their forefathers, Spain, immediately after assuming charge of the President of USA to court them in his dream of nation building.

Why should her mind fly at a galloping speed from football to Siddhartha and from Siddhartha to immigration at this hour when the football fever has been lashing the city in the wake of the much awaited game? She must sniff the festive air pervading this beautiful town at this moment throwing away all those incorrigible thoughts to the wind.

'Football is played in America by hands and the irony is that it's called Football.'

'Yes, the way the toilet is given a respectable epithet like restroom here.' She chuckled in her own noiseless way so that Siddhartha was not annoyed at her girlish giggles making a swipe at his intelligent wit.

She must sheathe her mind from the intermittent assault of that agony called Siddhartha. She maunders at a fast pace towards the old square area of the town.

Her intensified pace is suddenly halted by a rapturous roar from the stadium side, a tumultuous, titillating ovation by the spectators to something exciting. A tall, blonde girl with an engrossed look is seen coming from the opposite direction in equipollent pace, stopping for a while to look at the direction of that sound coming like thunders in continuous patches; she suddenly catches Gayatri by her arms, her strong clasp producing a sharp, radiating twinge in her hands. 'We've won.' There is something in that girl's wheezy, excited voice.

Gayatri is buoyed. She hugs that girl who is a total stranger to her in a bond of inexplicable camaraderie, her exuberance flowing to her flickering voice, 'Yes, we've won. Weeee-Have-Woo...o...nnn!'

✦ ✦ ✦

9

Abdullah is a new entrant in America who arrived just a few years back from Bangladesh. Immigration and Naturalization service of the USA had conducted a survey and found that a large number of immigrants had come from some particular countries while there was hardly any representation from a few tiny countries. On the basis of that survey it was decided to fix some quota for these countries for green card and as a first step, lottery was conducted among the green card aspirants of these countries.

To his utter amazement and delight Abdullah found that his name had come up in the lottery. He was lucky and to a certain extent clever to have included names of a number of distant cousins as his dependents in his green card. Six of his relatives landed up on the soil of America to eke out a living either as taxi drivers or as store clerks.

Gayatri once asked Abdullah, a news editor in their paper, the reason for bringing so many of his relatives here while they were not in a state of penury in their home country. Abdullah was forthright in his defense, 'They couldn't have earned so much in their home country. The taxi-driver boy sends 200 dollars per month to his parents. It maybe a pittance for this country but in terms of Bangladeshi Taka this amounts to 12000 which is a substantial sum. His parents are living in comfort with that additional money.'

Abdullah proclaims with pride that he is both a Bengali and a Muslim at the same time. His most desired city is Calcutta and the most favorite author is Sunil Gangopadhyaya, a strange choice for someone who is an avowed India-baiter. This year he along with Debi Ghosh and Amlan Biswas has formed Bengal Society in State College. *Saraswati* Puja was organized as their first venture with much fanfare, loudspeakers blaring out the hymns and sari-wearing svelte Bengali beauties gyrating to the accompaniment of beating drum.

Abdullah is not seen in office today. Gayatri has made some sesame laddoos with molasses, a delicacy of her place for Abdullah to savor, but he is nowhere to be seen.

During lunch-break, Abdullah arrived in a euphoric state, 'I was told that Every Thursday a fish market comes up near Susquehanna River. Oh *Boudi*, I just couldn't resist the temptation of a river fish and drove to that point in the morning. So many varieties of fish! I almost went mad. I bought a big one, cooked in ground mustard seeds, ate a delicious fish curry, kept some curry for you, and kept a few pieces in the deep freezer. Aha! What a day!'

'Did you go mad to have driven 100 miles for a meal of fish?'

'It was worth it boudi. Susquehanna is not my dear Padma, but still the fish was tasty. The smell of that fish market! I was sniffing all around and a make-believe Bangladesh was recreated in my senses.'

He is now gorging on the sesame laddoos like a child, eyes transfixed on the round, black objects of desire in total devotion.

'I haven't tasted meat for a long time. The meat sold in the departmental stores here are not halal meat. The chickens or the other animals are killed by applying electric shock and as per my religion that is haram and we are not supposed to eat that. There was an old Muslim man near the mosque who used to sell halal meat of home-reared animals. These days he shifted base and went elsewhere. What to do?'

A sigh is audible, a vivacious man suddenly morphing into a man in logjam.

'Why Babri Mosque was demolished in your country? Why so many communal riots in India? Are Muslims not safe in your country boudi?'

She just wanted to ask him, 'Why such irrelevant questions at this time and that too without provocation? We were discussing fish and meat, not human beings.' But she has never raised embarrassing issues like thousands of Hindu Bengalis migrating from Bangladesh to India due to persecution there. She has never talked about state-sponsored organized hounding of the Buddhist Chakmas in the Chittagong Hill Tract of his country.

'India is a diverse country.... There is co-existence of so many religions, so many languages and so many conflicting cultures. It's easy to arouse passions there...but the system has some inherent strength which won't allow it to get totally derailed....'

Her voice brims with pride while she speaks about her birth place. She is proud of India where she fondled with an innocent, vibrant childhood to move to an exciting maturity. She is proud of America where she waded through knee-deep rubbles of her marriage to clinch a life of her own.

And she is going to be glued to that pride and she is going to build armor around this pride like a fierce protagonist, rather than forsaking it at difficult moments as an escapist would like to do.

She has not met Greg for several days at a stretch. As for Gayatri and Greg and their story sessions, they are still stuck in that quagmire, the Vietnam War, hobbling out of it might take some time, a few days or a few weeks or a few months.

Natalie drags a chair to her side. Her irrepressible spirit is still there in her radiant smile, glazed eyes and throbbing voice, although her dull, sagging and somewhat porous skin tells a different story about her arrival in the not-too-flattering league of elderly women.

'How's your book progressing...? And how Greg's doing?'

'We're both stuck in the Vietnam War. There was a whirlwind, rapidly progressing tour through the First World War and the Second World War but one day just crashed at the Mekong Delta.... Not been able to get up and get on so far.... As far as Greg is concerned, I'm far away from the world of Greg. An impenetrable wall! He tells everything but at the end he tells nothing.'

'Yes.... Greg is highly emotional and introvert. Even after divorce, still clinging to the memory of that marriage. He's very attached to his schizophrenic brother. He hasn't moved on.... It might be the effect of homeschooling.'

'homeschooling?' A new revelation! She knows she need not prod Natalie for elaboration. Natalie has got great appetite for churning out a torrential flow of information. 'Many parents feel that the school system in America encourages bad behavior in children by making religion and God irrelevant for them. They want to keep their children at home and inculcate Christian values. There is also another set who want to protect their kids from the other unruly kinds.... Whatever, that made Greg a little recluse, a loner.'

Natalie's own construal of the events in Greg's life.

Gayatri and Natalie are on the way to attend the inauguration ceremony of Sayers' Science College, a new addition to the crowning glory of Penn State University. Sayers, a billionaire industrialist, is a product of this university. He is extremely indebted to this university for whatever he had achieved in his life and wants to give back something to his alma mater. He wrote to the President of the university about his desire and the President suggested that he might get them a science building with all the modern facilities for research and studies. Today the Sayers' Science building is ready with a life time endowment to carry on its desired purpose.

A majestic building with some of enviable state-of-art modern facilities now stands there as a souvenir of love. 'I understand you've three very beautiful children and you have decided not to leave anything for them...to spend all your wealth only for charity. I'm an India-born journalist with that scandalously terrible Indian habit of poking at personal lives.'

Mr. Sayers is a jolly good fellow, 'It's okay with me. I like those people who're curious and ask questions.... Yeah, I've three nice looking children and I love them too much to spoil them with wealth. If you love your kids, you leave nothing to them. Give back your wealth to the society which helps it to grow.'

'In my birthplace, we accumulate not only for ourselves but for all the future generations, visible and invisible ones. We're used to poverty. The plights of the have-nots do not seem to move us much. So, philanthropy is not a very popular word there...'

She confided to Natalie on her way back to the office.

Gayatri is in the lookout for new materials for making a story on an interesting topic for their paper. Myriad half-baked ideas swirl and stare in her mind to be abandoned later on. But she knows now for sure that this apparently not-too-grand function in Sayers' Building is going to give her enough matter for a full-blown story.

Gayatri must write on this facet of American life where the spirit of giving back something to the society flows quietly but indomitably under the citadel of materialism, palliating to a certain extent, the strident face of this Orwellian Big Brother.

When something is thought of, the entire universe conspires to make it happen. That is what Gayatri is forced to believe when she finds that Natalie has pointed out her fingers at the Bucke building 'This is the place where foreign scholars and students get information on the courses and other things. They're the ones who find out host families for the new arrivals from the other countries. Mr. Bucke was a student here and he could feel the plight of the foreign students who were confused, not knowing where to go. Mr. Bucke is a well-known entrepreneur now. The grandiose Bucke building is his gift to the university with an annual grant to carry on its activities.'

Then there stands the Sheffield building, an imposing structure in gray stone, where administrative activities are carried out. A football player's contribution to his alma mater!

Kern building is another of such buildings, the seat for research in biotechnology. Siddhartha used to sit there.

She wants to push Siddhartha out of her mind.

'You're invited to my house for dinner this evening if you're free. I'm calling Abdullah also.'

'Thank you.' Natalie seems to be glad. She is comfortable with spicy Indian food.

Natalie comes in the evening clutching two big Pepsi bottles in her hands; her plump body is awash with joy and spring in her gait carries that gaiety with unabashed fashion. Abdullah is equally happy; his boisterous, somewhat haughty manner has all the unmistakable signs of being flushed with joy at the prospect of a hearty sub-continental meal waiting to be served at his boudi's kitchen. Gayatri anticipates with worry that his tirade against the 'Big Brother' India is also going to be there in full swing in the dinner table to the consternation of the other guests, other guests not being familiar with the sub-continental politics have to look on distressingly at the two warring parties with similar skin texture, identical language and same food habit.

Berating India is his usual pastime and Gayatri is equally vehement in defending her birthplace.

'India is harsh with Bangladeshi immigrants who went there long time back. People are tortured and sent back by the Border Security Force, often forcibly, to Bangladesh.'

'Bangladeshis have been coming in hordes taking up all the vacant places and the flow is going on unabated. Yet you're talking of harassment of these people! In fact there has always been red carpet welcome for these ever-bulging vote-banks of the politicians in my birth-place Assam.'

'India thinks that she's the big boss of that area and she gave us independence.'

'India is the natural leader of the south Asian region because of her sheer size and economic strength. We had to go to war with Pakistan on that issue in 1971. But she doesn't assert her dominance anywhere. Your feeling is just born out of an unjustified and deep-rooted inferiority complex.'

'India would have annexed Bangladesh in 1972 if America didn't send the Seventh Fleet to the Indian Ocean during the War...'

Those internecine wars of words scoffed down in zeal would go on for hours together between these two friends and colleagues whenever opportunity arises in the form of both being alone in the office premises. This verbosity sometime appears to be a queer source of amusement for both of them and also an attempt to connect to their birthplace through this uncanny game of mud-slinging.

But today Abdullah is far removed from his usual belligerent mood, his mind is stuck in the aroma of spice floating from the kitchen and probably he wants to reel under a rare sub-continental demonstrative camaraderie at this moment in front of an American colleague.

Gayatri is busy in the kitchen making fish curry with star fruit, a dish savored by Abdullah. She hopes that Greg too likes her cooking. Greg is a last minute entry in her guest list for this informal rushed get-together in the evening due to insistence of her children.

'Let's call Greg. He's such a sweet guy.'

Gaurav's proposal is met with a big, approving grin from Katie.

'And whats about calling David? He finds our house 'refreshingly lively'. I am just quoting his words mom. Don't you agree that a little bit of music will make the evening spirited?'

Gayatri is waiting eagerly along with her children for the arrival of the other two guests in her home now.

Natalie and Abdullah's combined laughter has already filled the house with a cheerfulness she has so desperately been looking for these days to break the jinx of a stubborn, invisible orderliness planted in the family long time back.

✦

She feels being sapped and weary. Sleep was eluding her till midnight and when it was coming the sun was about to make a feeble appearance like a demure bride on the eastern horizon. She was again going back on a voyage to the not-too-distant past penitently as she had been doing in the last few years while trying to run away at the same time from everything through the motion of a deep sleep.

She looks forward to the aroma of a hot, piping coffee to get over the brewing exhaustion. The coffee-maker is in its place and her coffee-mug also stands arrogantly nearby. What is surprising is the neat, smug look of the dining-space. Then the sight of a bouquet with fresh, red roses in a bamboo-basket has caught her spell-bound for a minute. A close, stooping, torpid look at an ornately designed card with the writing in golden letters To Our Mom Who Is Special hanging by the side of the bouquet-basket makes to whir her mind instantly.

What the children are up to this morning?

Katie is there in the door-step of the kitchen with a glowing smile, fragrance of baked lamb meat wafting from the kitchen.

Her vigorous hug with a screaming 'Happy Mother's Day' is all too sudden. 'We're going to give you a very good lunch today. Gaurav is already on the job....' Katie's electrifying enthusiasm has already worked on her otherwise slothful brother and he has also come out from the kitchen to give his mother an effusive smile.

Mother's Day or Valentine Day are alien words for a woman brought up in the tradition of glorifying the dead, a tradition which entails to traversing the memory lane to drag the forgotten forefathers from the cupboard of a frazzled past for the purpose of that deification. She still reminiscences the way they had to observe every year the annual *shraaddha* days of their grandparents when all the uncles and aunts would gather at the ancestral house, offer day-long prayers and end up munching a whole lot of savories prepared for the occasion. It was believed that the souls of the deceased would come and participate in the entire exercise incognito. But in actual practice, it was a kind of reunion for the siblings in the family in the name of their departed parents who passed away years back.

The birth-days were never a very significant event to be cherished, most of the time they were just buried under a culturally crafted amnesia and on rare occasions when remembered mother would just pray silently for the child. Gayatri's grandmother would count her age in terms of the great earthquake which shook the state bringing in its wake a whole lot of devastation in 1897. But in the same society Lord Krishna's birthday has always been celebrated as a special day, a day of pure glory where merriment juxtaposed with divinity would sweep the country.

Birthdays were for the heavenly beings, not for the lesser mortals.

But that has changed very fast and Birthdays are big occasions now to be rejoiced for urban India. With it, a whole lot of other days like the Valentine Day or Mother's Day have also fiercely invaded into the recently exposed insularity of Indian psyche.

In her childhood, life in India was such a disorganized whole of conviviality that it did not need to squeeze into itself any special moment for a cloying celebration.

One day, probably the day is not too far off, she is going to tell her American children about this facet of their past and many other things which they have been carrying within themselves as mementos from their plaid heritage. Maybe they will understand. Maybe they won't.

She calls up Greg and tells him that she wants the day off; she is looking for a break from her hectic pace to laze around in her home with her kids. Greg sounds happy, 'Isn't it strange that both of us are thinking alike today? I'm also taking the day off. I'm going with Garry to the Penn Cave. He called up in the morning to suggest that we should go and I thought why not. It's a wonderful idea.'

Garry? Her own Gaurav? He wants to go out with Greg!

Bus No. 202. Gaurav is there standing in a queue to board it in the school campus. Then he catches her eyes. A faint smile plays on his young, impassive face. In a quick jerk he leaves that queue and fast veers towards her.

'You're coming to our office!'

He nods his head warily.

'You're going out with Greg.'

Again a look of being caught in a wrong act is being spread all over his face. Of late this boy of her has lost that earlier impassive veneer which has always been there clutching with a vengeance to his innocent face. So many times she used to despise that look, the look of being grave on that young face and so many times she just wanted that he dropped all his cautions to the wind to drool over small, trivial things in life.

'Isn't it exciting to make a quick plan like this and go out? I'm all for such fun. Come, I'm going to drop you in our office. Greg must be waiting for you there.'

She wants to reassure her son that everything is fine here; life does not move in the form of a straight line and it has a venerable place for wild pleasures too.

Suddenly as if on a cue she looks back and finds the elderly driver of the bus waiting patiently for Gaurav. She smiles warmly and waves at him. He also waves back and goes away inside the bus with a rare contemplation to drive those young boys and girls to their homes safely. He must have also murmured something like happy journey but nothing comes out from the purlieus of a closed bus. But she feels the vibrations of his never-uttered blessings at this moment.

'The mangled young body of my only son arrived in one afternoon, covered by a white sheet.... He was about to board the school-bus but the hurried driver had no time to wait. The bus was going full speed over my son's fallen body.... I decided on that very day that I was going to leave my paying job and be a school-bus driver to be of little help in the safe journey of our young ones....' He, the elderly looking driver working as a volunteer once narrated this incident and his mission to the parents in a parents-teachers get-together in the school.

She drops Gaurav in front of her office. Here he is, standing in front of her, tall and erect, shadow of Siddhartha is too obvious on his youthful face.

'Go and enjoy.'

He looks straight in her eyes. 'Dad called up yesterday.' She hears her own heartbeats clearly, a kind of dry, flat growl, growing menacingly inside.

'Dad is very angry with me... For not scoring good marks in exams. He feels that this music mania is going to finish me off.'

'What did you tell him?'

'Nothing. I just kept quiet. Had I argued he'd have screamed at me for not speaking Assamese fluently. But Mom, I felt so low, so miserable that I called up Greg and told him everything. You must be wondering why Greg of all people! It's because...Greg listens. Greg always listens to my problems, unlike my own Dad. When on an impulse I just told him that I felt like running away from this place he volunteered to take me to the Nitanny caves.'

'Very nice of him. It's really sweet of him.'

She feels load of pain welling up inside, filling up all the empty pores and rising to engulf her soul in an agonizing fury. Why should Siddhartha try to impose his premeditated choice on his son? Why can't he accept the fact that his son is in love with music and mathematics is a loathsome word for this young, obdurate mind? English is his mother-tongue, not Assamese. When is this arrogant man going to understand that love blossoms inside, respect blooms in the inner chord and loyalty or acquiescence flows inevitably from these twin towers of human feelings?

Siddhartha doesn't maintain any contact with her these days. This new vocal, somewhat mutinous Gayatri is certainly an anathema to his intractable, dogged ideas.

Anjali has come back from Assam a few days back and told her about the scandalous rumors flying back and forth there about Gayatri's character, her supposed to-be very colorful love life and poor Siddhartha's compulsion to depose his appalling wife in the process. Siddhartha's relatives in Assam were taking the lead in spreading those gossips, narrating and analyzing the events, as if the bizarre drama was unfolding in front of their eyes.

But Gayatri is unruffled by these tales particularly when her real life had to weather a storm of a monolithic proportion, when she had to walk through a rough patch of existence and she had seen betrayal in its most brutal form. Past comes and haunts her sometime in vulnerable moments, stubborn memories refuse to dissipate, and clinging emotions try to overwhelm her. But all these also remind her that inspite of the cruel blow of an undefined thing called destiny she is still a normal human being who strides ahead taking all the legacies, good or bad, of the past and emotions are still the strongest part of her consciousness.

Gaurav's long gait to disappear at the bend of the long winding corridor gives her immense happiness at this moment. In his broken, a little hoarse teenaged voice he is going to greet Gregory and both of them, Greg and Garry, will be lost in their world of new found alliance in the wilderness of Nitanny caves where prehistoric cavemen used to proliferate at some indeterminate point of time, leaving behind indelible mark through a series of beautiful, nifty art work. She wants the best of everything for both of them, the two sons, her own son and the son of Ethel.

Her eyes have still been burning with a peculiar sensation born out of sleep-deprivation of the last few nights. The entire town was smoldering with violence unheard of in the annals of whatever faint history the town has so far been carrying. Penn State won the football match and Wisconsin lost. Someone raised a slogan in praise of Wisconsin in the main square of Penn state. That innocuous thing put the town in flames. When you are in Penn State how dare you raise slogan for Wisconsin? The country which talks so intensely about individual freedom is fanatically passionate about loyalty. In one interview, Brad Pitt casually mentioned about his father going away to Australia during war time to escape being commissioned for Vietnam War. That innocent candidness of this otherwise popular actor caused such uproar that his popularity plummeted. He had to run to the media again for a denial of the entire episode.

There was so much pain, never felt before in that tiny, bountifully beautiful place. Everything happened so fast, almost in lightening speed, cops came and came the convoy of ambulances along with siren blaring vehicles. Who hackled whom and why have mostly remained unanswered. Some young boys were taken into custody and the sheriff of the town blamed alcohol for this odious situation.

Peter, one of the boys who raised slogan in favor of Wisconsin was a Colombian by birth. Why did Peter go so visibly against the popular wave on that day? His unabashed, open admiration for an opponent was actually an act of revolt against a country which robbed him of a childhood when he was in Colombia, his birthplace and a brow-beaten frail neighbor of America. Peter's own narration of the elegiac events of his life was heart-rending: The prime base of the Colombian economy was drug production and consumption. The huge drug cartels would audaciously move drug throughout the globe and the big neighbor, the USA, never had problem as such with this nefarious arrangement. But one day the entire equation went through an upheaval not thought of earlier when it was found that the Colombian drugs have found a flourishing market among the American youths in the bordering states and slowly making inroads in the heartland also.

America decided to swipe at the menace and bombed the poppy plants unceasingly for days together destroying all the other cultivation, including the food crops in the process and leaving an entire country wince in that macabre scene of ruin all around. Peter was the son of a rich farmer who owned a massive area of cultivated land where food crops occupied space along with bountiful cash crops. That indiscriminate bombing destroyed everything in Peter's family, crops, water, wealth. 'For me, Wisconsin is as bad as Penn State. They are both part of the same evil system which made us starve. Just to taunt all those Penn State supporters, all stupid blockheads, I screamed: Wisconsin, Hurray!!!

All other boys participating in the slogan-raising in favor of Wisconsin had their own tales to tell. Jidan was angry because America was blatantly and arrogantly anti-Arab siding all the time with a jingoistic Israel. There were some other boys who were just angry with someone, maybe their moms or dads or girlfriends, and wanted their venom swirling an entire populace.

Natalie makes a nice, though-provoking story on the entire episode of a weekend football game turning into a gory affair. But her pen stops for a while when she records Peter's views on America. 'Why should America be dubbed a villain when she was only trying to stop a scourge called drug?'

'Don't be a fanatic Natalie. What right do we have to bomb on the soil of a sovereign country when we're not going to tolerate such a spiteful act over our own land?'

Gayatri is surprised at this comment of a nationalist like Greg who usually never wanted to hear anything against America, not even the rational ones.

So many conflicting thoughts also play hide and seek in Gayatri's mind now. It is true that all the neighboring countries are uncomfortable with America; an unnerving feeling seems to be at play whenever America is mentioned to them. Pierre Trudou, the then President of Canada was once asked by a press reporter about his feelings for America. 'Oh, it's like lying by the side of a sleeping elephant. You're invariably under some kind of stress....'

Is it a deep-rooted inferiority complex arraigned as hatred against a very powerful neighbor? Possible. That reminds her of Abdullah who always assails India for each and every ill that afflicts his dear Bangladesh. For Abdullah, India is not a sleeping elephant but a fire-spewing demon out to devour all her tiny, innocent neighbors at the slightest opportunity. Pakistan had to build a fortified spy network like Inter Services Intelligence to protect herself from an antagonistic India.

Popular opinion in Nepal has been swayed so much against India that she has been blamed even for the mayhem in the Narayanhitti Palace where the king and his entire family perished.

India has always been castigated for her alleged villainy by her weak neighbors.

America might also be subjected to the same antagonistically biased scrutiny by her scraggy, envious neighbors whose own systems have been wrecked by their inner weaknesses.

But Peter of Colombia would never understand that. Abdullah won't buy that either and backlash against America or for that matter against India would go on forever.

On an impulse she has just dialed Abdullah's number. 'Hello boudi, Happy Holi! It's telepathy boudi. I was about to call you up and now it's you on the other side.' Abdullah sounds ecstatic as if Holi, the Hindu festival of color, has splurged color all around him. He maybe angry with India for some inexplicable reasons but he is certainly not angry with her, his loving Gayatri boudi.

She looks around. Some small sachets of color lie proudly over one of the cupboards. That is a gift sent by Anjali to Gaurav and Katie only a few days back. Suddenly Gayatri feels that this vast life with its timelessness is itself a big cause for celebration. She opens one of those sachets and starts sprinkling red color all around like a naughty child gamboling away in cheer playfulness when mother is looking elsewhere.

'Happy Holi!'

A bout of sudden joy has overwhelmed her completely.

✦ ✦ ✦

10

There has been a slow invasion of snow during the last few days and Ethel is particularly happy about the vanishing glow of the sun in that part of the country. The flow of tourists to the Allegheny forest would dwindle so much that her precious possessions, the Bald Eagles, would be left unharmed to flourish in the next summer. Her worries for the fast depleting wolves, exotic wild flora and fauna would also go away to a great extent.

These days she finds it difficult to move at a fast pace on the uneven forest track, her protruding belly has almost tied her down to her log house in the forest from where she has to keep a vigil on any sneaky movement that might be taking place during this brooding winter.

Before this area is turned into a white, lonesome, deadbeat desert, she went to her grandfather's grave to put freshly plucked flowers there, the last available supply of wild, scented flowers gathered and carried carefully by her nibble arms.

'You know grandpa, our Bald Eagles, wolves, green parrots, creepers, oak trees and all other things loved by you and me will be fine at the moment. By the time the lovely white sheet gives way to a haughtily red or a green pathway, all these lives would also be maturing to cope with a savaged civilization.'

She was going to abandon this bountiful life soon for a lonely existence in a human society for the sake of her child who was going to come to this world shortly. She was talking to her yet-to-be born child, not knowing that her bloated tummy was in fact carrying a load of two, about this huge, impregnated forest filled with her near and dear ones and her going away from all of them. She wanted to infuse into her unborn child all the elixir of love that she felt for this stirring forest and the dancing river.

'It's so surprising that a woman belonging to the first half of the last century could dream about communicating with her unborn child through her emotion. Medical science was not so developed at that time to tell that the fetus also reacts to the external sensations like the words of love or hate and flow of soothing music like we adults do in our everyday life.' Greg has become emotional about his mother talking to them when they were still in her womb, safely ensconced but raring to come out to the big, broad, beautiful world.

'You're amazed at the intuition of a woman who belonged only to the last century. In my country, when history was an unknown word, an epic called the Mahabharata was written. One yet-to-born child was supposed to learn some intriguing military skills from the mother's womb just by listening to what the great masters were telling to their royal disciples....'

She looks at Greg's face scouting hard to locate any sign of tedium. There seems to be none....

Ethel was happy about her pregnancy and imminent motherhood. Someone was coming to her life with dainty but stubborn footfalls to fill an overwhelming void.

Rudolf was born, a bonny baby with a whole lot of howling, the tired mother was about to close her weary eyes and then again a twisting pain with the announcement of the young nurse with her naughtily clanking voice about the arrival of another one. Oh! No! Not another one! She screamed in panic.

Ethel was an extremely dutiful mother to her two sons raising them with values, showering them with affection, dealing them with patience. But something went horribly wrong with Rudolf. He was always a trouble-maker, extremely impulsive or edgy, awfully protective of his mother and brother and invited wrath of everyone in the family and neighborhood.

Rudolf's shining eyes give out an impish grin to Gayatri from the framed photograph on Greg's table. 'You know Rudolf. You have seen him, heard him. That's why he's still here today. But I've removed photographs of my other family members from my desktop. A photograph may allow some prejudice to creep in. It may hinder your creative freedom. I don't want that to happen with your writing.'

She tries to close her moist eyes. Why should Greg have so much faith in her that he is leaving her with the freedom to draw portraits of his family members in her own ways? What'll happen if things go disgustingly wrong through some erroneous strokes flowing out of her prodigal thoughts?

One day Ethel came back to the town from her forest abode with a profusely enlarged belly. Her late mother's friend Juan was waiting to welcome her back into her arms. No question was asked about the would-be-baby's father. It was of no meaning to a loving person like Juan who was only too happy to offer a helping hand to her departed friend's daughter.

'When we grew up, she told us about our Dad being dead in the war-field in far-off Vietnam.... Ours was a happy family you know, my mom, stepdad, brother and me, our dog included.

'Stepdad? Ethel remarried? Oh, I remember now, Dr. Shakuntala Kundan once vaguely mentioned it....'

'Yeah. Ethel met this man, Albert, a Native American in a coffee-shop and she married him. He was a sweet man like most of those people of his time but a little bit lazy. He worked for a gas company, though most of the time he was at home. And my mother didn't mind to work hard for the family, sometime as store clerk, sometime as an accountant in a law firm.'

'Did those town-folks of Tionesta accept such a union between a white American woman and an American Indian at that time?'

'By the time we had grown up people must have got used to such a union. I've got no clue about the initial reaction. Mom never told us anything about it and I never dared to ask. Probably the town-folks didn't have much hope on someone like Ethel, an orphan girl who was mostly brought up in the Wild and got pregnant there. And I don't know why, Albert looked more like a White American than an American Indian with blond hair and pale-white skin.... He was Albert Amherst and our family became the Amherst family. We were called the Amherst kids in school. But everyone seemed to know that our real father had died fighting the Vietnam War. That saved us from a whole lot of sneering that otherwise would have come our way for having a Native American stepfather.'

'But you went for homeschooling. Am I right?'

'You're trying to jump the queue Gye.'

Greg is not angry. Rather an amused smile plays on his otherwise placid eyes.

'You're going to meet Albert soon.'

'Is he alive?'

'Yes. He's living in an old age home here.'

'When are you going to take me there?'

'Soon. Have some patience. Albert is hale and hearty and any day we can meet him. Now... Can we have some coffee?'

'Sure. I am making a rich, sugary one for us....'

'Thanks.' Greg's mind is surely not in coffee but drifting elsewhere. These days she can make out his mood swings, however subtle that might be, because of these prolonged interactive sessions.

'I feel like reading that great Indian epic Mahabharata...'

Gayatri's eyes are brightened by this sudden display of Greg's interest in something Indian. She is immensely happy and profoundly sad at the same time, a conflicting befuddling emotion which always comes to the fore whenever someone dear to her here shows even a remote interest in her lost birthplace. Since the last several years she has been trying to push that place from her awareness to the realm of oblivion so that her new-found abundant loyalty for America is not going to have a rival.

It maybe a baffling fear of sharing a finite space between two gigantic entities of her life when all she wants is to give whatever is available to America or probably it maybe an unconscious and silent attempt to take revenge on Siddhartha's precocious effort to thrust India on the people around.

The name India brings back myriad reactions: memory of a colorful childhood, memory of an absolute betrayal, of her umpteen efforts of getting away from this wonderful entity and also her failure to remain unruffled whenever India is mentioned.

'I've read English translation of Homer's Iliad and Odyssey and I feel that these epics pale if compared with the Indian epics the Ramayana and the Mahabharata in terms of maturity. The Mahabharata is very modern.'

'Do you sing?'

What a silly question! They were discussing grave issues of two countries, each on different plain touching different chords and here comes this pointless, irrelevant question from Greg.

'I don't but yes, I am a music lover. But why this question?'

'I was just wondering wherefrom your son Garry has inherited his passion for music....'

There is a pause.

'This morning I suggested to him that we should go to a concert. He said yes but on one condition, his mom should also come along. So Garry, Katie, you and me, we are all going to enjoy Bono. Ok?'

'Agreed.'

Her son wants her with him. Aha! Such a beautiful and profound sensation! She knows that tears have already welled up somewhere to fill a vacuum and she will soon be drenched in those bountiful feelings.

I'm sick of sorrow
I'm sick of the pain
I'm sick of hearing again and again
That there's gonna be peace on earth

Bono screams to a deaf world on something as earthy as human misery. His focus is on Africa, the so-called Dark Continent where hunger is the presiding deity and an omnipotent underdevelopment is the buzz word.

Bono and his wife lived in Ethiopia in a dilapidated refugee camp for a few days to see and inhale the desolate face of poverty and starvation from a close angle. Whatever he tells now, it flows from his heart. This is Greg's touching portrait of Bono in front of Gaurav and Katie, Gaurav's impassioned face has lapped up everything unwaveringly and Katie desperately tries to show through her vigorous eye movements that things are not beyond her grasp.

Gayatri remembers the nicely wrapped up gift box sent by her mother to her music-loving grandson in America whom the old lady saw long time back as a sweet, little trouble-maker who wanted to hold himself back from all the filth around and who must have grown up now as a suave, handsome young adult. Rows of CDs of different Assamese singers were neatly placed in the round, ornately carved wooden box like a pack of cards.

Gayatri wonders whether that famous song of Bhupen Hazarika, the music maestro, the wizard of word, will ever touch the inner chord of her son? O the old river Brahmaputra, why are you still flowing so steadfastly without a care when screams of depraved ones of the river-banks have reached you and filled the air with pain?

Gaurav has never seen the mighty river Brahmaputra; he has never sniffed the wild aroma of its divine, serpentine beauty. Will he ever comprehend these moving songs where the prodigious river Brahmaputra has been hovering as the backdrop in the land of the red river and the blue hills in a far off continent singing the tales of life? Music, a potent force, might demolish that mighty, impenetrable wall and push the frontiers of vision with zeal.

Music has its own unique, surreal language of life, love and hope.

✦

Their school was a majestic red-bricked building with a hat-like roof carrying with it the demeanor of an old, forlorn world. But the school campus was abuzz with the words of a raucous adolescent world, the fun-filled ambience there was in stark contrast with the brooding old building. Greg was a quiet child. But his brother Rudolf was really wild. One day Greg's class-mate Howard who was the tallest and the strongest boy in the class and who had a crooked, downward sloping eye came to him menacingly during a break and told him: You know you're a bastard. Your goddamned father must have been a nigger. And now a yucky stepfather!

He spit at a jet-setting speed to an empty area very theatrically in full view of the class. Greg cried in humiliation. A large-sized boy was there in front of him, almost challenging him to a duel and taunting him with the worst forms of verbal abuses. He cried like a helpless child. Most of the boys in the class giggled and the girls stared at him with sympathy. He loathed both.

While coming back from school he narrated everything to his mother. She listened with an unusual silence, her face turned pale. But Rudolf gave him a tight, agitated hug and told him in a keyed up voice: Don't worry. I'm going to take care of that scoundrel.

Next day he was sitting quietly inside the classroom during break fearing that the ruffian Howard might make an appearance any time and taunt him. Then he heard a scream, a loud one, a familiar shrieking sound. On an impulse he ran out and saw that Howard was on Rudolf kicking and thrashing him, puny Rudolf lying on the ground beneath a gigantic Howard and screaming and trying to kick back with a feeble ferocity. Greg couldn't resist himself.

'There I was with my ivory-carved pen thrusting at the right crooked eye of that ruffian Howard. It missed target but landed on his right cheek just below the eye. Blood was splashed all around. The next moment I could see the carved pen in Rudolf's right hand and a trickling of blood on the other. But the loud laughter of Rudolf could be heard in the entire field.'

The ivory-carved pen he was carrying had a story of its own. Stephen was from a very affluent family. He was the best sportsman in the school. During vacation, he would go for holidaying in the most exotic locales in the world and then brag a lot about those places when he returned. Greg was plain jealous of this boy.

That time he came from India and brought an exquisitely carved, emerald-encrusted ivory pen from India. At that time Greg was attracted to Jennie, the best looking girl in the class. One day he just gathered some courage and went to her 'Hi!' he greeted. She also replied warmly 'Hi! How are you doing?' Not bad for a first timer.

'Did you enjoy that dragon-fly watching trip yesterday?' She was effusive, 'Yeah, of course. That was great.' There was a big boost in his self-confidence.

But at that time Stephen came towards them flaunting his new exotic pen, green emeralds were sitting smugly on a pale ivory color. 'How pretty! Where did you get it?' The girl screamed in enthusiasm, her eyes dazzled at the sight of it and Greg was left totally ignored. 'Can you write with it?'

'Yeah, I can write.'

'Can I borrow from you sometime?' Her desperation to play with it was all too obvious.

'Yes. Sure.' Stephen's tone was one of outright victory mixed with some amount of wrapped up conceit. They strode together towards one corner of the corridor talking and laughing.

'I was fuming in anger, agony and all those predatory emotions usually associated with not having enough in life. I vowed then and there that I would rob him of that bastion of pride, the beautifully carved ivory pen.'

His intriguing mind was looking for an opportunity and Stephen himself was giving him that chance one day in a school trip when he changed his clothes for a swim-suit and went on to swim in a wild stream. There was none in the vicinity. Greg searched the shirt-pocket and there it was: the pale-white pen with splattering of green emeralds radiating vanity. He immediately grabbed it and put it in his pocket. The boys were on their way back home in the school bus; suddenly Stephen raised an alarm: 'Where's my pen? Where have I left it?' The class teacher after this tiresome trip was certainly not in a mood to take more.

'It's too late now Stephen. We can't go back and look for your pen.' The class teacher's voice was kind but firm.

Something happened to Stephen after that incident. He lost his earlier zest as if along with the pen a part of him also deserted him wholly. His unhappiness which Greg desired at one point of time so desperately did not make him happy either.

During that time, the annoying incident of Howard taunting him and his brother taking the cudgel on his behalf in an unequal combat where in a curious turn of events he appeared to have emerged victorious with the help of an ill-fated pen, took place.

'Our stepfather Albert who was a disciplinarian was wild with Rudolf for this incident. He was so furious that he slapped him repeatedly, one of his molar teeth which otherwise was also very weak fell off in the process. Do you care to believe that this tooth has been preserved in a jar till date by my brother?'

'Your brother is in an asylum. How can he preserve that?'

'I do it on his behalf. I know the day he comes out he may demand to have a look at his tooth, a relic of the foregone days.'

'Was Albert very tyrannical?'

'No, he was a staunch believer in propriety, discipline and social values.'

'Rudolf must have had resented that fiercely.'

'Rudolf resented the very existence of Albert in our life. He resented that his own father didn't return from the Vietnam War. Ultimately he weaved a very captivating story of Albert and America conspiring to eliminate his father, his own heroic role in saving his entire family, his ability to decode hidden messages transmitted from the universe. He felt that Albert had been staying with our family with a mission to annihilate us. He told me so many stories about Albert beating our mother to pulp. I never saw anything but I too believed him....'

Greg is silent for a while. Gayatri does not want to intrude at this murky silence where memory, introspection, pain, loss all get juxtaposed like some beautifully crafted exotic relic of foregone days.

'One day I could hear a suppressed sob coming out from my mother's room. Rudolf was fast asleep. I ran towards mom's room. I must save my mother from the tyranny of this man. The room was half open and the lights were on inside the room. I crouched and peeped inside. My move should be very swift so that the rascal stepfather won't get any reaction time. The huge stone which was collected some time back by my brother to hit Albert would be put to use. Then I saw a strange scene. My mother was curling up against Albert's hairy chest, his hands caressing her silky head, she was blabbering something.... He was killed by Paul McCarthy...a cold-blooded murder....' Then the sobbing again.

Greg sighed. A sigh of helplessness or bewilderment! His mother's vulnerability at that delicate moment of life, in a dimly lit bed room where emotions were pouring forth incessantly and he was ready with a huge stone to hit an unsuspecting villain of peace, must have still been etched in his mind.

'I crept back from my hiding place in slow motion to our bedroom in total silence. Later on when I tried to tell this to Rudolf he felt that Albert had wielded his magic power on me too.'

'Poor Rudolf!'

'Yes, poor Rudolf! He suffered on my account. The beautiful, long-lost ivory pen was found in his hand, and in that melee people surmised that it was he who had hurt the mighty Howard with a stolen pen. He was suspended from the school for a few days. And he didn't utter a word about my role in the entire episode.'

'You too kept quiet.'

A pall of gloom has suddenly descended on his face; he slowly nods in affirmation, 'Yes. I'm guilty Gye. Till date I couldn't forgive myself for my silence.'

'After a fortnight, Rudolf went back to his class; Howard also came back, the loser Howard, the fallen Howard, Howard with a black eye, the school boys teased him and he lost his sheen of might. He became unusually quiet. One day I went to Stephen and gave him back his beautiful pen. He looked at the pen for a moment without a flicker in his eyes as if it was a strange object and then threw it back to the garbage-bin with all the strengths in his young body.'

'All three boys involved suffered because of my petty greed...'

Greg seems to be embittered by that unpleasant memory associated with an episode happened some three decades back. The year was 1969, the year when for the first time in human history man landed on the moon.

The entire America was obsessed with the ghost of communism and Russia. The towns of America had trenches or some hidden, narrow, underground escape routes to get away from Russian bombings when it was going to come in future. The great event of an American man landing on moon happened at that time and the whole of America almost exploded in excitement. The communist Russia, the eternal enemy was sidetracked on one occasion! That baffling joy touched Greg's small town of Tionesta also. Tionesta was otherwise cut off from the rest of the world. The first time this town was really troubled was during the Vietnam War when dozens of her own young man had to go to this never-heard-before country and came back dead or maimed for life. However, the feat of America landing on the moon made the people of Tionesta happy. Tionesta was also little wary about some unknown but much talked-about enemy called Russia or a vague but viciously formidable entity called communism.

But for the people of Tionesta the most exciting and newsworthy news of the time was theft of an emerald-crusted ivory-pen of a young boy from an affluent family and bashing up of another boy, a supposed to be much-dreaded ruffian in the local middle school. The common culprit was one of the Amherst boys whose father disappeared mysteriously like hundreds of his compatriots in the Vietnam War.

Gayatri's mind flies back to India of her times, an era when they used to look at America as a land from the fairy tales, America's largesse in the form of food-aid for the poor countries was hurting her self-pride as a small girl and when Indira Gandhi as the dynamic, charismatic leader of a young nation blasted a nuclear bomb in an unknown desert village in northwest India, that fractured pride was almost restored. The Green Revolution, then the 1971 war and the decimation of Pakistan, an eternal enemy! The nation went crazy with a euphoria not seen earlier. Those were the egotistical moments for India and Gayatri was very much a part of that national vanity.

She recollects those moments now in bits and pieces as a flashback in the high drama of her life where America figured in the distant horizon as something like the Medusa dragon with rolling, fiery eyes out to devour. India was her dream if she had a dream at all. Now she is sitting in America and harboring an American dream.

'I don't know how I'm going to write about America in this book of yours Greg. I'm trying to paint a picture of a red-bricked two-storey house in Tionesta in my mind now where you had your childhood dreams and America was a vague entity. On the other hand, I had a very strong childhood image of this country as an all-pervasive being, an enigma of a sort....'

Greg has stood up and he is preparing to go out. He must be tired wandering in his own childhood which was filled with high drama of love, betrayal, jealousy, small intrigues, a war fought somewhere in the globe, so many, oh! so many things were happening together. If she looks back at her apparently staid childhood, many things were happening there too. She saw an enemy airplane hovering over her Guwahati sky, pursued relentlessly by some brightly lit, square-sized anti-aircraft guns: she was dragged by her mother towards an L shaped tunnel, the family was looking up to the sky with lots of trepidation, handkerchiefs firmly put between the teeth and woolen balls inside the ears.

She wants to tell Greg that this was the story of a war fought on her own soil, not the tale of a war fought elsewhere. At that night she asked her mother what that dreaded plane was for, what was its mission. Mother told her softly that it belonged to an enemy called Pakistan. 'What is Pakistan? Why is it angry with us?' Her mother was clearly irritated. 'Pakistan is bad, terribly bad, our enemy.'

When she was in Middle School, she coveted Trishna's butterfly shaped hair-clip. She hatched so many mental plans to steal it. At that time only, she was given a 4 Anna coin by her mother to buy some eatables during her Tiffin break. That was a fairly big amount for a Middle school kid. Her day was passed almost in a state of reverie, waiting for the school bell to ring at midday. She would rush out and buy her stuff before she was hustled away by the bigger girls in front of make-shift, mobile *chanachur* shop.

But when the desired time came she could not find her small, round 4 Anna coin which was lying there wispily in her school bag in the morning. It just vanished from the carefully selected place in the school bag like a magical disappearing act performed by some prolific magician.

She wants to tell Greg that her disappointment at not having the beautiful, daintily built hair-clip of Trishna was not much different from his craving for the ivory and emerald-crusted pen of Stephen or her distress at losing the 4 Anna coin is comparable to his losing everything on that day of the duel.

Losing something invariably causes a wound somewhere; this wound maybe an invisible one, but a lingering, surreptitious pain will always be there.

When Anjali told her about Siddhartha's second marriage, she felt that sneaky pain suddenly coming up through her veins. 'Why's your voice shaking my dear? You only showed him the doors when he wanted to come back?'

She wanted to tell Anjali that she was not playing a director-crafted role in a play or a cinema where she would scream at the top of her voice about erasing the memory of a traitor with whom she spent fifteen crucial years of her life. There was pain, but there were so many beautiful moments too in those fifteen years, tucked away cozily like some gorgeous, sleeping babies in the loving bosom of a fiercely protective mother.

Immediately after her marriage to Siddhartha, she found a home in this faraway land, a home totally and abysmally disorganized and how she built something out of that chaos like a skilful sculptor in a few days time is itself a story to be told and retold. Her favorite jaunts during that period to places like Goodwill or Salvation Army in look out for cheap, exotic, second-hand stuff was full of fun.

Once she picked up a small chair with a bending back, a chair which was donated by a 96 year-old lady to Goodwill, a chair which was loved by her so much that she spent most of the last days of her life sitting there, almost clinging on to its beautifully carved frail shoulders and when donated, her wish was that it should be given for purchase to a young woman about to start a home.

Whenever she was free in the evening waiting for Siddhartha to return, she would sit there and indulge in a reverie about things which were never going to happen like Siddhartha discussing matters of life with her as an associate, a collaborator in things to be done together, a dream team of husband and wife.

Those fifteen long years of her otherwise apparently sedate life cannot just be erased from her memory.

Anjali must have snapped her line.

A young woman had got married, with lots of dream in her wide, innocent eyes, to another handsome young man and then she had realized that her untainted, chaste dream was throttled at the hands of an alcoholic man. Will that fairy tale dream of living happily ever after, a reverie which all girls carry in their hearts be revived now with Siddhartha, a fiercely egocentric person or will it have a second, inglorious death? Gayatri wants to explore the mental space of Siddhartha's new wife, a stranger, at this moment. She is pained but certainly not jealous of that woman: a woman, embittered and embattled, deserves a good life.

'Naomi married that buffoon in the church yesterday.' Greg's voice quivers with a suppressed fury not usually seen in his composed demeanor.

'Forget it Greg. These things happen.'

She could clearly hear echo of Anjali's voice in her own crisp words.

✦

Gayatri is flanked by Azam on one hand and Abdullah on the other. Gayatri tells Greg gleefully, 'Look, this is Indian sub-continent, Pakistan, India and Bangladesh, Azam, me and Abdullah. I fought three wars with Azam and Abdullah was born after the last war. Three warring siblings.'

They have gathered to attend a party hosted by the university in honor of the foreign scholars. Azam is doing PhD in Environmental Science. His bubbling praise for General Pervez Musharraf is based on the contention that the Military Dictator is a much better ruler than most of the squalid, passionately dishonest politicians coming through the avowedly sacred democratic route. He talks about the glittering interiors of the official plane of Nawaz Sharif, solid gold crockery and cutlery shining with full glory at Tax-payers' expense; Benazir's era with her ten-percent husband was no less noteworthy in terms of corruption.

He criticizes the Indian politicians also for their royal lifestyle. 'What did you get during the long years of your so-called democracy...?'

'Do you agree with him, Gye?' It's Greg, out to put her in a difficult situation. She doesn't miss the mischievous grin on his face not usually seen in his sweet, cool exterior.

'He can speak whatever is there in his mind. It's his democratic right.' She retorts without much of a thought.

'She's smart.' It is Azam who laps up her snap with a good humored smile.

When the party is over she offers Azam a lift back home: a small, cozy, picture perfect house inside the university campus. 'Would you mind taking coffee with me?'

There is a kind of ungrudging sincerity in his voice which is difficult to resist.

It is a hot, steaming coffee, a nostalgic one, reminding her to sweet, piping tea brewed in her small, warm kitchen long time back for her and Siddhartha before bed time when the children were fast asleep and she was eager to share the tidbits of the day with her man.

'When my wife joins me next month, we're inviting you for dinner. Chicken biryani. Is that okay with you?'

'I'm making Malai Kofta.'

'I'm so happy today after I met you. I felt as if I met someone very close. I could talk to you in Hindi-Urdu mix dialect, about chicken biryani-malai kofta, about my country. But we always fight like cats and dogs on one issue or the other. I've one aunt in Amritsar in Punjab. Once, probably one or two years back, my father decided to visit her there. Then suddenly due to the infamous Kargil conflict, the Samjhauta Express, the train connecting our two countries got canceled. My father wept like a small child on that day. My aunt is his youngest sister, his darling, but they are far apart, a make-believe border stands as a barrier between the two of them. Today I've realized how futile, how useless our so-called animosity is....'

Greg too spoke about the American Civil War in the morning, a war which was about to divide a country at the altar of freedom, a memorable conflict for a cause which was ingrained deep in that voyage of Mayflower two centuries back. But it was fought with too much spilling of blood.

Greg's stepfather who was working in a gas company for some months of the year and had no apparent reason to be conversant with civil war or anything of that sort had talked at length to the boys on this topic. He even took the boys to Gettysburg, where 50000 people just perished in a span of few days, for a glimpse of the war relics.

Ethel was in her own world of nature. She shared that exclusive world with the boys whenever she got some respite from the grind of everyday life of doing numerous odd jobs in departmental stores and household chores.

The molar tooth of Rudolf which fell off as a result of Albert's tight slap on his face was preserved by Rudolf in a small jar in one corner of the boys' room. Till date Greg has not been able to make out the purpose of that concealed preservation. Once he just asked his brother about it. Rudolf had a very curious explanation: This tooth might assume human form one day and punish each and every villain in the drama of their life...

Rudolf was always beyond reason; hard hitting arguments which were never based on any logic would fly here and there to pin down his supposed enemies at any point of time.

One night Greg dreamt a vicious dream, a nightmare: he was swimming in a pool of water and the fallen crooked tooth of Rudolf assumed the form of a mammoth shark. A panicked and defenseless Greg screamed at the top of his voice. What a blunder it was!

When he opened his eyes the jar was laying on the floor, lid ajar and the tooth along with water forming a thin zigzag waterway was also on the same ground, Albert and Ethel standing there amidst that chaos, perplexed and somewhat sad. Albert did not take much time to react. He dragged Rudolf out of the bed and gave him a tight slap.

Rudolf gazed at the tooth for some time and then picked it up to put it back in the jar with an expression that nothing was amiss. There was not a single drop of tear in his dreary eyes.

'I was feeling terribly, terribly guilty Gye. It was me who opened up a closely guarded secret and made Rudolf suffer in the process in that night. But strangely enough, my brother was never bitter or angry with me for all those failings. He had a favorite whipping boy, his stepfather.'

'But what Ethel was doing all throughout? She should have intervened and sorted out any communication gap between the two. I'm a little bit confused Greg. Ethel was vibrant, enigmatic, a real beauty when she was wandering in the deep, dense darkness of Allegheny but as the wife of Albert or the Mom of Greg and Rudolf, she was inert, a lusterless woman. Please forgive me Greg for saying all these things about your mom. But I don't know how I'm going to depict your mother in my book.'

'Show her as a mother who was concerned about her sons. She was never passive, but didn't want to bring up her sons as rowdies. She was so happy when Albert took us to Gettysburg for a tour to the historical place...'

The affection for his mother was trickling through his blue-greenish, transparent eyes.

Gayatri does not feel the same way when she looks at Rudolf's pain, huge and borderless, smoldering a young, helpless boy. A word or two from his mother against a senseless discipline would have surely gone a long way towards healing an injured heart.

A person, who could feel so much for Allegheny and Allegheny's children and vouched so agitatedly for their cause, strangely remained calm to the dilemma faced by her own son.

'Are you coming to Gettysburg with me?'

A strange question; there must be some understanding with Gaurav, his dear Garry to go and visit that place and this is their ploy to involve her in this stimulating excursion. She was not averse to the idea of joining them.

The day was a hectic one with Greg's narration on his childhood followed by the stimulating dinner dates with Abdullah, Azam and others. When she reaches home after sharing a hot, invigorating coffee with Azam, she finds Siddhartha's voice on the answering machine. He wants to talk.

He sounds worn-out, drained and words have just listlessly been coming out to cause a storm in her mind, heart, body... everywhere.

'She was lonely. I also thought that it was better to have a companion. But things moved so fast that I couldn't even talk to you. There was simply no time. I went to India, met her in a marriage and married her the next day.'

Why does Siddhartha want to clear up now when he did not bother to tell her anything before simply vanishing with his young scientist lover to Chicago many years back? In the same way he did not offer her any explanation when he decided to come back to renew his authority over a structure which he still hoped to call home though it refused to open its otherwise fabulously welcoming portal to a stranger like him at that point of time.

It feels good to get an explanation, though an unsolicited one, when they are so far apart and they do not owe each other anything, not even apology. What Siddhartha has failed to understand is that as a wife she was mostly silent, but her silence clamored for more respect and it was brutally denied.

Siddhartha wants to take his children to Philadelphia for the Convention of Assamese People on 4th July where an Assamese from Boston would meet his counterpart from Las Vegas. Or an Assamese from Connecticut would share his feelings with another Assamese from Arkansas. A sweet but wasted effort to create a home away from home.

The inevitable process of Americanization for Siddhartha's wife would also begin on that day.

She broaches that topic to her children. 'Your Dad wants you with him there and I think you shouldn't disappoint him this time.' Her two children listen to her without any apparent sign of excitement. Even Katie, Siddhartha's Katyayani, is noticeably mum. Where have all those enthusiasms of that day when they packed off for a trip for the Nitanny Caves with Siddhartha and Nora vanished today?

Their mellowed look tells that they have grown up now. They are more sensitive to the feelings of their mother. Moreover, in all probabilities they don't want to be seen as a part of the new life of their father, a life built on the ruins of their beautiful togetherness.

'You aren't coming?' Katie's eyes try to find hers. She prays hard so that the storm brewing inside does not come out in the open.

'No...it's not possible for me to share space with your stepmom at this moment. It might take some time.... But you must accept her in your life. She came when I was actually out of his life. She never pushed me aside and made her way.'

The day the children leave for Philadelphia is a warm forenoon with a glowing sun making cryptic waves in a crispy air. She is in a state of inebriated sadness when they leave in a huff to avoid her confused, somewhat withdrawn gaze.

Two options are now available with her: To spend two quiet, lonely days in her desolate house or to go with Greg for an exotic trip to that quaint, historic town of Gettysburg. She can see two roads, hazy and surreptitious, lying in front of her and none of them may bring back any modicum of radiance to her life in the coming two limitless, expansive days.

Yesterday she told Greg about Gaurav's proposed trip to Philadelphia hoping that he would immediately cancel his Gettysburg excursion. But he just exclaimed 'Very good, Garry should enjoy in Philadelphia, a nice city, full of art galleries and a historical treasure trove.' And then went on to elaborate on the Gettysburg trip making it obvious that the two of them would be together in that enigmatic place where lives perished and a new America emerged engirdling a novel concept of freedom some one hundred and fifty years back.

When they leave this morning, a gleaming sunshine drowns the resting valley in its golden hues. Greg has been going at a breakneck speed. It is unusual for a sober person like Greg to be so wild in a sweet-scented autumn morning. She also maintains an impervious calm in the face of all these happenings like a colorful, sleeping valley being trapped into a golden-hued trance in the wee hours of the day and a speeding vehicle with two strangers in it weathering that curious magic spell.

Her eyes are burning at the moment. It was a sleepless night. Why she has come out today? Is it due to an intriguing desire to take revenge or to quench a suppressed longing to enjoy life to the fullest? Last night she looked at herself in the mirror, a deep, penetrating gaze at her beauty. 'You still have some time left for yourself Gayatri.' She muttered to herself.

Why should she not taste life and tread the forbidden path now? She is her own person and she doesn't owe anything to anyone. But why couldn't she tell her children that she was going out with Greg? A baffling coyness overpowered her the moment she opened her mouth for this bizarre truth.

What has been brewing inside her companion now? She looks at him. A handsome man with a kind, opaque face! He is an American and for him the heart and the body are two different entities, communication between the two is mostly closed. He might sleep with anyone in the evening and forget it like a mundane event in the eerie silence of the next morning. It could never be a searing experience for him like it would be for her. Why has he come out with her all alone? Is it a simple historic voyage or a pleasure trip?

Siddhartha must be on his way towards Philadelphia with his new bride to attend the Convention. Sometime she thinks that she is away from the penumbra of his agonizing memories. But in certain moment of life she knows that she has been cradling enough of those memories and emotions to be swayed with pain whenever he comes up to her in one form or the other. She cannot accept him back in her life but she cannot be indifferent to him either. What a strange feeling!

The person with whom she is now traveling is a total stranger to her. She knows so much about him, his childhood, lives and times of his ancestors but she is still miles away from this narrator's knotty, impenetrable thought process. Sometime he appears to be disarmingly candid, sometime little distant and most of the time he is not there at all.

What does he think of Gayatri? She wonders sometime. He has bared his past to a stranger like her. While talking to her he seemed to have been involved passionately in what he was doing but his eyes remained glued to something far away. His stares never touched her pale skin; his gawk never ever violated her beautiful, slim body. He must be having enough trust in her to have revealed a colorful, varied past. But it is all too obvious that he was not drawn to her. Trust and pull sometime occupy two different realms like two strangers living in the same place but never meeting each other.

Why did he invite her for a trip together to Gettysburg? Why was that invitation not extended to her children this time? When he seemed to be so concerned about his dear Garry's going through a plethora of conflicts during this tricky phase of adolescence at one point of time, why is he not asking a single question about him during this long journey through an undulating valley at the moment?

Manish called her up yesterday, 'Open your computer and see my wife's snaps.' He demanded raucously. A pretty girl with lots of jeweleries. The bright red bindi was somehow blending well with her blonde hair and blue eyes! 'Zion was looking forward to an Indian system of sat *phera* and wearing our mekhela chadar. Look, all the ladies in her family are wearing our dress. Even that obese grandmother of hers is also wearing one and it was such a problem to wrap that muga chadar on that plump body...' He was sounding roguishly euphoric and Gayatri's response was unabashedly muted.

Did he ever rifle through the sprawling memories of his earlier life with another woman who was long dead at that moment of another beginning?

'We've reached. Hotel Highway. Hope you like it. It should be ok. Nice and neat. I've booked a deluxe room for us...'

Greg leads the way, the key of the room dangling from his right hand index finger and Gayatri follows him coyly like a demure and thoroughly perplexed bride.

She labors under this strange feeling of going to the gallows at the moment, totally mesmerized, the hangman with a rope confidently leading the way.

✦ ✦ ✦

11

Augusto Renoir, 1841. One couple, a man and a woman taking shower, emotions seem to be playing hide and seek with varied colors on the canvas.

Katyayani is overwhelmed at the vast richness of the Philadelphia Art Museum. Gaurav is equally happy looking at this profuse display of colors. He finds a harmony between colors and music here.

Katie who has always been ebullient is somewhat sober today. She is in love with colors, painting has become her passion these days. She sculpted the images of the Jesus, Virgin Mary and the three shepherds during last Christmas from a bunch of dried wood. Simultaneously from a huge desiccated pumpkin, she also made a beautiful swing and put Lord Krishna and his three wives, sculpted from the same wood, inside that swing. She was making them outside, over a snow-covered white ground, conveniently putting them inside a glass cage.

State College Citizens' Forum organized a competition of decorating the foyers of the houses and Katie joined it. This riot of colors outside their home bagged the first prize. The day she was given that luminous trophy inside the Town hall by the Citizens' Forum, she called her beaming mother towards her side, gave her a big hug and handed it over to her. 'I owe everything to her.'

Now standing in this multi-storied majestic building, among all these monumental treasures, Katie's mind swiftly swings between her mother and her new-found-love for Art.

Gaurav also thinks that way. They are accompanied by their father but he has been sitting somewhere outside with a bored expression on his face.

'I hoped so much that my children would do well in academics and get admitted in an Ivy-League college. But both of you seemed to be interested in Music, Art kind of useless things. I spoke to your mother. But she's not bothered.'

His sigh with loads of disillusionment was palpably audible. The same disappointment was clearly visible during Convention when his bride, a young woman with lots of energy and with least inhibitions, went on to circulate in the crowd. She was belching out lots of melodious songs like the Jyoti Sangeet, Rabha Sangeet, Bhupendra Sangreet – all his mother's favorites and which have become, of late, his favorites too; all the soul-stirring songs of the Carpenter brother-sister duo of the 70s, then Madonna, Britney Spears, Shakira of the recent times also vied for space in her vibrating, vivacious voice.

His father looked helplessly dull in this melee where his new wife was hogging all the limelight. He was sitting there, yawning like an old haggard, the world seemed to be a lost place for him there.

In the art museum, he is relaxed but confused. He must have realized to his horror and then to his dismay that he is no longer in command of his life. Gaurav feels sorry for this stranger called father, insolence robbing him of everything including dignity at this stage of life when he should have been a buoyant bioscientist of the country and also a proud father of two lovable children.

It is good that their mother decided not to come this time with them. The shattered, lost look of their father would not have made her happy. Gaurav and Katie met Anjali Auntie this time at the Convention. Anjali Auntie is a fiercely proud woman and she has refused to talk to either Siddhartha or his new wife. For her, loyalty is a very big thing and hobnobbing with the betrayer of her best friend whose home fell apart like a pack of wobbly cards is just out of question.

For so many years in their childhood, their two families came together to the Convention in some fun-filled trips when they just stopped en route to have a bite at their favorite snacks, heated discussions on the latest election in India or something in Assam would keep the elders in a state of enlivenment. The kids were happy or excited being in that state of eternal flux in a never-ending kind of road trip to some far-off place in the name of Convention or whatever.

For them destination never mattered.

Gaurav felt a throbbing pain when he thought about those few eclectic years of his life, when both his parents were together and India was hovering like a never-ending entity wherever they went.

His father has always attempted, that too very brazenly, to impose his love for India on his children as if that love could be bequeathed on his off-springs and they would pull it further as sacred assignment. His mother's love for her place of birth is soft, sweet, melodious but obviously more reflective in the absence of that proselytizing mission of his dogmatic father. Whenever his mother browses through the net to get some news on Assam, a pristine glow usually spreads across her loving face.

It is a unique shine which is normally seen in the face of a devotee while at prayer in a church, mosque or a temple!

But his mother never told them that it was their divine duty to love that country. She left that choice entirely to them. And the quiet, intense, poignant love of his mother for her birthplace makes him also feel like falling for that place like a besotted lover.

Till this date he can recall clearly his Dad's voice, 'We won the World Cup Cricket in Sharjah in the year 1983. That was a glorious moment for all of us. This Sunday we're going to watch the video clippings of that match. Isn't that going to be fun?'

'I'm going to watch baseball game in our school on that day. I don't like cricket Dad.'

'Cricket is virtually the national game for our country. You cannot afford to dislike cricket son.'

'I hate cricket.'

He remembers both the sound and the pain of a powerfully virulent slap on soft, adolescent skin of his left cheek and his intense repeating of 'I hate cricket.' to the chagrin of a helplessly infuriated totalitarian person.

The rigid contours of life have changed dramatically in recent years. Gaurav fell in love with a classmate Paris. They spent so many moments together; he was belching out the old country numbers and she accompanied him on the guitar like an enchanted little angel.

'When we leave High School next year, we might go our separate ways. I might carve out a career in music and you in sports. But we might meet somewhere...we might catch up with the present with lots of new stories.' He suggested. She was little offended. 'Why should we go our separate ways? There's something so similar in our thought that we might stick to each other when we grow up.'

He visited her home one evening. Her mother was effusive with affection for both of them like any other mother in the world and offered them a bountiful of home-made goodies.

'So Garry, where do you belong to? I mean which country?'

'I'm from the USA.'

'No, your original country!'

'My parents were born in India.'

'Oh! You're an Indian! I guessed so but couldn't get the name of your country. My memory often fails me. India is a great country and you Indians are really doing well here, in our country....'

Gaurav was making a mental plan of stomping out of that house at that moment like a defiant child out to show his outrage. After keeping up the pretence of enjoying an evening, a gracious hospitality, for far too long in a friend's place, he just ran out of that claustrophobic environment once it was time to say a polite goodbye to an otherwise generous and kind lady.

Next day when he informed Paris, a girl very strongly attached to her family of father, mother and a younger brother and who invariably went to the church every Sunday, about their impending break up, she didn't contest his decision. One evening was more than enough to have convinced both of them that their dream of being together for life was just too far-fetched a dream to be realized. Till today Gaurav is amazed at their secret but unfulfiled desire to be together for life when teenagers of their time are in the distinct and inevitable mood to date, enjoy and conveniently forget everything.

Probably it was his parents' Indian genes which goaded him to think in terms of a permanent relationship though they themselves had to go their separate, irreconcilable ways in course of time. It was strange that even Paris, a girl brought up with typical American values in an archetypal American society where permanence in relationships has become more of an accident than a usual occurrence, should also think in a similar fashion though this feeling or hope was never expressed in words.

Since then he has stopped dating any other girl. A girl, petite and pretty, called Paris Smith has remained so doggedly etched in his mind that so long as she refuses to leave that place, no other girl can enter his territory.

Gaurav can feel tears welling up in his eyes.

'How are you Honey? How do you like Philadelphia?'

It is his mother on the other side of the telephone. The sound of a moving vehicle as she is talking has also been lurking in the background. 'I'm fine Mom. Philadelphia is a nice place. I'm enjoying.'

'We're coming back tomorrow.'

'Good to hear that. I'm also coming back tomorrow dear.'

Coming back tomorrow! Where had she gone?

Gaurav is little bit flabbergasted at his mother's apparent look of dejection during the last few days. He has wondered a number of times: Why his mother was not in her normal composed self? And no answer was forthcoming. Is it because her ex-husband had chosen to marry someone else? Gaurav wondered in silence.

When she could face the world so bravely at the time of his going away with another woman and when she could refuse his humiliating attempt at gate-crashing at a later date, Gaurav is sure that she would never bog down at this time of life too.

He is not going to intrude in the world of his mother's mind. She should be left to herself to rejoice, enjoy, mourn or get intimidated in that psychological world of her own.

But when he meets his mother the next day in State College, Gaurav is surprised to see her in a wrecked state as if a storm blows over her entire being and he is much relieved when Natalie comes to take them to another opera.

+

'...The first declaration of American independence was made in Philadelphia. Did you go to see the Independence Hall there? A historical landmark....'

Greg has already spoken enough on American history, on Boston Tea Party, on American spirit. In terms of time, it is just three hundred years, but America was a stirringly new concept, a Dream realized in a vast, virgin landscape far away from homeland Europe.

The glistening eyes of the children are spell-bound in unbridled amazement while listening to this epoch of American History from Greg. They must have heard these luscious stories of a Great American Dream umpteenth number of times in their class rooms in their growing up years and their indoctrination has been so thoroughly complete that they have already considered themselves to be an irrevocable part of that reverent Dream.

'We went to that Hall. The guide was explaining something but a child cried loudly and no one could hear anything. Such a cute, little baby! The guide was furious. She asked the mother to take away the baby immediately. Someone in the crowd suggested that the baby should stay back. The guide was so wild with anger that she left in a huff. Then a different group with another guide pushed us aside to start another round of story-telling.'

It is Katie. It is in her nature to interject and fill the void with irrelevant details. But today Gayatri finds this interlude refreshingly pleasing.

It seems Greg is carried away by the passion of America at the moment. She sometime feels that Greg wants to compensate for all the hatred harbored by his twin brother towards America and in this way they actually become inseparably intertwined to each other.

Though she has got enough weapons in her kitty to question American way of dealing with the world, the Little Man-Fat Boy combo was the ultimate, she doesn't want to wage a frontal attack on Greg's emotion and his love for his birth land. It is the birth land of her two dear children too.

She is immensely grateful to this country for all the opportunities provided to her at a time when she was desperately groping in the dark for a ray of light and suddenly, to her utter amazement, she could see light all around at the end of a winding tunnel.

'One thing sometime bothers me....'

Greg evades her gaze. He does it very often whenever she broaches some unsavory topic, particularly in respect of his enchantingly beautiful America.

'This country is the birth place of all liberal ideas like rights of the working class in the factories, equitable wages and so on and so forth...'

She tries to take a deep breath to gather her thoughts.

'It's strange that America, where all those revolutionary ideas were born, became avowedly anti-socialist. The way America repelled Marxism, it gives the feeling that a paranoid mother venomously threw away her baby to the wild.'

'What do you mean? A mother should not discard a wayward child...?'

'Aahaa...Greg, you've at least acknowledged that America is the breeding ground for such radically different ideas and she has only been trying to fob them off as something dangerous...'

'Why can't we have coffee?'

Children nod enthusiastically at this seemingly ordinary proposal of Greg for a cup of coffee, maybe with a brownie or a hot dog. They did not come to the world when this intense conflict between the two streams of thought was going on. Gayatri was only a teenager when the concept of a Star War was rocking the world of that time.

Gayatri suddenly remembers the stern, craggy face of Brezhnev as it was displayed on the front covers of all the newspapers of her time. He was standing by the side of a beaming Indira Gandhi after the 20 year treaty of friendship had been signed between these two countries, with no trace of smile or glee on his rutted look. In was in such a stark contrast to the affectionate, paternal look of Gorbachev, a leader who came to the world stage at a much later date with a face which was extending to a bare forehead where a gray-leaf-like spot was making a pattern. 'Look, he has this tamarind-leaf on his forehead!' Gayatri was screaming ecstatically. Siddhartha, who was concentrating on the news paper gave both Gayatri and Gorbachev's front-page photograph a consternating look and asked sternly, 'So what?'

Her soaring spirit dampened somewhat, 'No...I mean... my grandma always used to tell that people born with this kind of leaf-like birth mark were lucky. They were destined to accomplish something big in life.'

'Gorbachev and big things? Ha! He destroyed Russia by talking of all shits like Glasnost and Perestroika. Look, I never supported communism. I feel it goes against the basic human tenet to acquire and the very fundamental desire to be free. It's an artificial system. But this man was pumped up by America...do it do it, oh great man!...and then he was dumped unceremoniously when the work was done.'

The next day there was a news item in The New York Times about that mark of Gorbachev. The leaf like mark was due to a terrible car accident in his younger days which left this indelible scar on his forehead. Siddhartha was elated as if he had defeated his adversaries in a battle, this adversary might be his ever-submissive dull wife or a very faraway world leader named Gorbachev.

Is Gorbachev solely responsible for dissipation of the Soviet Union? The people there must have reeled under massive frustrations and Gorbachev was just a catalyst for transforming this collective wish for freedom into a reality. Gayatri felt tempted to tell all these things to Siddhartha at that time. Then she decided to incarcerate these thoughts to herself so that further antagonism inside her apparently orderly household on account of something as remote as the Soviet Union could be avoided.

America has again been going through a phase of severe recession and the state has once again jumped to the rescue of the notoriously riotous Wall Street financial market much to the embarrassment of the stern protagonist of the Free Economy policy. Similarly communism in China has flourished because of her going away from the conservative form of socialism, the deviations being manifested in the liberal flow of foreign investment and sudden rise of an entrepreneur class there. Russian leadership, on the other hand, had stuck to an old, inflexible system. This rigidity on their part sounded the death-knell for socialism on that soil long time back. Gorbachev just arrived there at that point of time in History to facilitate a safe burial for a system long dead.

All these thoughts keep on playing hide and seek in her mental world whenever she thinks about the socio-political-scenario around her. She remembers Tito, the charismatic leader of Yugoslavia and Indira Gandhi, the dynamic leader of the 3rd world who along with Nixon and Brezhnev once dominated the political landscape of the Globe. Gayatri had witnessed unfolding of these events in her teenage years. So many times her father discussed, in their dinner table, about the diplomatic stunts performed by the wily Kissinger and the way Kissinger and Nixon were snubbed by the equally crafty Indira Gandhi.

Gayatri's father talked of Long March in China, a seven-year-long journey through dense forests, uninhabited mountain terrains, by the committed leftist comrades under the leadership of Mao and Chou En Lai and he drew a parallel to the *Dandi March* where Mahatma Gandhi defied the unethical Salt Law of the British by undertaking a very long march to the Arabian Sea. The spirit behind both these innocuous marches was mobilization of the masses. Her father reasoned. Though it was difficult at times for the children to comprehend these world events, they never felt separated from a bigger, bustling world around.

Though a young Gayatri deliberately stayed away from whatever contained in her text-books during her school and college days and just managed to scrape through her promotional Exams, tits and bits of these discussions at the leisure time with her father kept her nourished. The stimulating information, which was stowed away indifferently somewhere during that period of her growing up, came to her rescue on many later occasions when Siddhartha attempted, rather unfairly, to impose his blatant, somewhat one-sided assessment of many issues on the family. She could get a foothold after her separation from Siddhartha only because she could look at life around her in a broad perspective which was a gift bequeathed innocuously under the garb of small talks by her father long time back in India.

Gayatri hopes that her protracted talks with Greg on several occasions might get accumulated in adolescent minds of her children too. She wants them to be like Greg who can narrate stories enigmatically interspersed with fascinating anecdotes.

She could discern this quality of Greg during their visit to Gettysburg.

Gettysburg: A turning-point in the annals of the history of a great country like America and strangely, a turning point in the life of a diminutive woman like her.

She surrendered herself fully, with body and soul, to a stranger in that historic town without delving much, at those moments, into the circumstances which propelled her to go through that pleasure-laden ordeal. For a woman like her who was brought up in a traditional family in the conservative setting of the 70s and 80s in India, this capitulation should not have been that easy.

A massive battle was fought on the soil of that momentous town in the year 1863. The Confederates tasted the first major defeat on the soil of Gettysburg with the killing of their twenty-nine Generals, all of them being astute war leaders.

Greg narrated those happenings which had taken place in that quaint town almost two centuries back to Gayatri as if he had witnessed all those events with his own eyes at that moment.

The battle at Gettysburg sounded the death-knell for the Confederate forces. They could never recover from this devastating setback inflicted by the carefully planned attack from their Northern opponents.

America remained as one nation.

On the eve of Christmas, one soldier, a survivor of the Gettysburg battle, wrote to his wife about a shadow that came in his dream the night before the battle was to start and whispered in his ears, 'I'm the death angel. I'll protect you from all kinds of destruction....' He survived though all his compatriots perished. 'I could live only due to the mercy of that death angel. Not a single troop from my regiment could withstand that devastation....'

Whoever could survive the ravages of that historical battle, came back home with a wrecked mind. They all wanted an end to this conflict. Immediately after this battle, President Lincoln rushed to Gettysburg, the place where an immense contradiction of a massive victory of one America over another America was recorded.

'It was a very strange kind of war. Look, that's the Culp Hill between the Seminary Hill and the Little Round Top, that small elevated black spot.... Two brothers fought with each other there, one fighting for the Confederate forces and the other for the Union. One for the slavery and the other against it....'

Gayatri tried to imagine two brothers fighting a duel some one hundred and fifty years back with gun-power on that piquant hill, almost invisible with naked eyes from the area where she was standing.

'There was a very long spell of hundred peaceful years before the Civil War in the country. That made some people restless. So, many of these people joined the war on either side without any conviction or belief about any particular ideology. They wanted some excitement in their otherwise drab life. The war was just an opportunity for them...'

Greg was jumping from one rock to another in a frenzied state to depict the events that happened so many years back in this charming little place.

At one point he took her to the old part of the township where bullet-marks had been preserved carefully on the old houses. 'Albert brought us here, me, Rudolf and Mom. We were asked to touch the holes. I was dreaming in my younger days that whenever I've kids of my own, I'd bring them here. But Naomi left me and my marriage collapsed....'

Whenever Naomi tumbled into their sphere of discussion earlier, Gayatyri never used to take it as an encroachment. But that day, when her limp body and mind have been kindled with fire of passion by the night before, she could not afford to be that magnanimous. Inwardly she cowered in pain.

'Going back to the question of insanity in the war, there was an old, decrepit war veteran who fired on anyone from his window who happened to pass that way during the battle of Gettysburg. He didn't have any foe or friend in the war; he wasn't bothered about the abolition or retention of slavery, but he was just carried away by the thrill of the war. Albert showed us the window from where that gruesome act was going on.'

They went to the Henderson Inn, an eating place since 1863 to have lunch. The ambience of the year 1863 has been painstakingly retained there. Waitresses were wearing ankle-length gown with frill, their heads were adorned with flowery caps. Waiters were also wearing colorful shirts, pants were held in their place by suspenders, black hat was decorating their heads.

'What do you want to have? General Jim Longstreet's food or General Sickles'...?' Gayatri looked at the Menu but her mind wandered like a gutsy wind blowing fiercely to be dissipated elsewhere. She was thinking about the passions in the night before and so many feelings like guilt, jealousy, love etc. aligned with that unusually stretched out brooding darkness. Her rebellious mind and body were consistently humming unity tunes in the night before, defying their mistress's desire to set them apart.

She wanted to gauge the feelings, the interplay of emotions of this American man sitting before her. Being American and being a man, it maybe possible for him to put his body and mind in two parallel lines ensuring them never to meet.

'You're looking worried. What's eating you up?'

She had to find out an escape route so that he should not get a whiff of what was actually going on in her mind at the moment. She was not going to afford him an opportunity to laugh at her very girlish emotions or her expectations at something so ordinary.

'Through your narratives, I could see only one person and that was Abraham Lincoln. He went back to Gettysburg after a massive victory. But he wasn't going there as a Hero, as a victor. Like a sage, he was talking of unity of fractured hearts. He reminded me of another person, our own Mahatma Gandhi who also spoke about love and union. When communal violence erupted just before and immediately after independence in 1947, he didn't celebrate independence but did penance for all those human miseries by abstaining from food and festivities. The Father of the Independence Movement was a very sad person at that historic moment like Abraham Lincoln being an unhappy person after the Civil War....'

A sigh of despair escaped her at that moment.

That despair was so consuming that while sitting here with her two lovely children and Greg around her, she feels its tentacles encircling her in a ferocious zeal.

✦ ✦ ✦

12

'One day when I opened my lunch-box, it was empty. I was upset, just too upset even to cry.'

Gayatri is amused. She also recollects her days in school when so many times the delicious stuff her mother made for her lunch just vanished as if some magician had played a trick there on her gullible food. She used to cry like an injured soul and the teacher would try to find a way out by arranging food from the lunch box of some other kid.

'The needle of suspicion immediately fell on Henry and his brother. This was the usual thing in our class. Whatever happened, it was an accepted thing that all blame should go to this duo. You might be curious to know why this was so. At that time we didn't have the capacity to ponder so deep. But later on we realized that it was because of their strange look which differentiated them from us. In my lunch-box case, one boy in the class even vouched to have seen Henry stealing the content during a short break.'

'You said that they were different from you in look. How were they different?'

'They had fair but rusty skin, thick lips and curly brown hair. They were always ridiculed by their class-mates for their exotic look. At that stage of life we were not in a position to accept and respect differences. But strangely it's not only the children but even the teachers were equally prejudiced about this difference...'

Gayatri tries to draw a mental picture of the two children, Henry and his brother. The identical twins with liquid, expansive eyes!

'Henry was dragged by the class teacher from his sitting place. A placard was made where it was written in capital letters I'M A THIEF. He was made to wear it round his neck and stand up in front of the class room for hours together.'

Somehow Gayatri is not in a psychological state to visualize such a cruel snap. She is not even going to attempt it.

'That evening Henry's still body was found hanging from the ceiling fan tied with a rope.... There was no suicide note but he seemed to be terribly upset. Next day the Principal of our school convened a meeting to mourn the death of one of the students. She elaborated Henry's many qualities like his quiet nature, his truthfulness. She sang a soulful song in his memory though she told in no uncertain terms that suicide was a sin and no true Christian should commit such a sin.

From among the class-mates, I stood up and told a few words in his praise: Henry was a handsome boy, both mentally and physically and precisely because of that he was chosen by God to be taken away at this early age....

There was so much pain in my voice that the entire school wept. I broke down completely when I ended my speech by drawing an imaginary cross over the upper part of my body. My heart was full both with pain and an unannounced feeling of pride at my capacity to talk something good for a fellow who was not of our types.

When I entered my class room with that swollen pride, I met Henry's brother, Jimmy, on the doorway. And what a face it was! It was burnt with so much rage like hot, amber coal shooting a burst of annoyance towards me through his squint eyes. My vanity evaporated instantly in the thin air.

My brother Rudolf came to me surreptitiously. He whispered in my ears, 'I had eaten your lunch yesterday....' I was horrified, 'Why didn't you tell yesterday? Look, your action had taken away one innocent soul.'

'So what? I wanted to punish Albert.'

'Albert? How does Albert come into the picture here?'

'Look, Albert is one of them.... All of them should be punished...'

It was my turn to be stunned, confused and pained. That evening I narrated everything to my Mom Ethel. With a highly injured feeling, she rushed to the school next day to apprise the school about what had actually happened so that the poor boy Henry could be absolved of all the blame he was getting on the last day of his life and even on death he could be respectfully rehabilitated. But the Principal looked at her in amazement as if she had gone out of her mind and very sweetly suggested that she should keep quiet.

'We've always been nice to them. I mean We Americans.'

'What do you mean by We Americans? Aren't they Americans? They were here when Columbus came to this country....'

'I understand your feelings Mrs. Amherst....'

Another cryptic remark! A cagey smile was flowing out of her thin, wavy lips.

'Mr. Amherst, my husband is also an American Indian....'

Ethel wanted to sound very blunt. She did not want to continue with this outer trapping of modesty which the other lady was conniving to use to farther her way of thinking.

'Your children are very sweet, well-bred...they're white American kids....'

She was adamant.

'You go back home Mrs. Amherst. Your son did no wrong. He's a well-behaved boy...'

'Ethel had a very strong sense of justice or fair play. She decided to withdraw her two sons from that school where the first lesson in fragmentation was taught. She was horrified. That is thc background of our going to Home School...'

'Wow, Ethel was really brave. She was prepared to put her own guilty son in a delicate position for the sake of justice.'

'Remember, she used to think like this at a time when people were shot dead for believing and raising this issue of equality. Even I'm not to be excused from this blame of pampering my elder brother's wayward ways. When I knew that my brother was responsible for the disappeared lunch-box, I should have immediately informed my teachers and other class-mates. I chose to remain quiet and took the easier way out by telling my Mom....'

'My Mom made another very grave mistake in one of those days when she was seriously contemplating about going for home-schooling. She told us about the circumstances under which our biological father had to give up his life. Since then Paul McCarthy joined as a very prominent figure in Rudolf's ever-increasing list of adversaries. During that period, Paul McCarthy came to our school. He talked about human rights, the right of an individual to be free, explained lucidly about the need to have a peaceful world and America's role in ensuring all those ideals. He was about to finish his lectures. Rudolf stood up and screamed at the top of his voice: Lies.... He is telling all lies.... He is a big hypocrite.... The world doesn't need America.... The world would be a far better place without America and without this captain of all lies: Paul McCarthy.... For a moment, there was a pin-drop silence in the lecture hall. The usual smirk in Paul McCarthy's face had also disappeared for a minute or so. But he quickly regained his composure and started talking.

The principal of the school who was so confident about Rudolf's innocence a few days back was livid with anger this time. She called Ethel and informed her coldly that Rudolf had been suspended from the school for a few days on account of bad behavior. My mom must have heaved a sigh of relief and went ahead with her decision to put Rudolf under homeschooling though sparing me for the time being from this home-schooling thing.'

Gayatri could clearly hear a bit of disappointment ringing through Greg's voice for an impending calamity called homeschooling for which a teenager like him who wanted to be in the big, broad, naughty world of a school had to be prepared.

Gayatri looks at the outside world through the huge, transparent glass of the window. The town is agog with enthusiasm for the Annual Homecoming of the university. The festivities can be felt from her glass-caged office. They have seeped adamantly inside her cocooned world like the fresh rays of the morning sun on a summery day in an oriental country. Mr. Sayers, the billionaire industrialist on a specially bedecked Mercedes is going to lead the procession of people on beautifully decorated carriages and vehicles. So many people, young and old alike, have come to this small university town to shower their love on an institute from which they started their exciting journey in life.

Homecoming! A journey towards home! Such a pleasant word!

'This forced separation between me and Rudolf made him more aggressive. So far, we were doing most of the work together. Suddenly, I'm not there with him. He devised an undefined enemy called America to give vent to his pent up feelings. My mom made a real blunder of telling him about the massacre in Mekong Delta. Whatever little faith he had on the mankind had totally gone.... I wasn't-too-happy about leaving Rudolf behind. There was an indeterminate emptiness inside me. That year my grade in the class also came down drastically. The class-teacher informed Ethel that I lacked concentration and I might be suffering from some attention deficiency syndrome.... Ethel did not take these suggestions kindly. She felt that both her kids would be driven to the brink of lunacy by that heartless school with its merciless teachers. With the support and encouragement of Albert she pulled me also out of the school and homeschooling started in right earnest for both of us. She became the teacher. I missed my school, class-mates and innumerable chaos associated with them. But I was happy to be with Rudolf....'

Greg has been telling about his life incessantly, without a pause. And suddenly a bizarre thought occurs to her. Is she ever going to be a part of this story in view of her spending a few intimate moments with the chief protagonist of the drama?

She must have been harboring an illusion when she should have known that this is as ordinary an event as enjoying an opera in the city hall. But Greg is an emotional person and all his physical actions are very strongly embedded in his emotional planet. But his lover! What was her name? She tries hard to remember. That woman has become an insignificant entity for this story where otherwise even the minutest details involving all the nitty-gritty of lives find a mention.

What could he do if she, as the story writer, gives that woman a very prominent place in defiance to the wishes of the catalyst? It's her story and she may do that. She might add that piquant Night in Gettysburg where she surrendered herself completely and unconditionally to him as a crucial moment of juxtaposition between love and denial.

Gayatri feels like hurting herself for even remotely indulging in such ineffectual thoughts. She wants to admonish her errant mind.

'I want to meet your stepfather Albert.'

She tries to divert her thought.

'Yes, of course. You should meet him. He stays in an Old-Age Home; not very far from here.... Rudolf was in a terrible state of mind after Ethel's death. She died quite young like most of the other members of her family due to a sudden illness. After her death when Rudolf was virtually uncontrollable, I had started blaming Albert for all this mess. Poor Albert! He didn't protest. Albert conceded that his method of dealing with the boys might have been wrong but he didn't have any ill-motive. I have erred Greg. Please forgive me. Albert pleaded like a small child many a times, but I was always rude to him...

Greg suddenly gets up and commands 'Let's go'.

The destination seems to be so clear that she hasn't bothered to ask any question and follows him to meet that enigmatic character of the story: Albert Amherst.

Darkness has been descending slowly over the Oakland Old Age Home residential colony. The entire area looks like an inscrutable place being gripped by the last vestige of a fugitive day-light. The large blue glass-caged swimming-pool is in sync with the green, undulating valley around. The symmetrical houses stand there as if they have posed with glee to be clicked for picture.

There is a note hung in the door-knob of Albert's house. 'Greg, I'm in Tennis-Court. Come there.'

Albert is a tall, huge man with a seemingly kind face. His eyes zeroes on Gayatri, a grin beams through his slightly opaque green-blue eyes surrounded by sagging eye-lids. He stands there like a giant watching the two of them with curiosity. Then without much of a warning he gives her a bear-hug, 'I've heard a lot about you from my son. Today is a very good day for me. I have defeated almost everyone in the game. Nora is going to be my partner in the Mixed Doubles. She's going to play such a superb game...'

Nora! Nora! Gayatri wants to scream in anguish.

His admiring eyes are on a thin, old, likeable woman with bubbling enthusiasm who must have been a stunner in her younger days. With her body-hugging T-shirt and Shorts ensconced comfortably on her wrinkled skin, she is all set to play her game in her twilight years. The same woman Gayatri met in one of those days in Dr. Shakuntala Kundan's clinic when she came with Rudolf there.

'If we can win this Mixed Doubles, our Oakland Community Service is going to give us a free trip to Miami. I'm looking forward to this win!'

This old lady is dreaming about a trip to Miami. Gayatri's mother in India is planning a trip to Haridwar for a pilgrimage. Her lease of life as far as the enjoyment quotient is concerned is over in this world. She has contemplated a grand re-union with the Maker and also with her husband after her death somewhere in the outer world. In every letter, she writes to her daughter, 'I am counting my leftover days here.. Your father's soul has been calling me from there.'

This nebulous thing called there has always been referred to by her mother after the death of her husband and no one raises any question on this undefined term.

Gayatri has made a mental picture of her mother with her lost, frail look in her completely white attire which has become her trade-mark since the death of her husband as if colors have vanished from her life with his passing away. Her colorless life is in sharp contrast with the vibrant look of this old widow whose enthusiasm for the proposed journey to Miami is diametrically opposed to the yearning of Gayatri's mother for a pilgrimage to Haridwar.

This lady's enviable zest for life is strangely opposed to the other lady's passion for death.

But this name! Nora! Why couldn't she choose another name from the innumerable options available? A nice and kind woman like her should have had another name.

People have gathered in the Community Centre for a feast. It happens very often there. A huge statue made of paraffin of St. Nicholas with a hat and a stick, the effervescent Santa Claus for the kids, stands there in full regalia. 'I've made it.' Gayatri could discern a tone of pride, a sense of gratification in Albert's voice.

One very old lady comes in faltering steps towards them with a broad smile playing in her thin lips. 'Hi Albert! We're making a plan to go for trekking on coming Sunday. That day is Deer Hunting Day. Please come with us with your gun.'

'Deer Hunting Day...?' Albert is visibly very excited at this plan. Then suddenly he looks sad. 'You know Gayathri, the ever-increasing deer population has caused a havoc in our state of Pennsylvania. The Government has fixed a day for gunning down deer.... But I can't take up gun against this animal. Ethel's memory, you see....'

Albert's voice is soaked in so much emotion that he almost sounds like crying. Nora clasps his hands, pates his back to soothe him and the other lady who was so thrilled about deer-hunting till a few minutes back says an inaudible sorry to this huge man as if she is in a state of shock for this turn of events.

Then Nora's feeble hands catch hold of Albert's bulky waist and gently push him towards the dance-floor. A popular song of the 50s is being played by a band. Albert's giant-like body tries to sway itself rhythmically with this tune though poor Nora finds it difficult to keep pace with the beat.

'I've arthritis.' Nora utters it so gently as if she is talking about possessing something precious.

'I know you're going to have a great time in Miami.' Greg quips with a twinkle in his eyes.

'How did you like my stepfather?'

Though Greg's hands are firmly on the steering wheel and the huge car has not been rushed impetuously, she can feel that his mind is not on the road ahead in this homeward journey.

'His look tallies well with my imagination. A huge man with a kind face.'

'My Dad's last letter must be with Albert.'

'It's your wild imagination Greg. Ethel might have destroyed it. Or she might have misplaced it somewhere. So many years have passed...'

'No, she's not going to misplace the last letter written by the first man in her life. She wasn't going to throw this away. She must have told Albert to keep quiet about it till such time he got a more reliable hand to pass it on.'

'Why are you looking for this letter Greg? Why are you still holding a grudge against Paul McCarthy? So many years have passed!'

'I want to protect a great concept called America from such imposters. America is a unique concept based on freedom and enterprise. However, what Paul McCarthy was doing in Vietnam was a total anti-thesis of what America stood for....'

Greg trembles in an uncontrollable ire. It is essential to shift his focus from the large things to the very ordinary at the moment.

'Hey Greg! What are your plans for the Christmas?...You know what.... I really admire your system of sending photo-albums to the relatives during this festival. You may not visit your relatives for decades, but you can keep in touch with all, through this small gesture.... Someone has put on weight; someone has added some gray hair or a few lines here and there. It's like updating the profile...'

'I do not have anyone. Whose photograph can I send Gye? The only brother I have is in a lunatic asylum. The only wife I had a few years back, has become someone else's wife. ...Whose photograph, tell me, whose photograph I'm going to send...?'

There is so much desperation in his voice that Gayatri feels like cuddling him like a child. This person, this apparently confident person needs reassurance, a dollop of comfort.

'The situation may change next Christmas. You maybe having someone very near...your own....'

She was about to finish the sentence when suddenly she throws up everything inside the car. 'I'm sorry Greg. Your new car...let me clean...'

'It's okay. I'll do that.'

An unusual calm bordering on annoyance in his voice!

When she is dropped in front of her house, there is no exchange of farewell greetings. Without looking at her, he drives away, probably very far, his blank stares being fixed on an empty horizon.

✦

Gayatri has just reached the clinic at the appointed hour. Traffic is generally chaotic at this time of the day when everyone simply rushes to the workplace. Her inward tension vies for a space with the palpable stress outside while her eyes are glued to the road ahead and her hands fixed on the steering wheel.

When Greg left the job and vanished from the town without a word, she also decided to come this far. Martha too advised her to listen to her own mind. 'It's your body sweetheart. You've got absolute right to take any decision about it.'

She tries to look deep inside and fathom her own feelings. Does she want to announce to the world that she is free to take any decision about her life? No, she is not going to put any question to herself at this time when she has already spent so many sleepless nights in seeking answers to innumerable questions, the nights smoldered by guilt about those heretically passionate moments in the historic town of Gettysburg.

Where has Greg scampered off and why? And that too in this crucial juncture when a life was unfolding inside her womb? In some weaker moments she told everything to Natalie and Martha. Natalie was as reassuring as an old comforting friend and told her that nothing was amiss. Life threw challenges and the beauty of life was to take up all those challenges in their strides. 'Yes, it's your life and you're free to take any decision. But it shouldn't go against your conscience. Conscience is a very big thing Gye. No one can run away from it. Not even the mighty ones.'

Martha was cool about abortion. 'Go ahead. I don't see anything wrong here. Why should you take a load on your body, mind and soul all alone if you are unprepared to carry it...?'

Dr. Johnson's abortion clinic reminds her to Dr. Mrs. Kundan's clinic. There she went to re-build a fractured life and here she has come to destroy one. She remembers the bronze idol of the goddess Kali looking down in a pensive fierceness at all the troubled souls in Mrs. Kundan's tastefully decorated chamber and Mrs. Kundan talking about creation and destruction both being embodied in the same goddess. She was elaborating how destruction contained seeds of creation as well. That was Indian philosophy in pristine form where contradictions co-exist beautifully like Siamese twins. But at this moment Gayatri is not sure how the impending doom of her baby in the protective warmth of her womb is going to carry any hope for creation.

That incongruity so nicely illustrated by Mrs. Kundan in the context of her then splintered life simply refuses to fit in her present existence.

The man enters the premise coolly and leaves with equal calm.

This is the price he should pay for killing lives. Whoever indulges in anti-catholic activities would meet a similar fate. That is the note the killer leaves on the table of Dr. Johnson. There is no sound of gun-shots, no apparent struggle; the suave operator gives away no cause for immediate suspicion and he melts away swiftly and anonymously among the morning crowd.

Martha tries to drag Gayatri out of that clinic and she follows her like a zombie. At the same time Martha tries to give an idea about the physical attributes of the killer. 'He's tall, slim and pallid with curly hair. He had a kind face. Must be a Hispanic...' Gayatri doesn't remember anything about that man. The entire episode happened in such a diabolical pace that she probably passed through an amnesic feat to block that miasma of a pre-meditated murder in front of her eyes.

An act of destruction to avenge another act of annihilation!

Last evening Gaurav sang an Australian ballad in the huge auditorium in the University's Bucke Building. The enormity of his voice dawned on the spell-bound crowd and they seemed to have soaked in the gravity of the moment. It was a rebellion against war coated in the aching words of a maimed soldier: Then a big Turkish shell knocked me ass overhead/And when I awoke in my hospital bed/I saw what it had done/Never knew were worse things than dying there...

A man who thought there could never be a worse thing than death had to swallow this bulging pain of being a crippled. Death would have been a far more welcoming proposition than this pitiable existence for this young soldier. Gaurav's grandiose voice was conveying this potent emotion so well that the entire hall was soon drowned in a sea of expansive grief.

And sitting here today in the Dr. Johnson's clinic Gayatri also feels that this horrendous existence of hers where she has been welcoming the destruction of an innocent life is far worse than death itself. And finally when she reaches home with the life of her yet-to-be-born child intact she howls and howls like a baby in an abundant feeling of relief.

Good news have been pouring of late without much of a fanfare, almost like some preplanned conspiratorial cosmic design to prove that when life plunges into a depth of sadness, good things also come in profusion. The billionaire industrialist Mr. Sayers was so impressed with Gaurav's rendering of the plight of a wounded soldier through his music that he offered him a gift voucher worth several hundred dollars and a free ticket to a country of his choice. Gayatri has been offered the editorship of Greg's paper by the new owner who bought the paper from Greg just before he decided to vanish. Another prestigious newspaper America Today has also requested her to contribute a weekly column to their paper. It is an exultant time for her at the professional level.

But there are enough parallel scars carefully wrapped up inside her indefatigable heart.

She asked Natalie about this strange paradox of Greg going away at a time when she was hoping that he would be there to shield her from all the travails of life. It was a hope nurtured by his obvious concerns displayed on innumerable occasions to her and her family, a flickering hope which had snow-balled into a thickening desperation in course of time and then dazed to the ground by the same intense betrayal. 'He was supposed to make a film on the concentration camp of Berga where his grandfather perished.... Maybe because of that...or maybe some such reason...'

Both of them knew that it wasn't true. Greg ran away from her and the unborn child and any amount of attempt to coat this elopement with dignity would be futile.

But how she is going to paint this act of Greg or Greg as a person in her book? The book is going to be her baby and she is free to portray him either as a villain out to destroy things or as a hero pursuing all sorts of noble vocations or an ordinary human being who might go away or stay back as per convenience. She can paint him as a weakling also, a feeble indecisive character who might run away at the slightest provocation. She is not going to write a biography; it is a novel where wild imaginations may run amok.

But she is looking for a plausible answer to the vexed question which has been agitating her mind for very long, 'Why did Greg go away?'

Natalie is busy scouting for an agent and an editor for Gayatri's book, a book still growing inside her like a kicking fetus, undaunted by the colossal setback of the story-teller deserting it at the climax point. She is not sure where she is going to start her story: at the Allegheny forest when young, enigmatic Ethel chasing a forest dream or start with Greg as the inheritor of a complex litany of interwoven events with her ink tracing his life in a backward movement?

Vanishing of Greg was so sudden and unexpected that she is still in a fix with the last part of the incomplete story staring starkly at her face. She should have been prepared for this sudden twist of events like so many other things that have happened this way earlier in her life.

As the writer of the story, she can fully control its destiny. But she cannot control the real events which will follow their own surreal design and may even go haywire. Truth sometimes becomes as baffling as fiction.

Martha has been coming to her as frequently as possible during the last few days to enthuse her. She is thrilled at the news of Gayatri being offered the editorship of the only daily paper of the town. Otherwise, Martha is awfully busy these days. She is asked by the university authority to mobilize the new African-American students of the university and make them acclimatize with the alien environment.

'The number of such students has almost halved this time compared to the last year.' Martha informs with a mellowed voice.

'Why so?'

Gayatri expects a barrage of white-bashing profanities from Martha.

'The university conducted a survey recently and found that the most intelligent students were from the Jewish community followed by the students of the European origin and then by the Indian Hindus. The university decided that the Jews, Europeans and the Indian Hindus would be given preference in awarding admission and fellowship.'

'Don't you think it is discriminatory?'

'No, why? How'll the university survive if the corporate sponsorship is not forthcoming? The captains of industry look for brain power and the university is a machine to produce that.'

Martha, who wants to talk about prejudices so often, does not find anything wrong here.

She further adds some interesting anecdotes on the university life. The number of girls in this fall semester outnumbers boys in a big way in Penn State. During weekends the girls compete with one another for grabbing a Date and the failed ones have to go to the pubs and other such places in a huge girlie group.

Siddhartha also called up in between. He was furious with McDonald for apparently mixing beef-fat in the potato-chips, a blasphemous act deserved to be condemned. He was planning to file a suit against this fast-food-giant for their obvious attempt at hurting the religious sentiment of an important religious minority of this country. He opened his feelings to his children with the hope that they would also be equally scornful about this injustice meted out to them and their beliefs. The children listened to their Dad impassively without any outward sign of being affected. Why should they react? Their small world has remained unperturbed by this innocuous act of potato chips being mixed with beef fat somewhere.

Natalie is deeply immersed in her research on the feelings of intense alienation harbored by the Muslim community in the western society and a disinclined Gayatri has also been roped into it. Natalie has not told anything but it does not require any streak of imagination to know that her friend is trying to associate her with a project to woo her away from all the worries which have been plaguing her of late.

'If you look back, you won't get anything called a Muslim world or a Christian world or any such medieval polarization before the First World War period. A modern Turkey emerged during that time only. But then the western strategists started harping on the divisions so elaborately for their own gains that people became alert and alarmed. Pakistan was designed by the westerners to weaken the Indian sub-continent. Israel was thrust on an area where there was no Jewish presence for very long. Dominant western existence was ensured in the oil-rich Middle East. All these factors encouraged jingoism, alienation, separatism and terrorism.... You see Natalie, whatever you sow, you reap. It was the British who backed the thesis that the Hindus and the Muslims were separate nations so that Pakistan could be created conveniently. Now there are bomb-blasts in the heart of London....'

'Yeah Gye, we can add all these things in our write-up. Look, when two brains are put together, the result is fabulous....'

It is amazing that Natalie has already amassed enough information to explicate her theory of alienation of the Muslims in Europe or America.

Sangati is a tiny township in France in the mouth of English Channel. Red Cross had built four temporary shelters for people who have been camping there for months together in the hope of crossing to England through four dangerously difficult routes via English Channel. Fear of death from electric shock, fear of death from speeding train inside the tunnel, fear of death from heavily armed security personnel! Death has spawned a web everywhere there!

This has always been explained to the inmates of the shelter homes in the Red Cross so that they go back without undertaking this potentially life-taking exercise. But those shelter homes in the midst of a potato crop were always teeming with people. For them that was the only way to escape an otherwise a sure death from hunger lurking snugly in their home land.

Jamal was a bright student from Algeria. He topped a French university in his discipline. But he could not get a seat in the PhD course just because he was not a naturally born French national. A dismayed Jamal wanted to move to England where equal opportunities were supposed to be offered to citizens and immigrants alike in matters of education. But migration to that country was not an easy job. An undeterred Jamal wanted to try his luck through English Channel. He tried forty one times to cross the tunnel covering twenty-two acres surface area where a speeding train moved between two neighboring countries. He failed each time.

When he finally succeeded in this life endangering exercise, he realized to his horror that while he was safe on the top of the speeding train, his other family members had also arrived by the same train, all frozen and dead inside a perishable-carrying-cold-storage van. England where human dignity was supposed to be cherished did not bother to give the dead people a decent burial. They were left to be devoured by wild animals. Jamal felt so terrible that all his great English dreams got crashed at that ghastly sight. He became a rabid anti-west.

West became an entity against whom he raised a revolt of guns and words.

Gayatri listened carefully to Natalie's views. She finds a whole lot of truth in her friend's analysis of this gaping distance between the separatist minds and an indifferent mainstream. Who would understand the pain of rejection better than herself?

A fire burns inside her, slowly and leisurely.

This prolonged flame might engulf her sometime before she shakes herself out of its grip. She must learn the trick of redirecting that macabre fire at something more volatile than that sweet, little, trusting heart of hers.

The murderer of Dr. Johnson who wanted to avenge destruction by another act of vehement annihilation must also be reeling under some pain of denial. This was apparently an act to uphold a faith, his endearingly beautiful faith. But why should this fabulously insecure man feel that his faith is as weak as his own feeble self and needs a wand of protection from his highly corrugated spirit?

Last few days Gayatri has been reading that fascinating book 'Tuesdays with Morrie', a book which cherishes life for its myriad hues of possibilities. This is not a book of fiction or a biography but a book which sings paeans to life. Morrie, a renowned Professor in one of the American universities, was diagnosed as having a serious ailment with not even the faintest hope of recovery. One of his favorite students would go to Morrie on every Tuesday and he would talk about the beauty of the world.

The book was the last gift Greg gave to her a few days before he left and it was lying in one of her cupboards indifferently till she picked it up one day to see what was there inside. Then an intense journey of bonhomie between her wilting soul and a dying person who sings the most beautiful song of life began.

Morrie's zest for life is so contagious that she is touched, stirred and awakened from slumber.

When she has still been reeling under the impact of all those positive vibes emanating from the philosophy of a dying man, she suddenly remembers the murderer of Dr. Johnson. What a terrible waste!

'Why did you go to Dr. Johnson's clinic mom?'

It is her turn to be utterly surprised at Gaurav's question. She decides not to answer him.

'...I saw you hurrying and scurrying in that melee...like a very frightened soul...under the glare of TV cameras.... Mom, Tell me.... Why should you want to kill someone who can't defend itself? ...I didn't expect this from you, Mom...of all people....'

Gayatri has failed to find any trace of annoyance in Gaurav's calm demeanor in spite of her intent probing in his deep, impassive eyes.

A formidable bond has interminably and seamlessly been formed between these two people at that fragile moment of time.

✦ ✦ ✦

13

Martha Stuart's show has been going on in the Food Channel. Gayatri has been sitting leisurely on her long sofa, hands and feet overstretched, eyes glued to the idiot box but her mind with a myriad imaginations has been wandering on a different plane. Yesterday was a hectic day. Time passed in a tempestuous speed in that forebodingly spirited city at this time of the day when they, she and her two curious children, decided to be onlookers in a human drama in one of its expanded parts, known as the Alice island.

New York has always been enigma for her with its dirt, noise and a profusion of feckless chaos. It is so diabolically opposed to what the rest of America stands for with certain amount of mess staring at any visitor's face! She feels like going back there to breathe in the aroma of that jumble when the boringly uniform landscapes of a sleek America spanning across the entire country of a continental proportion starts gawking exasperatingly at her.

Once Siddhartha was accosted by a fierce looking youth when he was walking through a narrow lane of the city on his way to the hotel where his university was putting him up for striking some business deals with a biotech firm.

'Please give me everything whatever you have. Don't try to act smart.' Siddhartha had to shell out his wristwatch, gold chain, his diamond-studded gold wedding ring, three hundred dollar bills and the T-shirt he was wearing on that summery day. The only saving grace was the credit card that remained ensconced cozily in his back pocket after all those dizzying pace of events. The receptionist in the hotel was not flabbergasted when Siddhartha entered the hotel bare-chested; tell-tale signs of being heckled were all too obvious to be ignored. The apparently indifferent receptionist in the hotel lobby just told him, 'In this city, it's better not to venture out much in the evening. It might be dangerous, you know. People get killed here....'

Next time they came to New York to enjoy a Broadway play with the children, 'Miss Saigon'. The children shrieked in pleasure to the discomfiture of their father when a plane landed on the stage.

New York brought back all those memories when a huffing and puffing Gayatri was roaming around yesterday in a shambling gait with her two children in the melee of the inimitable Time Square. It was almost a replay of the past. The jostling crowd with their craving to snatch some moments of glory in front of the camera was still there like that of the last time. Siddhartha told them about the desire of some men and women, walking past the camera, to talk to their intimate people through media in that chaotic push and pull. It happened mostly in the dawn when Good Morning America or some such program was beamed.

This time too she found that nothing much had changed there in that broad sea of humanity. The beggars with guitars or mandolins in their hands, near the Statue of Liberty, asked for alms when she came with Siddhartha. They were still there this time too like the statue itself to announce the invincibility of something eternal.

Before her marriage to John, Kenny lived in New York. Kenny recounted her growing up years in New York with lots of fondness. 'Sometime I feel like running away from this sleepy university town to that highly vibrant city of New York. Our house was very near to that of Helliwel, the Mafia don. Once I saw him standing in front of his house, a very rare occasion. I went near him and asked him why his photographs were always splashed on the newspapers. Are you very famous? That was my silly question. He laughed heartily and replied: Yes girl, I'm. But infamously famous.'

Whenever Gayatri went to New York she would tell Kenny, 'Hey, I'm going to your city.' On the other end of the telephone she would shriek in delight 'Gosh, I am so jealous. Enjoy.'

Once during Christmas time they went to see the huge Christmas tree near the Rockefeller Centre. It was decorated with all kinds of colors like a blooming Indian bride with her finery on her wedding day. This time also they took a round there, the aridity of the landscape there at this time of the year was striking with the barren Christmas tree looking down at all the visitors. Gayatri felt a strong pull towards this abandoned beauty as if in this desolate state also it was radiating a pride which no one could see during a pampered Christmas season.

The same city was attacked and destruction was unleashed on its multihued populace on a fateful day called 9/11. The city took it upon itself to come back to life with a fierce fortitude not usually obvious on a normal day. Gayatri took the children to Ground Zero to show how life could rebound on a plinth of mass destruction. It was like her own life which was conspired to be raged to the ground in one fine morning when Siddhartha announced his decision to leave her. She collapsed but bounced back later on with the support of some very kind people like Martha, Shakuntala, Lara, Kenny, Natalie, Greg! Yes Greg! Her own Greg, Gregory Amherst! But he also decided to go in his own way.

But yesterday she had a special purpose to come to New York. She wanted to take her children, who were once thrilled at the stories of escapades of a little girl called Alice in a wonderland, to Alice Island: another wonderfully lofty joist in this country where many such exotic tales can be weaved.

From 1890 to 1920, daily average five thousand people entered America from Europe through Alice Island. A huge inflow of human beings in terms of numbers! In terms of aspiration, pain and other quotients of human emotions it was not less loaded. America with her vast landscape and awesome resources welcomed that massive White influx, an amazing wealth in terms of human resource, with open arms. After their landing in that desolate island, a health check up was done and they were rehabilitated in different parts of America. Their names and physical attributes were recorded carefully in a register as a part of that health check up not knowing that these insignificant figures would provide emotional succor to a generation desperate to know about their roots at a much later date.

Till 60s Americans were not bothered about their root. They were so well-entrenched in their comfort zone of being only Americans that they never raised the issues like how and why they came to this land of affluence till that period. But then a new generation of Americans wanted to come out of that cocoon and look backward to know more about their forefathers than the desultory knowledge of their simply stepping into the shores of this country.

It is an emotional voyage towards an indeterminate past, not known and not seen!

Gayatri was trying to explain to her children about this new craze among the Americans to flock to Alice Island.

The Melting Pot is an undeniable truth in American society. Gayatri had made her children read a poem of Emma Lazarus inscribed on the edifice of the Statue of Liberty:

Give me your tired, your poor,
Your huddled masses yearning to breathe free,
The Wretched refuge of your teeming shore.
Send these, the homeless, tempest tossed to me,
I lift my lamp beside my golden door.

The Melting Pot, Israel Jengwin's book on America became the perfect epithet for this country that became a refuge for so many millions across the world.

'I've brought both of you to this place for one reason...to see yourself that people are desperate to know about their root.... Look, so many people have come here to unflinchingly peep at their past. But you don't have to go to an island to find out about your ancestors or flip through worn out pages of any book to know about their emotions. Your past is very much alive in India. You can go there any time to know more about yourself....'

Garry, her own Gaurav was noticeably quiet. But that should not deter her from baring her heart to him.

'Son, you are not an isolated identity. Your mind, body and soul have inherited quite a deal from the past. If you acknowledge that, your acceptance of India is not going to contradict your present identity as an American. When all other fellow Americans are flocking to the Alice Island to find out their root, why should you lag behind? ...You asked me once about where to go with the big, fat gift-voucher from Mr. Sayers, I wasn't ready with the answer that day. Today I'm ready to tell you that you should go to India.'

She paused for a while.

'Decision is entirely yours.'

Where did the multicolored cuisines of Martha Stuart vanish? She is not even aware when she has switched over to 'Whose Line Is It Anyway' show along with her truant Remote. Brad Sherwood, one of the show-presenters is singing a song, his own love ballad, as requested by one young member of the audience. He has to put a meaningless word Niroshi after every sentence. And who can stop Sherwood now? As if he was waiting with readymade lyrics for a song to be sung at this moment, he just took off.

He'll take his beloved Niroshi,
To the river Gaa-shi,
Where they'll cook some brioshi
And across the Pacific O-shi'
To put some 'Suntan lo-shi'.

There are roars of laughter from the audience and must be from the unseen viewers also. Gayatri could not contain her glee as this abrupt display of wit by an erudite player in the field. She opened the TV for Martha Stuart show and now finds herself in this delightful program. Whatever happens, happens for the good. Her mother's simple explanation for anything that has gone wrong! It was very easy for a fatalist like her mother or for any other Indian lady of her generation to accept life as it was. If life became very difficult, they thought it was destiny or the fruit of the previous birth's karma and sometime decided to take it as a good omen. They could take so many travails of life like this and wait patiently for a better day to arrive.

At this moment when she has been wavering between two insignificant television shows, Gayatri also wants to take solace by thinking that the turn of her life's events, even this ordinary act of going from one program to another without conscious knowledge, maybe happening for the good. She could laugh to her heart's content like a maniac and that's what she needs the most at this hour.

She decides to speak to Martha, her friend about her adventures in the Alice Island.

'This Alice Land will talk about the history of only fair-skinned people. Nothing has been recorded about the emotions of colored people who were brought forcibly like some caged animals to this country for sheer exploitation and torture. Where'll we go to find that truth?'

'Don't feel that way, Martha. Your tales are recorded in literature, in the pages of some chronicles. The value of all such writings is not less than what is available in the Alice Island's records.'

She has to tell more to assuage her friend's injured feelings.

'Look, it's not only your people who had to face this scourge called racial hatred. In the year 1943 in the state of Bengal in India, three million people perished in a famine. While these unfortunate souls were awaiting a long-drawn-out silent death in one corner of India, ships carrying wheat consignment from Australia were passing through the Bay of Bengal for an aborted war effort in the Balkan. So many persons appealed to Churchill, the war hero and the great statesman of the world at that time, for diverting this food grain for the famine-ravaged people. He refused to do anything. Nearly seven-million perished in the world due to racial hatred of Hitler and at the same time three-million died in my country due to similar prejudices of Churchill. But why should we always look back and harbor pain and hatred? It's time that we should look ahead...'

Martha's pensive mood is slowly lifted, a smile plays on her eyes, understanding and compassion taking over the place of a never-ending agitation.

Gayatri meets Natalie in the office the next morning.

Gayatri could read an impish twinkling in her round, blue eyes. 'My friend Claudia went to the Alice Island with lots of hope. She found out that her forefathers, a man and a woman, entered America after murdering a number of people in Prussia. America welcomed them with open arms. Poor Claudia! She's simply aghast.'

Natalie giggles like a teenager at this perceived plight of Claudia.

Natalie's eyes are now transfixed on the computer screen.

'So.... Garry has finally agreed to go to India? When you called me up last night I was damn happy....' Natalie has not raised her head.

'Yes, he has agreed. My persuasion probably worked.'

'Look, it's mutual. You have also agreed to retain the baby in your womb because of his urging.'

How can she make Natalie understand that Gaurav interceded on behalf of an abandoned soul only because he could see his reflection in that innocent being? Both have swallowed the intense pain of rejection of their fathers. She has also perched herself on the same plinth and felt the same pain for herself.

She is jerked back into the present by the loud ringing of the telephone on her desk.

'Hello Gayathri, it's Jimmy here.... Hope you know me from Greg...'

Jimmy? Is it really Jimmy on the other side of the telephone? And Greg! Does he have any news about Greg? Her heart leaps with joy.

'Yeah Jimmy. Henry and Jimmy' She bit her lips. What has she done? 'I'm so sorry, Jimmy. I had no desire to hurt you. Henry's name cropped up whenever Greg mentioned about you and in my mind the two persons became one entity. He used to speak a lot about you. Tell me what can I do for you?'

'I'm looking for Greg. Where has he vanished? He once told me, not too long ago, whenever he was not traceable, I should contact you to know his whereabouts. He's in that habit of vanishing sometime. When his wife left him, he went into this kind of hibernation....'

'I really don't know where Greg has gone. He has virtually gone with the wind. Dissipated, I should say...'

'Then I need to see you Gayathri. It's urgent.'

This is Jimmy in front of her eyes in her office room. A replica of an image that she developed in her mind long time back when Greg narrated a story of his childhood! Sometime imagination and reality strangely merge.

'Greg's stepdad Albert was my uncle, my Dad's elder brother. Ethel used to maintain a very warm relationship with my family. Time was different then. We were very poor, virtually on the edge of the society, living in a kind of ghetto. She didn't want to tell others because that might have made her two adorable sons an object of ridicule. Albert's mother was also a white lady and her son was born after a relationship with my grandfather when she came to work among our community. Later on, she married someone her family wanted. Probably, a Jesuit doctor working somewhere in India. My grandfather married a lady from his community. Albert was brought up in a white household, his grandparents' place, almost like an abandoned child. But when he grew up, he sought out his father's family and contact was re-established.'

Greg's stepfather Albert a blood relation of Jimmy and Henry and Albert's mother a white American! A curious sub-plot inside a plot! That explains Albert's Caucasian features and the confusion of the people of Tionesta about the intriguing origin of Ethel's second husband. They knew for sure that something was amiss there, otherwise who would have married an unwed mother of two! But they couldn't find out his exact blood-line, though there must have been lot of whispers in the community about his atypical origin.

It is her turn to be stunned. 'Did Greg know about it?'

'Hmm, I think so. We've never discussed. He knew that Ethel had used to visit us very often. Sometime with Uncle Albert and sometime alone. She shared a very good rapport with my mother.'

There is a pause now. Jimmy has come in search of something, a truth or a void or a man called Greg: all rolled into one for Gayatri at the moment.

'Greg's mom left a letter with me, must be an important piece of paper. I'm going away to the Far East in the work of the church. I don't know when I'm returning. I'm looking for the rightful heir to this letter. Rudolf must still be in the Rehab.... I wonder where should I leave this...'

Jimmy is visibly distressed at this disappearance of a dear friend when he was to go away to a far-off place in search of a spiritual quest.

'In a few days time you'll find the rightful heir...'

She was eager to show more exuberance but her wiggly voice was loath to cede more than what was necessary to convey a meaning. She is not sure whether that really conveyed anything at all. Her impulsive hands slowly caress her bloated belly. When an opportunity to announce the arrival of a new life to the immediate family members of the child dangles so salaciously in front of her eyes, she is about to let it go.

Jimmy is not looking at her but nodding his head inscrutably, suddenly he slips an envelope in her hand. 'It's for you. Before her death aunt Ethel handed over this with a request that her two sons should never see this. Once probably she revealed a part of the contents to her sons, but it made Rudolf very violent. Greg also looked confused. She decided to keep quiet after that.... It has always been a load on me...this envelope...I don't know what is there inside and I'm not keen to know either. But you open it and see what is there before it's too late...Ethel's soul will be happy.'

There has been unusual warmth in his hands when he clasps her hands for sometime before saying bye to her. She knew in an instant that an incessant tie had been formed between the two at that moment itself, a bond of understanding and compassion transcending all the barriers.

Jimmy has started hurtling away towards the door as if he is in a tremendous hurry.

'I'm very happy to meet you Gayatri.'

Jimmy's voice from the other end of the room, when he is about to go out, sounds very faint from a curious blend of pain and relief. Then she could hear his words again, loaded with lot of din and wafting like small bubbles towards her, 'I'll be the godfather of your child. I'll always be praying for the child wherever I stay....'

Here is a man who lost his brother because of a treachery perpetrated by Ethel's tempestuous son and he still clings to Ethel's love and trust like a truly merciful saint.

Very slowly she opens the grayish envelope and draws out a paper, slender and tinged with brownish color. The faded, hurriedly written words speak about a night when in one forgotten corners of the world a ghastly incident was staged at the behest of a person who is about to pledge a noble life for the citizens of the world: It is drizzling out here. The alluvial soil of Mekong Delta is draped in a strange red color...you can see blood everywhere.... I can clearly see a kind of wild exuberance coming out from the face of Paul McCarthy.... He was virtually dancing over these dead bodies like a maniac. A demonic dance over helpless, unarmed people.... I'm going to raise my voice soon. But this vengeful man might do anything.... My dear, you pray for me. I want to see my child....'

Gayatri clutches the diminutive but extremely weighty envelope with lot of passion as a tribute to a person who has been connected, in some way, to her unborn child. The paper is invaluable. She cannot afford to run away like a coward at this moment when history is going to be recast in an entirely different way.

Your granny will cuddle you with all the strengths that she can summon from her frail, worn out body and plant kisses all over your face. She longed to see you. She would take you to a photograph of her dead husband and go on telling to that snap: 'Look, he's your grandson, our daughter's son and he's coming back to us. Please give him enough of your good-wishes so that he goes ahead in life.' ...Your granny believes that your grandpa's spirit has heard all and seen all from a remote, invisible and somewhat mysterious land. Never question her beliefs. She may feel hurt if you try to make her see reason. Then you'll be taken to the Puja Ghar. She would ask from God a very long life for you, the years to be counted in terms of the number of hairs she has over her scalp.

You would be taken to your numerous uncles and aunts. They might also come in groups as per their own convenience and without any prior appointment. So much food would be forced down your throat. You are also not supposed to think much about encroaching their time or territory. You'd be aghast at the sight of new, fast moving and sleek vehicles plying over some pock marked roads in a gusto. You'll see more of such contrasting pictures elsewhere there too. India lives not only in the urban elite areas but also in the dusty, unwinding roads of the villages, in the paddy fields or in the schools where children can look up and see the sky through the innumerable holes of the roof. India exists in both the worlds and if you want to know the country, you must know both these overlapping entities....

Gayatri has been telling her son about the country of his ancestors in bits and pieces during the last several days. He has been listening intently without much of a fuss and without asking questions.

Gayatri's work has increased manifold after she has taken over as the Editor of the paper where she was earlier a staff member and used to write some assigned pieces. Here she has to oversee everything, from the contents to the sponsorship.

One day she goes to meet Albert in the Old Age Home. Albert in his usual jocular manner asks her about Greg: Where have you managed to hide yourself and Greg all these days?

Then on a more solemn tone he tells her how he has been trying to contact Greg frantically. The emails are never replied back.

'Should we talk to someone? If something has happened to him.... It never occurred to me earlier...'

There is so much force in her words, words buoyed by a raging despair.

Albert stares at her, a huge man almost looking down at her with a face contorted with pain. She could read dollops of empathy floating in those watery eyes presaging a storm. 'He is seen. With his former wife Naomi, in many places including Berga.... They've been roaming around in all the holocaust locations. One of my friends sent me a video-clipping of Greg and Naomi dancing to the disco beat of the Gloria Gaynor song in front of the Work sets you free sign at the entrance of a notorious holocaust site. He must have celebrated the survival of the clan even when his grandfather perished there....'

She could feel a nudge, a soft touch of his wrinkled skin over her left hand, 'I'm sorry dear. I didn't mean to tell you. Nora would kill me if she knows that I've told you about him.'

'I'm carrying his baby.'

'I know it. He told me.'

'But why should he go away?'

'I want to be absolutely frank with you. Greg, this stupid Greg loves Naomi and no one else. He regrets that he would have to father a child from someone he never ever loved...I am quoting him only...'

Gayatri has sensed that blood has been oozing out to her face making it unusually warm and radiant. Strangely she feels relieved too of a burden she has so far been carrying inside her about an illusion called love. It was such a knotty burden that the entire feeling had been encircling her inner self like a serpent holding on to its prey. With a sudden thud, that grip is gone and she is free to soar high in an infinitely limitless space.

'Look at the irony! You have a Nora with you who has brought forth a fresh breeze of hope in your life. Another Nora came to my life long time back bringing in her wake a devastating cyclone of destruction. I survived that. While going through the process of coping up, I realized that I was possessed by immense self-love. I could never destroy myself. I'm grateful to My Nora for making me realize that.'

Alber looks straight in her eyes, a deep and penetrating gaze. 'My Nora is very ill. I don't know how long she's going to survive. She has decided to shift to an apartment inside this Old-Age-Home where she could take the help of a caretaker.'

'I'm sorry to hear it Albert. Your love might cure her of her illness. You never know. Love is such a powerful a force.'

'Thank you dear. We were very happy together in Miami. When Ethel passed away, I thought I had lost everything. Then this Nora came. You are very right. She gave me a new lease of life.'

Nora looks pale, her color matching with the pallid whiteness of the bed sheet where she has been sleeping listlessly. Her thin hands are lying over her belly. It is far removed from the scene when on another time the same hands were clutching the fat waist of Albert and they were dancing away in glory.

Gayatri could feel the warmth of her teardrops falling liberally from her eyes down the cheeks.

In the lobby a TV program catches her attention. The anchor is in an effervescent mood asking questions to his victim, a handsome, suave man in his 60s or 70s, a dynamic person who is effectively tackling a barrage of questions on issues concerning future of America. A familiar face!

'What America thinks today, the world will think tomorrow.' The person has told so wryly as if he has made an inevitable declaration.

There is a pause, a small recess to breathe-in some freshness inside; the effect of this effort is evident in his face which glows like amber in excitement. 'Everyone has acknowledged the great American ethics of justice, equality and liberty and her commitment to a free society. My dream is to make this edifice of trust more robust for millions of people across the globe.'

There is a pause again, with a gleeful expression and then this look turns into a more somber one. 'We're passing through a lean phase; a phase marked by job loss, downswing, and general gloom. But I can assure you, in all earnestness that it's going to be over soon. We, the great Americans, are going to put all our efforts to ascend again. May God bless us in our endeavor!'

Paul McCarthy! It's him. She saw some of his other interviews somewhere. A glowing, unassuming smile plays on his lips and eyes.

'He's going to become our President. He has been far ahead of John Edmond in the popularity rating. This clever guy! During Primaries he almost decimated his rivals by his look, personality and an apparent sincerity. John Edmond is a powerful speaker, a highly knowledgeable person. But he appears to be arrogant. So, it's natural that this person is going to edge out his rival by a huge margin.'

'People have been lapping up his enthusiasm, particularly in this distressing time of recession. Do you share this passion Albert?'

'I share Ethel's sorrow of losing her husband in far-off Vietnam.'

'And the two, this enthusiasm for Paul McCarthy's vision for America and Ethel's sorrow, do not co-exist. Right?'

Albert once again looks straight at her, his deep, brooding gaze. But there is something intimidating in his look.

'Do you know how much I loved my Ethel? You don't know.'

Gayatri coyly brought out an envelope, gray and brownish and pulled out an equally soiled paper from inside. 'My conscience will prick me if I just sit over this letter sent long time back by Greg's Dad from a battle-field.'

Albert does not take much time in finishing this letter as if he is in a tearing hurry to gorge down everything. His twisted face shows pain, maybe for his boys' biological father or for so many other unfortunate souls on that bizarre night. His quietude is daunting, somewhat nerve-wrecking.

'Ethel left this letter with Jimmy.'

She told Albert with lot of contemplation.

'Jimmy is your nephew.'

She added further to proceed with her conversation.

'You know everything about this family. Greg has told you enough. Or it might be Jimmy himself. Whatever.... Ethel left this letter with someone she can trust and that was Jimmy. Jimmy, in turn, has handed over to you. Ethel's trust in Jimmy is transferred to you Gayatri. It must have been Ethel's wish. She has maneuvered even after her death to send it to the right person.'

Gayatri could not find any trace of humor in Albert's deadpan expression.

'Since this letter is here with us, let's act fast.'

'Paul McCarthy is a popular leader with a clean image and a very long, unblemished political career.'

'Are you scared?'

'No, I'm worried.... About you...'

'...I'm going to fuck her dead body. He was laughing like a maniac. This rogue called Paul McCarthy. In front of all of us he undressed the dead body and played with the breasts... everyone kept quiet. Some cheered Paul. The lone exception was Mel, my buddy Mel Blanc. He mumbled something, very feebly and then kept quiet...'

'Mel Blanc! He maybe a good contact point.'

Albert leads her to the Recreation Room where computers lie in a row in covered cubicles. He goes inside one empty cabin and quickly opens the Internet. His nimble fingers somehow catch hold of a site on Vietnam War...Paul McCarthy's platoon, Mario, Neal, Denis, Andrew, Pearl, Osco, Mel.... The cursor is now at Mel. Mel Blanc, a veteran of Vietnam War. Fought heroically and lost one leg. He is settled in Pittsburgh, owns an opera house and proud father of four children.

'Hi Mel! Gayatri here. Did you know someone called Andrew who was with you in Vietnam?'

She tries to calm herself. She will have to tell a lie, a big one at this time for a bigger cause. 'I'm his daughter-in-law.' She looks at Albert. He smiles indulgently; his eyes plead her to go on.

'Andrew sent a mail to Ethel, his fiancée. That devastating mail is with me now. Mel, should we leave the destiny of this great country in the hands of a rogue called Paul McCarthy?'

'Forget about it Gayaa....'

'Why should we forget, Mel? If you give me one convincing reason for forgetting all that had happened in that terrible night in Mekong Delta, I might ask my conscience to be at peace.' Her voice is devoid of any trace of excitement.

There is a pause on the other side and then the words pour forth inconsolably, inexorably as if these were held back for so many years together by some impediment and now that barricade is gone forever.

It is a live telecast; Gayatri is flanked by Mel Blanc. Mel tells so many things relentlessly and so much repressed anger has been oozing out from his serene face.

'Andrew was shot dead in front of the platoon members. The dead body was dumped in the nearby backwater lagoon. Andrew was a thorn in the flesh. He used to protest against Paul McCarthy's high-handedness. Paul was livid. After killing him, Paul was screaming: Look at his imprudence. I'm so happy that I could teach him a lesson. His bastard son or daughter should also be finished likewise. How much I would've liked to do that...'

Mel lowers his gaze. His eyes are filled with tears.

It is now Gayatri's turn to read out from the letter. She is doing it with an impassioned voice. The anchor of the program, Edward's face is furrowed with lots of emotions, 'Intercourse with a dead body? Horrible, horrible...!'

'Yes, it was like that. He laughed and laughed: It is easier to rape a dead body than a living woman here. A living woman can always conspire along with those commies. Not a dead woman. Come and join me my boys....'

'Why did you want to make this letter public now? The effected people kept quiet for long. Suddenly you woke up and came here to tell American people that one of their favorite contenders for the post of American President is not a man to be trusted.'

Edward's question was already looming large over that large spectrum of American viewers. A letter written long back and mysteriously retrieved by an Asian-origin woman implicates a person at a time when the whole of America is actually looking up to that person as a savior before an impending doom.

Gayatri had already braced herself for such a question.

'I'm indebted to America. It has given me honor, life and opportunity to stand on my feet. America is the birthplace of my two dear children. This great land is the native land of my child who is playing in my womb. Our America, my America and yours is in a crisis now, the crisis of the danger of falling into a wrong hand. We must resist it by all possible means. However, keeping up the tradition of this country, I would like to say that Mr. McCarthy should be given a fair chance of defending himself. He may give his version of the story....'

American news channels have picked up this sensational disclosure; so many new revelations come up about McCarthy! Some other guilt-ridden members of the same platoon have also come on TV and supported Mel Blanc's story. There is a swell of public protest. 'Paul be punished.... McCarthy is a killer.... We don't want such a villain as our leader....' They scream.

Paul McCarthy comes on TV. He looks devastated. 'Please forgive me. All this is true. I'm so sorry...for Andrews' family, for all the helpless people of that night....' He is crying, crying like a small child in need of succor, his wrinkled hands pacing up and down over his face.

Gayatri's telephone has been buzzing incessantly, one congratulatory call after another keeps her on her toes the whole day. Anjali is particularly ecstatic, 'Hey, I've announced to all and sundry who care to listen that I'm your friend. A few days back some people in a Bihu get-together in New Jersey were condemning you. They felt that you had set a bad moral precedent for our community by opting to be an unwed mother. But before anyone could actually defend you, two people virtually jumped on their feet to come to your rescue. One was...Guess...Ha...Ha...Siddhartha Borthakur, your ex-husband and the other one was Manish. Siddhartha shouted as if all people there were deaf: Stop all these nonsense! She's is bold. She has the courage to stand up for her conviction.... Manish was equally emphatic in his support to you.... After that there was an avalanche of support for you....'

Kenny, John, Martha, Natalie, Abdullah, Azam and all her friends in the Effective Communication class have called up to congratulate her.

Jacob Archer is seen on the television screen. A dry, spindly face without a trace of life! He has always been a blind supporter of Paul McCarthy. He would have been the Secretary of State if McCarthy were elected President. 'A shadowy past should not have been dragged to decide the present and the future. War invariably means violation of human rights. When your enemies, with fire weapons about to roar, surround you in a war-zone, how can you think about great emotions like love and life? Paul McCarthy would have made a very suitable President for this great country. But he is a conscientious person and would never ever try to elevate himself till the time his name is cleared of all these indictment. He has decided to withdraw himself from this Presidential race.'

It is going to be a bright morning where slanting rays of a glistening-apple-like sun stares discreetly at her and all other morning-walkers from a distant corner of the sky. The elderly lady whom Gayatri bumps into almost every day in the morning, goes ahead of her with the usual cultivated slow pace, clutching as usual in her right hand the chain of her pet dog and a paper-bag of dog-wastes in her glove-fitted left hand to be deposited at the dustbin a few meters away. Suddenly she looks back, stops on her track for well over a minute and tells Gayatri in a whispering, faint tone, 'You've really done a great job for us. You've saved America from a total disaster.'

Without waiting for a polite reciprocation, the old lady goes ahead with her daily chore of throwing away the dirt from her hand, her playful dog in tether following her in tow.

✦

Gaurav's voice is weighed down by lots of excitement during his sudden brush with this exotic land of his forefathers.

'The river Brahmaputra is like a sea, so huge, so majestic. Life with all its varieties is a beautiful medley of enthusiasm. Lots of things can be done here....'

Gaurav is touched by a sense of responsibility. Her son has grown up.

Last evening Katie showed to Gayatri her latest painting, a golden woman in a black backdrop emitting light like a divine being, eyes wincing with pain but face showing a kind of resolute determination. A hazy golden glow is within her grip and a ray scurries back to the womb taking the shape of a sleeping child inside.

'It's you.' Katie declared in a soft voice.

'You know I'm going to be mom again.'

She can now expect to see annoyance taking over Katie's radiant expression. 'I know. Garry told me. You also told about it on the TV that day. So what? I'll have a little bro...' Katie's face retains the same glow.

'Greg deserted me and the baby.'

'That's Greg's problem mama, not yours. He ran away, not you.'

This evening Katie is going to Philadelphia to take part in an art exhibition with a team of her classmates riding a Greyhound Bus. She hasn't betrayed any sign of getting exhausted or bored while painstakingly packing her art materials and putting all the heavy canvases with the consummate skill of a vigorous young woman.

Her Katie, Siddhartha's Katyayani, has grown up.

After bidding Katie an effusive farewell through hugs and kisses for this short but potentially life-changing journey towards a pulsating future, Gayatri strides back to the coffee house in the main square of the town.

She receives a warm greeting from everyone there on her arrival.

'We have more people than some of the States in the USA. But we, the people of Washington, do not have representation either in the Senate or in the House of Representatives. This is an injustice.'

The elderly looking person with a kind, rotund face seems to be really pinched by this alienation of his mega city from the electoral process.

'Our country was born on the issue of No Taxation without Representation. There should be a reverse Boston Tea Party now. We, the residents of Washington, should tell the Queen of England that she should take us back.' The anguish of another aged person is obvious.

She is going to write about this feeling of the Washingtonians in the next issue of her paper. The last issue was devoted to the Ground Zero and the design of the Twin Towers. Why should you conceive a lackluster design without any uniqueness? Either you keep the old design intact or build one which is going to be a befitting reply to a brazen destroyer like Bin Laden. But the latest owner of the paper is not happy about these new topics being covered. A woman from State College got a million dollar in the television show *Who Wants To Be a Millionaire* but that news was relegated to the back page. He asked for an explanation and she told him clearly that readers of this small town also looked for varieties and they needed to be pampered with news from the world.

In the evening when she prepares her supper, Katie calls her up to tell that the portrait created by her about a mysteriously hallowed woman has drawn widespread acclaim. 'You know Mom. They all said that this might go a long way like the Mona Lisa....'

'My blessings are with you, my child....' She should have been there with her to share and cherish her moments of laurels.

Today she is going to call up Garry, her Gaurav to tell that she is going to be there with him for helping him out in his vision, his dream for the place of his forefathers. She will mobilize some people to work for that place.

She remembers Jennet King who is involved in the rehabilitation of refugees in El Salvador, a place wrecked by so much turmoil. Once she went there for some work and amidst sounds of bomb blasts she was offered coconut water by a household. A glass of coconut water and that made this frail lady to fall for the place and the people!

Gratitude is a very big thing and one should never shy away from it.

Gayatri must tell this to her son so that he feels indebted to India, a place from where he has been carrying a whole lot of values and attitudes in his mind and heart. She has always been indebted to America which gave her enough space to grow as a human being, as a person to reckon with in her own right. She is grateful to Siddhartha who gave her this opportunity, an opening which was a dreadful proposition at one point of time, to grow in an embattled zone of life without any armor of protection.

She wants to extend this logic of gratefulness to Greg also at some stronger moments and then immediately withdraws herself from such a lofty and idealistically merciful situation. Probably at some future date she will be compassionate enough to take a magnanimous view of this proportion when their child grows up and her heart wells up with affection and pride for this young person.

Her reverie has been broken by a sudden and fast-paced shrill sound outside. Her neighbor Maria screams like a maniac at someone: '...You shirkers, we've all lost jobs because of you and here you've been paid hefty bonus out of tax-payers money! Aren't you ashamed of enjoying at our cost...?'

Gayatri could clearly see the elongated face of Maria and the severely shriveled frame, crushed under a bout of super-imposed shame, of her boyfriend, a middle-level executive in Lehman Brothers, from the balcony of her house. Maria has recently lost her job. Out-of-work Maria's outpourings heard from Gayatri's home are an everyday occurring phenomenon. One day this boyfriend of hers would just simply walk out of her domain to get rid of all these tantrums thrown. She would then be left all alone to fend for herself in this distressing time.

But there are also a few who have taken this setback of losing jobs in its stride to carve out something new for their otherwise humdrum existence. One day, David, Kenny and John's adorable son called her up from nowhere, 'Hi Gye, David here. I've come to a very cute island in the South Pacific....'

'What for?' She wanted to ask, but restrained herself. Kenny's son must be carrying that indomitable gene of his parents to roam around and explore the world. Good! Before she could say anything he almost screamed out in delight, 'I lost my job in that medicine firm. Initially it was shocking. But then I thought why not use the savings and see the world? This is a God-sent opportunity.... I went to so many places as back-packer....'

So, she was not wrong in surmising that this boy of John and Kenny had been carrying the parental gene of exploring the world.

'You know why I remembered you today! I met a man of my age here who also lost his job in Lockheed Martin and he was sun-bathing here on the beach. One day, one wing of his company got closed. This wing was making preparation to build F16 Aircrafts. They were hoping that India would buy their products. But their hopes were dashed when India bought from Russia some other fighter-planes, MIG or something.... He along with many others in the company lost their jobs. When India was mentioned I remembered you, looked for your Phone number and decided to call you up. Look, it's such an eye-opener. We Americans always think that our action in America affects job-market in other countries. But a decision by India affected lives of so many people in a giant aeronautical company in far-off America. My vision would have remained myopic had my firm decided not to get rid of me. I'd have continued to live in that belief that America was insular and America could decide everything for the rest of the world and not vice-versa.... Anyway, how are you? Are you keeping in touch with my old gal, my Mom?'

On the one hand, there is this staggering lot of depressed people who have been making a beeline to the psychiatrists after losing their jobs and on the other hand, there are the likes of David who have taken this trouncing as an opportunity to add a new dimension to their lives around. She has recently read an article somewhere about an American investment banker coaching football in Congo after being laid off in Wall Street crisis. He has been living in a dusty village in far-off Congo, among some impoverished people. The radiant face of that person with a beaming smile had touched her while she was going through that write-up.

It's a warm Sunday morning. The incessant ringing of the telephone forces her to leave the bed though she wants to lie down for some more time. It is Siddhartha on the other side, 'How are you? ...Have you heard H-1B Visa fee has been hiked?'

'I read somewhere...'

'Do you know what they are going to do with the increased revenue? They'll create a fund for war-effort elsewhere! Ridiculous! What do you feel?'

'I didn't think much about it....'

'They know that it'll affect the inflow of professionals. They need us more than we need them at this distressing time of the day. Foolish people...!'

With lot of effort, she desists herself from asking him to explicitly define those hazy terms 'We' and 'They' in the context of his perpetual existence in America. The excitement and agitation in his voice is reciprocated by her lukewarm and feeble words.

She has suddenly been over-powered by a jaded feeling, a murky sensation not there earlier with her in the bright, weekend morning. She opens the door of the kitchen to check if sufficient provisions are there for preparing a frugal brunch of rice, lentil and a vegetable curry. These days she doesn't feel like cooking and eating in the absence of Garry and Katie at this sprawling house but the blooming of another quiet life inside her body almost compels her to give up that reticence and go for providing for that tranquil entity.

But as soon as she decides on the menu for her lunch, her eyes immediately falls on the happy and rotund figurine of the Laughing Buddha otherwise peacefully settled in one corner of her living room, a gift by Greg on the day of her house-warming party. She was informed, rather casually, by Greg that this small statue must face the front door of the house to attract eclectic flow of positive energy, a Chinese belief nourished for centuries under Feng-shui.

She could feel an indiscernible movement of that statuette as if it has shifted its focus from the front door towards indoors with wide stares directed at her. A shiver goes down her spine at this bizarre turn of events. She wants to scream but sound seems to have eluded her as it happened so many other times. Suddenly so much quiet has dawned on the near-empty house!

And at that very moment she could see that the front door has opened and a very familiar hand is seen clutching at the half-opened door like a clinging serpent making a semi-circular posture there. That hand, thin, pinkish and slender with puckered skin on the long fingers...they moved very fast on the computer keyboard in the office and they moved very tenderly on her delicate skin in a close room in Gettysburg.

Greg! It's Greg. He has already moved inside leaving behind the half-closed door.

'Why are you here Greg?'

'I'm so sorry Gye. I know I don't even deserve forgiveness. I ran away.'

'No Greg, you shouldn't ask for forgiveness. You didn't promise anything to me...'

'I thought that I loved only Naomi and there couldn't be a place for any other woman in my life. But you proved me wrong. I couldn't run away from truth when in a different place, far away from you, I realized how much I loved you and how much I wanted this baby of ours....'

The shrunken Greg with a gaunt face stands in front of her, stooping low with an enormous burden of guilt. She wants to probe deep into his blue eyes but his eyes are mysteriously hazy staring away at nowhere. Somehow the look of the Laughing Buddha and Greg's looks are so much alike that they seemed to have borrowed each other's eyes at the moment to befuddle her.

'I saw you in front of Dr. Johnson's clinic on that fateful day among numerous other people on the television screen. Martha almost dragged you out on that day. I thought everything was over. All my hopes got totally dashed and I cried inconsolably for our baby. Then this Paul McCarthy episode happened. In front of a million viewers, with a glowing face, you spoke about our son. I felt so relieved that I cried again. I want to come back to you Gaayaathri if you accept me back in your life. I can't live without you and this baby of ours....'

There has been an incessant bout of sobs. She feels like holding his stooping body at the seraglio of her turbulent bosom.

'I thought about a name also for our son. Once you told me that Yoga stands for union between mind and body or connection between soul and God. Our son will be called Yoga, a bridge between the Orient and the West, a bond between you and me....'

'We can take our child to Gettysburg. He'll touch all those bullet-marks on the houses of the old township there, like you did during your childhood trip with Albert, and feel about an era of American history. That was your dream Greg....'

There has been ceaseless pouring of words from Greg and Gayatri could not find an opening in between to put her words for a proposed dream-trip to Gettysburg though she has already rehashed that speech in her mental world. But she has got no regret on that account as she is going to get enough time for telling lot of things to him in the days to come.

He stands near her but his voice has that uncanny aura of being at a mystifying distance, words carried on the crest of some waltzing waves. She is not in a position to resist the urge to rush to this long lost friend so that she can deposit all her worries, all her turbulent thoughts in his wide, hairy chest for good and cry her heart out.

But why should there be so much blazing-charcoal-like heat in his heaving bosom which is almost going to incinerate her to ashes? She shudders in panic, 'Oh Greg! Go away. I can't stand this anymore....'

'Poor girl! She's running high fever....'

She could feel a soothing touch, a silky feeling engulfing her and a voice so sweet that she wants to run away from the clutches of an intimidating darkness to the direction of that sugary voice.

Slowly she opens her eyes and finds herself in the loving arms of Shakuntala Kundan. 'Door was open. You were standing in a state of trance with that fat gentleman, I mean the Laughing Buddha, in your hand. You were muttering something incoherently...I made you to lie down on the sofa and put some ice on your forehead. How are you feeling honey...?'

She looks around. The nauseating giddy feeling is no longer there. A familiar person, a bespectacled, podgy figure is sitting on another sofa grinning at her, 'Hi, I'm Rudolf....'

'Greg's brother! We met.'

Her voice is feeble, words are still incoherent.

'Rudolf is my guest these days. Thankfully, he is released from the rehab or the hospital or the asylum, whatever you choose to call it. He wants to help me as a caregiver in my clinic. Since he himself went through so much trauma, he'd be in a better position to understand another person's pain...I also felt that you would be glad to see a happy, healthy Rudolf. Looking at your bright face, I can say that I wasn't wrong in assuming that...

'Let her take some rest Shakun. She's not well....'

'I'm making a soup for her. A spinach soup is going to do her a lot of good. She can't take any medicine in this condition. Poor girl!'

'I'm so sorry Gye.'

It is her turn to be perplexed. She is face to face with the brother of Greg. There is so little similarity between the two that Rudolf couldn't evoke any memory of Greg in her mind.

'Sorry for what?'

'My brother had caused so much pain to you. He's not a bad guy. But we had an insecure childhood. I went outwardly mad and he became a recluse, a loner. He is scared of commitment.'

Rudolf has put a brake to his words. He is now looking at her. But she is in a hurry to hear the rest of the story and trying to put up a brave front so that Rudolf feels encouraged to go on.

'He thinks he loves Naomi a lot. But I doubt that. He was adamant that I stayed with him when he married Naomi. Naomi was scared of my presence and demanded my removal from the house. It was so natural on her part to do so. Greg refused to relent. But when Naomi left the house, he promptly sent me to the asylum.... Today in this state of fever, you were uttering his name and I felt terribly guilty....'

Rudolf, who once spoke about some hidden enemies, about coded messages being sent by the CIA or KGB against him, about America hatching conspiracy against the entire world, is now talking about diffidence being infused in their early life. She could never imagine that the flabby and lovable guy whom she met at Dr. Shakuntala's clinic a few years back and who was supposed to be consigned only to a mental asylum in her proposed book could come out from that incarceration to share his views about his childhood with Greg to give another dimension to the story.

Another exhilarating twist in the convoluted drama called life!

Rudolf's presence is so soothing that she starts feeling much better. She is in a reclining position on the long, black, leathery sofa, her hands lying casually over her protruding belly without any tangible effort being made to hide this aberration. Rudolf pulls a chair to sit near her. This comforting proximity with Greg's brother has brought back all lost cheers like a refreshing breeze rejuvenating a sagging spirit.

'Last time when I saw you, you were like a volcano spitting out fires against America. This time you are like a mist spray over a beautiful mountain, placid and calm.'

'You're a writer. So you have described my two different states in a poetic fashion. I do not deserve all those niceties, Gaayaa. The truth is that I was a psychotic. I was a patient. With treatment I have recovered....'

Such a candid admission from someone so remotely connected to her life!

'You must be wondering what brought me back to this state from a brink of total disaster. It's not those red-white tablets or the so-called counseling sessions with the psychotherapists.... It's Shakuntala's care, her affection and love that did the trick.

She was so patient with all my tantrums. She went on talking for hours together like an elder sister in the hospital with the special permission of the hospital authority. It was a therapy, but she did that with a lot of concern....'

Shakuntala enters the room with three bowls of hot, piping soup on a tiny tray, her eyes totally engrossed on the enticing sight of the sparklingly green liquid and her lissome body makes a swinging movement under the weight of a repressed joy.

She helps Gayatri in gulping down the liquid in small amounts like a mother taking care of her child in distress.

'Rudolf is thrilled that he's going to be an uncle soon. Albert is equally excited about becoming a grandfather. Your child will have a very affectionate uncle and a very loving grandfather, dear. With such people around, he's not going to miss his Dad. Who knows his Dad may also come back one day.'

Gayatri's eyes are welled with tears. When life takes away something, it also gives back so much in profusion. But loss is mourned more than the gain cherished. Only a few moments back, she was dreaming of Greg and his homecoming and now she is beguiled into immersing in another reverie, a trance she wants to lap up.

✦ ✦ ✦

14

<u>*In the year 2040*</u>

He stands on the steps of the Lincoln Memorial. The historic Memorial grounds are full of enthusiastic crowd. They have been cheering at him as if he is going to churn out a magical recipe for their country at this time of the day when their world has shrunk to an utter state of despair.

Yoga Amherst, the young and handsome President of America is a worried man these days with an all-pervasive hunger, staggering unemployment and rapidly declining income staring starkly on the home turf and the world's top-notch super-power China posing serious threat to the very existence of this country on the external domain. But he knows that all is not lost. The rapid depletion of ice-cover over the polar region, a fall out of the much-dreaded global warming has thrown up very interesting probabilities, a kind of virtual windfall not only for America but for all the five countries in the Arctic region. The vast untapped reservoir of energy sources and precious metals lying untouched in that virgin area for millions of years are going to enrich all these five

Arctic countries in such a massive way that they might together become a mighty power-house in the near future.

There is going to be mounds of riches on a mountain of disaster. A beautifully contrived contradiction weaved by an unseen hand called destiny!

Russia has already moved her troops around an under-water mountain ridge believed to have contained a huge amount of oil and gas, to claim it for herself.

Canada is in an offensive mood to establish her monopoly over the Northwest Passage, the Arctic sea route which has recently been cleared of ice-cover. Who won't do that when that sea-route linking the Atlantic and Pacific Oceans is going to shorten the distance between Japan and Europe by well over seven thousand kms? America is slightly intrigued by this twist of events when a cordial neighbor has almost turned into a bitter foe.

As the new President of this country he is dead against going back to the Cold War era of mutual distrust or arms-build up. He needs to marshal enough negotiating skill to ensure American presence in the Arctic and he is certain to wrap it up in America's favor. Of course, he is not averse to the idea of flexing his muscles as a last resort if Canada and Russia refuse to budge from their belligerent posture.

There cannot be a very bitter conflict on ideological account in this world now as had happened in the cold-war age since all ideologies more or less had failed at the critical crossroads of human history. Rigid socialism failed in the Soviet Union. And so did rigid capitalism in the USA or Europe. Even the modified socialism of China has faced severe challenges from the Maoists there though she wants to camouflage the tell-tale signs of the strains behind the iron curtain. But Yoga Amherst is a statesman and a politician. He has to harp on ideological differences to bring home message of hope to the masses.

He looks around. A vast sea of people jostles for space in front of him and he must infuse spirit in this confluence of humanity.

The time has come! The time to act! The Red Dragon has breathed out its fire sweeping the world with terror. It has destroyed the pillars of democracy and freedom across vast parts of Asia, like what the Soviets did almost a century back. My dear Americans, the world scenario has changed! And that too by a huge margin! China has replaced us in terms of economic and military strength. But at the cost of civil liberty and human right! Friends, brothers, sisters and all of my dear Americans, the time has come for the great nation of the United States of America to redeem its lost glory and strengthen the foundations of democracy across the planet.

We have been passing through a phase of severe financial and resource crunch. But that too will pass, I'm sure. Almost 32 years back when the charismatic Barack Obama took office of the President of this great country, America was reeling under a depression no less than ours and with the threat of terrorism no less fearful than now what is sponsored by China. But that too was overcome in course of time by this great land of Washington, Jefferson, Roosevelt, Lincoln and scores of other iconic leaders who blessed her soil.

We, the Americans are not only going to overcome the gloom but restore the multihued glory of America in the world sphere and as I take the oath of office and secrecy as the President of the USA, I swear by the name of God that I along with you shall endeavor the historic feat of achieving American grandeur.

He could clearly hear thunderous applause invading the air.

Looking at the glowing faces of the vast multitude of crowd around, he could make out that he has largely been successful in instilling hope, the ultimate elixir of life, in the fluttering hearts of these people with his words.

Whenever Yoga Amherst, the young statesman of the country loses heart, he looks at the photograph of his mother and involves in an intimate but silent dialogue with her. She died just after giving him birth and it was Uncle Rudolf who brought him up with the tender care of brother, mother and father, all rolled into one. He gave up everything which might have interfered in Yoga's upbringing including his nascent dream of involving with Dr. Kundan's social work. Yoga can clearly see him now among the enthusiastic crowd waving at him and holding onto his weak and decrepit body with a quiet dignity to prevent his fall amidst that surge of humanity.

His sister Katie must have been glued to the television to have a peek at the much-awaited festivity. She has been away in Cairo in connection with the World Art Exhibition organized amongst the pyramids to save these priceless heritages from the brink of ruin in the wake of the deserts turning into vast wetlands.

As wife, Emmy has been equally supportive of her husband in his different ventures. Though she has always been busy in setting up a comfortable home for him and the kids, Noah and Keanu, she has become an integral part of his public life as well. Today also she stands here near him with her mauve colored self-designed outfit waving at people with a beaming smile.

Yoga Amherst, the 50th President of America has ignited the flames of passions of a dormant nation not only during this victory speech but also during the long and exhaustive campaigns spanning over almost a year. His uncle who had toiled hard to bring him up has been instrumental in implanting this combative spirit in him and his undying love for this great country. He was almost speechless when one day Dr. Shakuntala Kundan, the octogenarian social worker, told him about how Uncle Rudolf used to pour venom on America in his younger days when he was reeling under a severe psychological trauma.

That intense hatred had turned into an obsessive love for his country in his matured years as he could come out of a serpent-like clutch of a massive feeling of diffidence under her tutelage and care.

One day, during the heyday of his campaign, Natalie, his mom's friend, came rushing towards him in Penn State's large auditorium when he just finished his lecture on his vision for a future America and amidst thunderous clapping of the onlookers she stealthily slipped some crumpled papers into his hands. Her wrinkled hands clasped his; there was a kind of entreaty in her small, round, endearing eyes, 'She left them in her office laptop and that laptop was handed over to me after her sudden death by the next editor. This half-finished document, the true story of a family in America, was occupying a space there. Before the laptop was sent to the junkyard, I retrieved the document and waited till I met you. Please don't throw it away dear. You'll find the story fascinating. Your mom was an amazing person....'

He won the much predictable poll to match the charged expectations of the vast multitudes of American people who have started looking up to him as the savior of their lost splendor.

Today the historic day has come to deliver a promise, show a dream and initiate drive to steer America out of this morass.

Last night he opened his mother's half-finished manuscript and America draped in her mottled finery came surreptitiously towards him like a charmed beauty. The story of a family in America was almost progressing concurrently with the chronicles of America, edges merging effortlessly in many areas. He got to know his father, the enigmatic Gregory Amherst, who left him much before his birth and his half-brother Garry who went out in search of his root in India through the writings of her mother. The slushy-life stories of both Garry and Greg also seemed to have merged in their gory deaths in two different places of the same continent almost at the same time.

Gaurav was taken on his feet through a splatter of mud towards the near-empty river bank in the wee hours where dark and orange colors were playing hide and seek in the sky and a faint, dainty moon was trying desperately to show her presence in that tussle of colors.

'What have you been doing here? Who has sent you to our place?'

The short, stout boy in olive camouflaged military uniform stood there on the huge, hard, uneven rock stroking the dangling gun hung carelessly over his right shoulder, his tightening gazes were trying to find out something on Gaurav's fear-laden face.

'You are unnecessarily worried. My mother who was born in this part of the country asked me to come here and do something good for this place. This huge river island needs to be protected from the fury of the river Brahmaputra. I am working among the people. I'm not spy. I'm not anyone's agent....'

'You've incited people against us. When we went to clear the jungle, some people who never dared to question our authority earlier,

didn't allow us to do so. They had the audacity to tell us that tree-felling was bad.... We don't encourage any opposition.... Our high-command pronounced death sentence on you....'

Gaurav's young face cringed in panic at the impending doom to befall on him shortly. He didn't want to die so early, he wanted to do so many things here and one day go back and open a music band in America when work would get a momentum in this place. But he knew there was no hope.

'What you are waiting for? He should be finished off immediately. He is a threat to our survival....'

A familiar, hoarse voice. He looked back. The contractor, a bald, lean guy with a deceptively kind face who was going to build an embankment before the coming monsoon, an annual ritual at a staggering cost, and which was going to be devoured by the river as usual, was standing behind. Gaurav mobilized people against the construction of a weak, shoddy embankment, a far worse scenario than an open island left at the mercy of nature!

Lot of money was pouring forth for the development of the river island. It was coming and by some queer force of magic it was draining out without leaving any trace of its existence on the rugged exterior of the landmass.

Then this handsome lad from some alien land arrived and tried to talk people out of inertia. He became their voice, their eyes and their new-awakened consciousness. Can we? They asked in sheer disbelief and when assured of their potent force lying inside them like a sleeping genie, they joined him in the protest against injustice.

People were telling this boy about the militants and their dream of an independent country in this neglected and deprived northeast part of India. He had also come here for unleashing an economic emancipation. In his naiveté he couldn't find any apparent conflict of interest between his mission and that of the militants. Both of them dreamt of freedom.

One day, the contractor came to his thatched, humble house which had become his abode here to tell him to budge off. 'Otherwise be prepared to face the music....' His impassive face was not betraying any emotion.

'Don't waste time on him. Just finish him off....'

This labyrinthine confluence of interest between an oppressor who was siphoning off money meant for development and some young boys who renounced home and hearth vowing to fight back that exploitative oppression was baffling for this young man from another country even at the last moment of his truncated life.

They surged towards him menacingly and this young man from another continent stood there, transfixed and frozen like a statue.

His bullet-ridden body mutilated beyond recognition was found in that spot by a village woman who came there to collect firewood.

She screamed, jumped up and down as if she had gone out of her mind and the news quickly spread like a wildfire in that river island.

Yoga shuddered under the impact of a strange confluence of panic at the plight of a vulnerable boy who happened to be his elder brother and also a concurrent moving desire to save him from the clutches of those brutal elements.

Yoga flipped through the pages quickly to shake himself off from that wretched feeling and then by some strange coincidence his gaze fixed on another story, the last days of his lost father seen through the eyes of his dead mother:

The American journalist was made to walk several kms blindfolded, and when he reached a house and was made to sit on the cobbled floor, he was thoroughly exhausted.

The news of an American journalist being abducted and kept as a hostage in far-off Afghanistan was planted with so much meticulous details by the group which did the mischief that it sent a shock wave to the entire western world. The idea was to create a buzz in the media and in the minds of the common people about the might of that fundamentalist force. Or it maybe a strange way to wage a venomous tirade against anything even remotely connected with the privileged world by these disgruntled and ruthless elements camouflaged under the banner of a structured religion though that religion has got nothing to do with their evil design.

Mr. Gregory Amherst was warned several times by the pro-establishment forces not to venture out in the countryside at that critical juncture when the numerous splintered terrorist groups were running the show in the rural areas. But Greg as he was popularly called was adamant. How could he write something on a country if he did not dare to mingle with the real life there? He went to several places and everywhere he was made to feel like an ordinary person. But then one day he was accosted by a group of young turbaned men, 'Why are you roaming around here? Are you a spy?'

'No, I'm a journalist from America....'

Greg was flabbergasted but he was not panicked.

'Oh an American...!'

Greg could see a mixture of glee and loathing in their voice: joy of getting an American catch so easily and the manifestation of their general revulsion for the Americans as a whole extended to one of their vulnerable members.

The fate of Gregory Amherst was sealed then and there itself without his consent or comprehension about the eerie design of events deliberated elsewhere.

The macabre scene of that cruel execution was first telecast on Al-Jajeera television. Later on that was picked up by all the channels all over the world as the hottest news of the day.

Like a sacrificial lamb in a Hindu temple in India, he was dragged to the scene and he was forced to bow his head so that the huge machete could be put forcefully over the arched neck. His face cringed in fear before the sharp blades went through his stooping body.

Blood flowed liberally like streams of wild current.

These two ghoulish scenes which took place three decades back in close proximity in two unrelated situations flashed through his mind several times while Yoga was preparing his maiden victory speech last evening and these two macabre deaths sent chill down his spines. Though happened many years back, he somehow felt responsible for perishing of two innocent souls of Americans somewhere on the globe.

As President of this country now he strives to reinvent America as the supreme power through collective force of the American people where no one will ever dare to mess up with American lives.

During his campaign, he could see the disillusioned faces of vast multitude of people desperate to ride again on the galloping horse of success. In utter desperation they have found out numerous whipping boys. Some have identified China as the enemy number one; others have put all the blame on the immigrants of Asian and African origin, some others, particularly the rural folks of the southern states, and the inheritors of the legacy of the Bible belt hold the other faith people responsible for the present mess.

'During the hopeless phase of my depression, I was holding America responsible for all my woes. Hitler singled out the Jews and told his depressed countrymen: They are to be blamed for your problems. When people are down, you can tell them anything, they'll it lap. As the new President of this great nation, you should talk to them about hope, about rebuilding....'

Uncle Rudolf told him last evening and when he finished reading about how his own Dad and half-brother met their tragic ends, he could find a harmonization of thought between him and his octogenarian uncle. Instead of whipping up a mass hysteria against an enemy, he would try to talk about the inherent strength of a nation.

China's stride is achieved at the expense of her dispensable human resources. Huge dams which have enabled generation of electricity at dirt cheap rate there have taken away lives of millions of people and displaced an equally staggering number mercilessly. The cries and agonies of those throttled voices could not come out of a carefully laid down totalitarian frontier.

American people should not look forward to a development based on cruelty. There might have been transgressions in the international arena in the past, some intrigues here and there or some wars fought on foreign soil, but the country paid a very heavy price for all those needless misadventures.

His country did not dare to question China on human rights violation or authoritarianism simply because that Asian super-power provided a vast market for the American capital to flourish. It was a win-win situation for quite a long time when American capital flowed there and Chinese goods made with the severely underpaid exploited labor supplied an incessant flow of cheap goods to the American consumers.

But that opulence or supremacy achieved at the cost of a denuded virtue did not prove to be eternal. It was not in accordance with what the original American Dream stood for.

It has been a lesson that the edifice of a future American greatness is to be built on justice and harmony.

'Mr. President, what is your strength? How do you propose to lift this depressed state out of this gloom?'

An elderly person with a thin, pointed face has started the deliberation.

The interactive session with the common American people has just started. It was the idea of the new President to break away from the traditions of delivering just a victory speech and then interacting only with a select audience under the full glare of security people. He wants to reach out to all.

'My strength is my confidence and my belief in all of you. If we all join hands and revive the great American Dream of becoming the greatest nation on earth, no one not even our enemy, can stop us from realizing our mission. But it is to be built on the sanctuary of love and not on the citadel of human misery. End doesn't justify means....'

'What is your message to all of us on this day?'

A young boy standing just near the podium asked him in all earnestness. He looks at the boy: young, lean and muscular with a mop of golden hair glittering on the top of his round head and a sun-burnt craggy face.

'The Americans are not to lose hope. Nothing is lost. This downswing is just a temporary phase in our nation's history. We should be grateful to the almighty that we were His chosen children for two full centuries. We failed Him for some reason but we are going to bounce back with bursting glory with His blessings soon.'

'You started your speech with pouring venom against the Red Dragon...!'

'No, I was just stating the facts. There is absolutely no time to sit in our ivory tower and relax. But my intention is not to create panic either. We Americans have the ability to deal with any eventuality and we would overcome this as a nation. I was talking of establishing American Dominance in the world. But aggression as a means to achieve that objective is ruled out. Complete isolation as we used to do in the earlier phase of our history as a means to conserve and enhance strength is also not possible. We'll go for some strategic alliances in the world scene. But on the internal front we should be very strong as a nation. I'm not ashamed or embarrassed to tell that we are going to offer help to those industries which are down for the time being but showing signs of revival. Complete non-intervention as a strategy had failed. If we use tax-payers' money for the good of the tax-payers, no one should dare to condemn us. What is the use of that money lying in our coffers if it can't bring smile to our people?'

'How do you want to deal with Chinese hegemony?'

This is a middle-aged lady concerned with the Chinese expansion like many others in this country.

'Not by weakening them but by making us stronger. We'll have to surpass them in economic might. We have the resources. We have the freedom. What we need is a strong will power to mobilize whatever we have with us.'

The young girl with a very pretty face asks the new President with an excited voice.

'Mr. President, you are talking about undoing the past mistakes. Do you agree with the view that accepting the

Darwinian thesis as the origin of human-beings was a huge mistake? It negates creationism. Are our forefathers, Adam and Eve, monkeys?'

'Young lady, what do you want in life? How does it matter that your forefathers were monkeys or evolved human-beings so long as your belly is full, your heart is appreciative of what you have as an American and you're content with life...?'

There are lots of applauses.

'Our problem started when we became too liberal. People came in hordes and our jobs were taken away. The same people waged an internal war here by demolishing twin towers. They built a mosque in the same sight a few years later....'

The pretty girl has been telling in the same fervor of innocent excitement. Yoga looks at the girl's unsullied face; the gullible face of his baby-daughter comes to the fore.

'American history is based on the saga of assimilation, an incredible story of a melting pot. Our entire heritage is built on the blood and sweat of all such talented immigrants. A mosque stands with pride near the Ground Zero. It stands as a testimony to a great concept called America. We should all be very proud of this unique concept. Otherwise there would not be any difference between us and some narrow-minded bigots. Even those people who applauded demolition of the Bamian Buddha in Afghanistan are now remorseful. But they can't undo the past.... They're trying to rebuild something there... We didn't do anything of that sort....'

He pauses for a while. He wants to be brutally candid.

'This mighty country fell because we all started assuming arrogantly at some point of time that we owned the world and we could dictate terms of peace or strife to others. It backfired.

So, it's the time to take stock of our blunders and take a combined pledge that we're not going to repeat our mistakes. China through her very active role in world politics has started committing exactly the same mistakes and I can very clearly see her fall in the near future. America should prepare herself to fill the vacuum. In the same breath, I'd like to assure you that there'll be no compromise on the issue of upholding American Honor and we'll do everything to safeguard our interests in the global arena.'

Yoga has got down from the podium causing almost a pandemonium of sort among the security people. He wants to break down all barriers and reach out to his people, particularly to this young girl so that all present here and all those glued to the televisions are reassured about their future which they are going to build together.

The girl is very near him. With a face flushed with affection and excitement she proceeds at a quick pace towards him as if she is going to give the new President a big hug and as the People's President he is not going to mind it either.

The entire sequence of events have moved at such a lightening pace that when the girl was being dragged away and he was cordoned off by a huge contingent of security people, he could hardly see the falling figure of Uncle Rudolf.

Katie could see the girl striding ahead on the television screen with great force and in the next instant she could see the shining revolver being pulled out. While Katie screams in horror in a state of utter helplessness in far-off Cairo, she could see the old, stooping body of Uncle Rudolf covering Yoga and blocking the girl's galloping stride. Before someone could make out what has actually been happening, the bullet coming in dizzying speed goes straight into the feeble upper limb of Uncle Rudolf. Among a sea of humanity his collapsing body rests on someone's shoulders, his right hand going up and his posture reminds Katie of the invincible Statue of Liberty braving all odds for centuries in the Stratton Island.

Katie screams out in horror at the ghastly death of her very dear Rudolf Uncle.

She feels relieved that Yoga Amherst, her half-brother and the young and charismatic President of America could be saved from a doom so assiduously planned for him. It would have spelled a catastrophe for the entire country at this time of a faint hue of hope when a moribund nation has started seeing a dream through the alluring eyes of this new leader.

There is enough debate now on television about how a girl could enter the area with a firearm in tow. Some people talk of a Chinese conspiracy; others about a Canadian or a Russian game-plan for destabilization so that they could establish hegemony in the Arctic region.

Katie is going to conclude her mother's half-finished story with the full account of the fall of indomitable Rudolf Amherst, a frail old man and the awesome rise of the doughty American spirit with that memorable fall in this important crossroad of human history.

She could see an undaunted Yoga, among a sea of humanity, mourning and commemorating in the same breath, a hero's last glorious voyage to eternity.

✦ ✦ ✦

Leena Sarma is an officer with the Indian Railways and currently working as GM, Centre for Railway Information System, New Delhi. She is a well-known novelist from Assam with eight novels to her credit. *A Melody in the Wilderness* is her first English novel. Widely traveled, the writer developed the plot keeping America at the backdrop.